A STRANGE STATE OF AFFAIRS

Copyright © 2025 Simon MacDonald

The moral right of the author has been asserted.

Apart from any fair dealing for the purposes of research or private study, or criticism or review, as permitted under the Copyright, Designs and Patents Act 1988, this publication may only be reproduced, stored or transmitted, in any form or by any means, with the prior permission in writing of the publishers, or in the case of reprographic reproduction in accordance with the terms of licences issued by the Copyright Licensing Agency. Enquiries concerning reproduction outside those terms should be sent to the publishers.

The manufacturer's authorised representative in the EU for product safety is Authorised Rep Compliance Ltd, 71 Lower Baggot Street, Dublin D02 P593 Ireland
(www.arccompliance.com)

This is a work of fiction. Names, characters, businesses, places, events and incidents are either the products of the author's imagination or used in a fictitious manner. Any resemblance to actual persons, living or dead, or actual events is purely coincidental.

Troubador Publishing Ltd
Unit E2 Airfield Business Park,
Harrison Road, Market Harborough,
Leicestershire. LE16 7UL
Tel: 0116 2792299
Email: books@troubador.co.uk
Web: www.troubador.co.uk

ISBN 978-1-83628-426-0

British Library Cataloguing in Publication Data.
A catalogue record for this book is available from the British Library.

Printed and bound by CPI Group (UK) Ltd, Croydon, CR0 4YY
Typeset in 11pt Minion Pro by Troubador Publishing Ltd, Leicester, UK

A STRANGE STATE OF AFFAIRS

Simon MacDonald

This book is dedicated to my family – those no longer with us and those who remain.

CHAPTER 1

As Samuel Bartholomew McAllister walked around the garden of the old family home in the damp chill of an October morning in 2018 he looked up at the house and recalled what it had been like in happier times. Born there in 1959 and now approaching sixty years of age he thought back to his childhood, a mostly happy childhood with the house full of laughter, music and the aroma of his mother's cooking, apart that is from the days when the house was full of his father's frequent moaning, complaining and petulance. The house had remained largely unchanged since his childhood days but had now become a depressing and unloved place after years of neglect. He was there to meet his brother Duncan and Emma his sister. It was a sad day, their mother Bridget McAllister had passed away the previous day, a little inconveniently for Sam, as today, the start of a new academic week, he was due to introduce his year ten English class to George Orwell's dystopian novel *Nineteen-Eighty-Four*, one of the books they would be studying for their English Literature GCSE the following year. Mr. Smedley-Barrington, the headmaster, had been sympathetic to Sam's predicament despite being telephoned at seven-thirty that morning to be advised that Sam wouldn't be in school that day, an inconveniently timed telephone call that resulted in Mr. Smedley-Barrington's egg being boiled for eight and a half minutes instead of the usual six. Nevertheless, he had generously told Sam to take the week off as compassionate leave to sort his affairs out. George Orwell would have to wait a week.

He approached the summer house at the bottom of the garden, kicking the dry sycamore leaves on the lawn as he walked slowly up to the rotten wooden door. The summer house was a substantial structure about fifteen feet square, built of breeze blocks with a pitched tiled roof and large windows, which were still adorned with the car stickers he had fixed to them as a schoolboy. He pushed the door open and entered, somehow expecting it to look the same as it had all those years ago. The table and chairs, the piano, the paperbacks on the bookshelf and the old lawnmowers were all gone. Gone also was the aroma of incense sticks, cigarette smoke and coffee that he remembered. Now the summer house smelt musty and damp.

As a teenager in the 1970s the summer house had become his haven, his sanctuary. He had escaped there to listen to his records, play the piano and smoke his brother's dog-ends that had been left in the ashtray machined from an old lorry piston. Occasionally he'd entertained girlfriends in the summer house, not that he'd had many, usually with the embarrassing results only to be expected from an inexperienced spotty-faced youth.

Now forty-five years later the summer house was derelict, the roof was falling in and the window frames rotten and draughty, the only inhabitants now insects and rodents. They didn't care if the roof leaked and the building had become neglected and unloved. Nobody seemed to care anymore.

He thought of happier times in the summer house in the 1970s as a teenager. He had loved the seventies – the cars, the music, the politics and the fashion and he often thought how perfect his life was back then. He'd forgotten the three-day weeks, the strikes, the roaring inflation, the oil crisis and the power cuts; to a teenager things like that were irrelevant. It was a decade that seemed to go on forever. In 1970 as an eleven-year-old he was still at junior school and by the end of the decade he was twenty-one. So much had happened during the intervening years – he'd left school, discovered girls, learnt to drive, started earning money and met his future wife, Morag. They had been at secondary school together, although took little notice of each other then, but when they met a few years later in a local pub, Sam's attention was drawn to her immediately. As a teenager he had a vision of the girl of his dreams – long blonde hair, wearing jeans, a white cheesecloth shirt, desert boots and an Afghan-coat and back then in 1977 in the bar of the Rose and Crown there she sat, a vision of loveliness meeting all the requirements. Their friendship blossomed and they were married four years later in 1981. So much for the decade that seemed to last forever, since then his life had passed by alarmingly quickly. He raised his arms and brushed aside some large cobwebs dangling from the ceiling as he moved towards the open door. He walked out, breathed the fresh autumn air and pulled the summer house door closed.

Walking slowly back across the lawn towards the house he paused to look at the old family home. Fifty-seven Stonebridge Road was a mid-1950s detached house with a large back garden, and although no doubt comfortable in the fifties, the house hadn't changed much at all over the years. With the passing of several decades the garden had become neglected and equally as depressing as the house itself. The large lawn, once lovingly manicured, was now overgrown and weeds and creepers encroached onto the once beautiful rockery that surrounded it. Sycamore and silver birch trees, once regularly pruned, had been left neglected for years and at the bottom of the garden the branches of the trees on both sides almost met in the middle, forming a canopy over the old summer house. Sam then looked up at the imposing neighbouring house of red brick, which was as equally run-down and neglected as his old family home, the two properties being separated by a rotten wooden fence. A sudden gust of wind blew the leaves around his feet in a circular motion releasing a lovely earthy autumnal aroma. A shiver went down his spine as he watched the circling leaves moving across the lawn towards a gap in the broken fence, as if he were being drawn with them towards the house next door, compelled to follow by some unseen force. He thought of his visits to the house as a schoolboy and the old neighbour Reginald Ramsbottom long since dead. He had been a strange man, although a gentleman in the true sense of the word who had never shown anyone any malice. He was a bachelor, had owned a jeweller's shop in Northumberland and had been an old family friend and a customer of Sam's father who had also worked in the jewellery trade. Reginald Ramsbottom sold his shop in the 1960s and decided to move to Lincolnshire with his elderly mother who hadn't really wanted to relocate to Lincolnshire and passed away shortly after the move in protest. After the death of his mother Reginald Ramsbottom had become a recluse and rather eccentric. He had a strange religion, or at least everyone else thought it was strange. He'd belonged to a peculiar American religious sect called the Church of… something or other, some strange name, worshipped a God called Yahweh and no doubt filled the church coffers with lots of his hard-earned cash for the privilege of being one of the flock, no doubt required to donate a percentage of his earnings to "The Brotherhood" or the "Fellowship" or whatever it was they proudly referred to themselves as, probably enabling the recipient a life of luxury on some exotic island thanks to the naivety of his followers. The house was now inhabited by Sam's brother, Duncan McAllister, who had inherited the property from Mr. Ramsbottom twenty years earlier and had eerily left the house exactly the same as when he'd lived there. Sam continued to walk slowly back towards the old family home, thinking of his mother and what had appeared to have been an unfulfilled and mostly dreary life. She was ninety-four when she died, having survived her husband Bernard by six years, and had belonged to the generation that believed that bicarbonate of soda and Mackenzie's smelling salts cured most common ailments, the generation that considered the woman's place to be in the home. She had been a dedicated and hard-working housewife, her life taken up with bringing up her three children, cleaning and cooking, the usual domestic chores and always ensuring that a meal was on the table when her husband arrived home from work, often late in the evenings, resulting in his dinner being kept in the oven for several hours and probably quite unappetising but was nevertheless consumed without gratitude.

She had met her future husband, Bernard McAllister, during the Second World War in the Kent village where she was born. Having left school she had worked on the telephone exchange in the village Post Office. She often recalled how Bernard, who was stationed at a barracks nearby and had driven a Churchill tank, would regularly park the monstrosity outside the Post Office, which was situated at a crossroads, jump out, enter the Post Office and purchase a single stamp. The next time he was passing he would do the same, no doubt in an attempt to impress the young Bridget. His attempts to impress appeared to have been successful and Bridget and Bernard McAllister were married in 1946 after the war. They had three children, Emma their first, Duncan 18 months later and ten years later Sam, who had always considered himself a mistake considering the age gap between himself and his two older siblings. Because of the large age difference Sam had grown up almost as an only child, Emma and Duncan being away at college in London most of the time and only returning home to Lincolnshire for the end-of-term holidays.

As a teenager Sam had approached his mother on the subject of his existence. 'Why did you leave it so late to have a third child? Was I a mistake?' he had once asked.

'Certainly not,' she'd replied, putting on her posh voice. 'You're very special.'

Sam didn't feel special, he felt like a mistake, and many years later when he and Morag produced Bridget and Bernard's only grandchild Alistair McAllister, Sam considered the prospect of having another child in ten years' time with horror. *Surely people don't do that out of choice,* he thought, *I must have been unplanned, a mistake, a result of failed coitus interruptus.*

Since an early age Sam had developed a fascination with words and the English language, often referring to his dictionary for meanings and definitions of words. As a boy, when he had pondered on the subject of his existence he'd looked up "mistake" in his dictionary – *"mistake – an error of judgement or a misconception"*. That word conception! He must have been unplanned, an error of judgement, otherwise he wouldn't have been conceived. He'd looked up "conception" in the dictionary – *"act of conceiving, the fertilization of the ovum and the beginning of the growth of the embryo in the womb, thing conceived"*. Not wanting to think of himself as a *"thing conceived"* or a *"mistake"* he had put the dictionary away before becoming more depressed, convinced that he shouldn't really be here at all.

Sam arrived at the back door, which opened into the long, narrow kitchen, and stepped inside. The kitchen felt cold and damp and the air was stale, the windows having rarely been opened over the years for fear of flies entering. One of the few improvements made to the house was in the late 1960s when the kitchen was modernised, indeed that updated kitchen was still there over fifty years later, desperately in need of being updated again. It still had the original white wall tiles, now dirty and cracked, the hard and brittle linoleum flooring, the framed car pictures on the wall given free with petrol in the 1960s, the aging, dirty and rusting domestic appliances and the tired-looking grubby cupboards and drawers that were lined with scraps of old wallpaper and full of chipped crockery and tarnished silver cutlery.

He walked from the kitchen into the adjoining room, known as the breakfast room, a small but equally grubby room with a table and four chairs, threadbare carpet and dust-covered yellow venetian blinds at the window. One end of the blinds was hanging down at an angle of about sixty degrees, precariously balanced on the top of a large dust covered cactus on the windowsill. On the table was his mother's 1950s medical book, once owned by her mother before her, which they'd both used to look up their ailments. Next to the book was the ubiquitous brown bottle of Mackenzie's smelling salts.

As he looked around the breakfast room he was transported back to his school days when he would sit at that very table for his breakfast, often with his father, something he usually tried to avoid as conversations were often difficult and usually ended up with his father asking embarrassing questions. As he stared at the table he remembered one morning in particular:

'What did you do at school yesterday?' his father had asked.

'Nothing much,' he'd replied, not wanting to be drawn

into a lengthy and boring conversation with his father, which usually started with a lecture beginning with "When I was your age..."

'What's on the agenda today, son?'

'Nothing much.'

'Don't remember doing that subject when I was at school. What's that all about then?'

Sam had been about to reply with another "nothing much" but decided to ignore the question. He'd put a large spoonful of marmalade on his toast and had been about to spread it when came the usual reprimand from his father –
'You've got enough there for two slices.'

Sam had continued to spread it then folded the slice of toast in half and pushed it flat with the palm of his hand so marmalade oozed out from the edges onto the plate.

His father had looked on in despair and tutted. 'Don't know what the matter is with the youth of today; rebellious, no respect and no manners. I hope you're not going to waste all that marmalade, money doesn't grow on trees you know. On the subject of money, have you had any thoughts on what you're going to do when you leave school, any thoughts of a career?'

'I'm doing rather well at biology at the moment, it's very interesting and I have thought about going into medicine, maybe becoming a doctor.'

'That would be wonderful, Sam. If you get into medical school I'll buy you a new car on your 21st birthday.'

'A new Lotus Europa?'

'If that's what you want.'

'A black Lotus Europa in John Player Special colours with the gold pin stripes.'

'Er... yes.'

Sam had noticed the slight hesitation and had begun to doubt his abilities to achieve this objective and thought his father had probably had the same thought otherwise he wouldn't have made this wild offer in the first place. He didn't usually agree to part with money so casually. In any case his 21st birthday was six years away. That seemed like a lifetime. He couldn't wait that long.

'Dentistry,' his father had suggested. 'That's another good career with plenty of money, or accountancy. My cousin was a helicopter instructor, marvellous job he had, until he crashed that is. He went all over the world.'

Sam had sighed as he scraped up the large pile of marmalade that had dropped onto his plate and transferred it to the last mouthful of toast. Now totally confused – doctor, dentist, accountant, helicopter instructor, what was he to do?

'Actually I've thought of joining the police.'

'WHAT! I should jolly well hope not!' exclaimed his father, who had an ardent dislike for the constabulary, particularly the traffic variety. He'd waved an envelope in his hand. 'I've just opened this, it arrived this morning. It's a court summons for speeding. That's it now, I've already got ten points on my licence. I'll get a ban.'

'How fast this time?' Sam had asked timidly.

'One hundred and five over a quarter mile stretch of a single carriageway in Norfolk.'

His father had started to smile, a sure sign he was about to relive the exciting events that had resulted in the unfortunate summons.

'I was in the Jag and had just left a jeweller's in Great

Yarmouth with a boot full of samples, rings and watches, thousands of pounds' worth of stock, and noticed I was being followed by a Ford Capri, typical villain's car. We got on the Acle straight, thought I'd open the taps to shake him off and we had a bit of a ding-dong for a few miles. It turned out to be an unmarked police car, one of those 3-litre jobs. He started flashing his lights, came past me and the back window lit up – "Police Stop". Bloody swines. Don't you talk to me about joining the police.'

Sam had been about to discuss the benefits of a police career when he'd noticed his father staring at the letter, chewing rather aggressively on his toast and clenching his fists, so he had dropped the subject. Instead he'd gazed out of the window at the trees swaying in the wind and became mesmerized by the sound of the rain beating on the window and drifted off into one of his daydreams, considering that the prospect of joining the traffic police and stopping his father for speeding or some other offence did hold some appeal…

Constable Samuel McAllister was sitting in his Rover patrol car, parked in a farm entrance with his colleague Constable Ivor Nickalotz, enjoying the peace of the countryside, watching the barley moving gently in a light breeze and listening to the song of skylarks high above. Suddenly two cars drove by approaching the village, followed by a white flash of a car overtaking them at speed. A horn sounded, not a melodious friendly tootle, but a horn blown with vigour and aggression. Sam watched as the white Jaguar MK2 moved abruptly back

to the left, having overtaken the two cars, just before it reached an oncoming tractor. The white Jaguar entered the village still travelling at considerable speed. Sam started the Rover and set off in pursuit with blue lights and sirens. He caught the white Jaguar, which had slowed down and pulled into a driveway. Sam stopped, blocking the driveway, and walked towards the car, its chrome wire wheels glinting in the sun.

'Oh, it's you,' said the driver with a look of relief on his face.

'Is this your car sir?' said Sam.

'Of course it's my car, you bloody idiot.'

'There's no need to take that attitude,' said Sam.

'You know very well it's my car you fool, you've been in it enough times. I used to take you to school in it not that long ago.'

'I only recall one occasion when you drove me to school in this, reluctantly as I remember. It was raining and you didn't want to get it wet, "damn nuisance" you said as I recall. Rather exuberant driving back there, sir, overtaking two cars as you approached an oncoming tractor and just before you reached the 30mph limit. Rather pointless really, wasn't it? Can I see your licence please, sir?' His father opened his wallet and handed Sam his licence. 'Is this still your current address shown on your licence, sir?'

'You're having a laugh, boy, you know bloody well it's my current address. You used to live here not that long ago and I'm parked on the blasted driveway. Have you got nothing better to do? You're wasting my time, your time and police time. Shouldn't you be out catching criminals?'

Sam's colleague, who had been checking the car's details, walked up to assist Sam. 'Have you got an awkward one here?'

'No, he's just got a bit of an attitude. I'm letting you off with a warning on this occasion, sir, just watch it in future...

His father's voice had ended Sam's dreamy thoughts. 'Are you daydreaming again? I suppose I'd better give you a lift to school, Sam, it's pouring with rain. I'll get the car wet. Damn nuisance.'

CHAPTER 2

Childhood thoughts ended abruptly with the sound of a key turning in the front door followed by footsteps in the hallway and the blurred outline of three figures approaching the frosted glass in the kitchen door. The door opened and Emma and her husband Kendrick entered followed by Duncan. Emma's entrance was accompanied by the usual soundtrack of the jingling bells that adorned her bracelets, her earrings and small bells attached to her handbag, the jingling sound reminding Sam of the approach of a court jester or morris dancer. The other distinctive sound of her approach was the clip-clop of her stilettos on the parquet floor. As always she was smartly and colourfully dressed, her long hair, once blonde, now greying gracefully, tied back in a ponytail still giving her a youthful appearance, denying her age approaching seventy.

She was followed into the kitchen by her husband Kendrick, a tall stocky man who usually dressed in black, always wore a waistcoat with a gold pocket watch on a chain and a Homburg hat whatever the weather. He oozed charisma. His short black hair was starting to turn grey. He had a greying goatee beard, spoke in a soft Scottish accent and, apart from the accent, always reminded Sam of Orson Wells.

Duncan, by contrast, was always dressed rather scruffily. His usual attire consisted of badly creased black trousers, white shirts with frayed cuffs and worn-out collars and a dirty old sports jacket, garments that he considered quite normal but which Sam thought gave him the appearance of a 1970s Burton's shop window manikin. Sam often despaired at his brother's dress sense, or lack of it, and today was no exception, as today being windy and damp, he was wearing his dirty fawn-coloured raincoat, which together with his dishevelled black hair gave him a strong resemblance to Lieutenant Columbo.

As Duncan followed Kendrick and Emma into the kitchen he started mumbling softly 'oh dear', an annoying habit of his when he couldn't think of anything worthwhile to say. He had taken the loss of their mother harder than Emma and Sam. Living next door he had had a closer relationship with her, spending more time with her, preparing her meals and making her life as comfortable as possible in her final years.

The mood was subdued and conversation difficult. Emma broke the silence. 'We're going to look through some papers and start to sort things out. There are people we need to notify of Mum's death. Kendrick's going to sort out the bills that need to be paid, notify the bank and sort out her pension. Things like that.'

'Oh dear,' said Duncan.

'Righty ho,' said Sam.

As Duncan, Emma and Kendrick left the kitchen and disappeared into the front room Sam started to follow but felt in the way, a little surplus to requirements and not required for the task ahead. He paused by the door of the lounge, which was the back room of the house. The door was closed. He hadn't been in the room for many years and as he opened the door he was greeted by a musty, damp aroma. The room was in darkness. He fumbled for the light switch. A ceiling light with three low-wattage bulbs gave a dull glow. The room hadn't been used much since his father's death six years earlier and the curtains had been permanently closed. It was a large 'L'-shaped room, which housed Bernard's collection of pianos and organs he'd acquired over the years. These included a huge Steinway concert grand piano, two upright pianos and two Hammond organs. The grand piano dominated the entire room and one had to squeeze by it sideways to gain access to the other parts of the room. As one walked round the 90-degree corner of the 'L'-shaped room and looked ahead, a large mirror taking up the entire end wall gave the illusion of a long corridor containing yet more pianos.

Bernard, his father, had been an accomplished classical and jazz pianist and had spent most of his many years of retirement in the lounge, also known as the piano room, playing his beloved Steinway grand piano, only leaving the room for a visit to the bathroom or when summoned by Bridget when his lunch or tea was ready. Occasionally she would enter the room (coughing first so as not to startle him) with a cup of tea or coffee and whisper in his ear 'drink for you, dear,' to which he would merely grunt in acknowledgement whilst continuing to play. The relentless piano playing went on for years. Sam remembered as a schoolboy being serenaded to sleep to the tones of Chopin and Liszt as his bedroom was immediately above the piano room. Occasionally there would be a break in the proceedings whilst his father stopped to relax with a whisky and cigar, only to resume a little later, continuing into the small hours, the evening usually being concluded with a rendition of "Lullaby of Birdland".

As a young boy, if Sam entered the room to bid his father goodnight, as he was required to do, he would stand by his side as he continued playing until he reached the end of the piece. Sam was having lessons himself and could read music well so he could follow the music being played, but he occasionally lost his place. Stopping and restarting was not an option for Bernard and, being determined to reach the end, he would shout "Turn, turn!" to Sam as an instruction to turn the page of music so that he might continue playing without having to pause to turn the page himself. If Sam accidentally turned two pages by mistake, piano keys would be thumped and his father would shout "you've ruined it! Now I'll have to start again". As time passed and Sam's knowledge of his father's repertoire increased, he began to recognise the stage of the piece being played and would time his entry to the room during the final few bars of the piece to avoid a lengthy wait or a reprimand for turning the pages incorrectly. Since his father's death six years earlier the room had fallen silent and the pianos and piles of music had gathered cobwebs and thick layers of dust.

Sam looked around the room which, like everything

else in the house, seemed to have remained exactly the same since his childhood. His gaze fell on the large tiled fireplace. It hadn't been used for many years but had been laid with screwed-up newspaper and twigs, the newspaper now brown with age and sprinkled with soot that had fallen down the chimney. On the mantelpiece was a 1950s electric clock, which no longer worked. His father had always been reluctant to disturb it to correct the time when the hour changed in the autumn for fear it would stop working, so rather confusingly it only displayed the correct time for six months of the year. Ironically, now it didn't work anyway. He flicked the switch to turn on the wall lights on either side of the fireplace, they didn't work either. Nothing seemed to work anymore. Sam looked at his father's old armchair in front of the fireplace and the chair opposite where he'd sat nearly forty years earlier on the eve of his wedding to Morag. He'd returned home late after a night out with Duncan and some friends to find his father sitting in front of the fire with a cigar and a large glass of whisky.

'Ah, Sam, you're back. Have a good evening? Your last evening of freedom.' He'd chuckled. 'It's your big day tomorrow then. Fancy A scotch?'

His father had then started talking in a strange way, rather like Noel Coward, a sure sign the conversation was to become serious – 'Come and sit beside me, upon the chair, before the fire. I'll get you a drink.'

Sam sat down by the fire, if it could be called a fire, two lumps of wet coal smouldering away underneath a damp green log with water and sap oozing from each end of the log and hissing as the liquid dropped onto a small flame in the coal. Suddenly the flame grew longer and started to roar as some gas within the coal escaped and ignited, producing an intense bright light and a brief burst of warmth before fizzling out. After this brief moment of excitement the fire had returned to its former state. Sam had become mesmerised by the hissing sound and his head had started to spin with the effects of the alcohol consumed during the evening. He'd continued to gaze into the fire and had noticed a woodlouse walking on top of the log, rather like a sailor walking on the upturned hull of a ship, waiting to be rescued before it sank into the icy depths of the ocean. Having probably been woken from its slumber from within a crack in the log the woodlouse had run one way, then the other, as it had desperately tried to avoid the growing flames and falling into the apocalyptic fire below. The prospect of a rescue was out of the question. Sam's father had been waging a personal war with woodlice in the house for years and had probably tossed it into the fire earlier. Sam hoped it would escape from what seemed certain death by suddenly leaping to safety and returning to thrive in some other part of the dark, damp room. As he'd sat there gazing into the fire he had compared himself to the woodlouse. The following day, he would also be escaping, escaping this stuffy, depressing house and his parents, to be with Morag in their new home, their independence and their new life together.

His father returned from the cocktail cabinet and handed Sam a glass of whisky, his hand shaking.

'Now then, Sam, there's something I want to talk to you about. I want to talk about ladies.'

'Ladies?'

'Yes, Sam – ladies.'

Oh my God, *thought Sam*. It's the birds and the bees talk. Please no, don't let it be that, for heaven's sake, I'm twenty-two.

'Er, yes, the ladies,' his father had continued rather nervously. 'Now er... yes well... you know what it's all about, don't you?'

'I don't know what you mean,' Sam had said, thinking he'd make this as difficult and embarrassing as possible for his father.

'The ladies,' repeated his father, who was now starting to perspire. 'You know all about the monthlies, don't you?'

'I don't know what you mean,' repeated Sam.

'The ladies and their monthlies – the time of the month,' said his father, raising his voice slightly in frustration.

'You mean when Aunt Flo comes a visiting?'

'Who the hell is Aunt Flo?' his father had shouted.

'That's a euphemism, and don't shout, you'll wake Mother.'

'Look, I'm talking about women trouble, the time of the month. Periods.'

'Yes, I know. The musician on the bicycle – the minstrel cycle,' Sam had said, starting to slur his words.

'No. The menstrual cycle, Sam.'

'That's what I said. I knew it had something to do with cycles, like the lunar cycle – comes round once a month.'

'Yes, well you have to be a bit understanding you see, at certain times of the month, gentle, not too demanding – they can get a bit, well, a bit touchy about that sort of thing.'

'What sort of thing?' Sam had asked.

'Well, physical things, that sort of thing, you know,' his father had said, winking at Sam.

'Bendy flex?' asked Sam.

'Bendy what?'

'Bendy flex. It's rhyming slang for sex.'

'I don't know what you mean, why don't you talk proper English? You're supposed to be a blasted English teacher.'

'Why don't you get to the point?'

'Look, this isn't easy for me, Sam.'

'It's not easy for me either. I haven't got a clue what you mean. Are you talking about Oedipus Rex? That's rhyming slang for sex as well by the way.'

'I don't know what you're talking about, boy.'

'This conversation's going round in circles. It started with me not knowing what you were talking about, now you don't know what I'm talking about. Shall we call it a night?' asked Sam.

His father sighed. 'Yes, I suppose so,' he conceded, frustrated that what he had intended to be a serious father-to-son conversation had turned out to be such a farce.

Sam had looked down again into the fire. There were no more flames, no smoke, it had fizzled out, but he noticed movement in the ash. The woodlouse had managed to flee what seemed certain death and was scrambling across the ash towards the front of the grate and freedom. Well done, thought Sam.

'I know all about that sort of thing' he said. He winked at his father, finished his whisky and walked towards the door. As he opened the door he looked back at his father. He was blushing, shaking his head, a cigar in one hand and a trembling whisky glass in the other.

'Goodnight,' said Sam.

The room had fallen silent many years ago, the aroma of log fires and his father's cigars long since gone, now replaced with the musty smell of a deserted, dusty and unloved room, a room that had become unused but still full of memories. Sam often wondered why he recalled so many conversations in such detail, conversations that had taken place so long ago. He remembered the smallest details of his past. He remembered some of his school friends' telephone numbers, even his mother's Co-op dividend number she used to give every time he went shopping with her as a small child at the local Co-op. Everyone has memories but his childhood memories seemed so vivid, so tangible, as if he was reliving them almost in real time.

He wondered what would happen to the house and its contents. He supposed it would have to be cleared and the house sold, which would be the normal course of events. Maybe a builder would renovate it and modernise it to make way for new occupants, so the house could live on in other people's lives.

As he walked slowly back towards the door he turned and looked again into the cold dimly lit room and for some inexplicable reason looked at his father's empty chair and said, 'Goodnight'.

He switched off the light, left the room and shut the door.

CHAPTER 3

There was the sound of rustling paper as Sam entered the front room. Emma was sorting through a pile of letters and paperwork on the large table, tearing off addresses and personal information from documents she had removed from the dusty wooden bureau that stood in the corner of the room.

'I'll take this pile home with me for shredding,' she said, 'and this pile of paper can be thrown out.'

'Recycled,' murmured Kendrick who had a passion for correctness and recycling.

'Quite correct, Kendrick. Recycled,' replied Emma.

Sam grunted in approval, walked towards the large front window and stood by Duncan, who was staring out of the window with a glazed, vacant expression on his face, his hands in his pockets jingling his keys rather annoyingly as he repeatedly said 'oh dear'. Sam stood by his side looking out at the passing traffic.

Kendrick was sitting in an armchair making notes in a notebook. He was a psychiatrist and a little older than Emma, who had worked as his secretary in Edinburgh for many years before they married and moved to London. He was a man of few words (unless they concerned correctness or recycling) but always appeared to Sam to be observing others and writing in his notebook.

Sam viewed psychiatrists with suspicion, almost a fear that went back to his college days. Some of his college friends had studied psychology and sociology and at break times he had often thought they were watching him, studying his movements and using him as subject matter for some bizarre research or a project they were undertaking. They used to write in notebooks too. It always used to give him an uneasy feeling, the feeling that he was being assessed or scrutinised. Kendrick stopped writing, looked up at Sam over the top of his half moon reading glasses then looked down and started making more notes. Sam shivered and looked around the room.

During his childhood in the 1960s it had always been a warm and cosy room but now, decades later, had become a dark, dismal and depressing place to be and the decor had remained exactly the same as it had been during his childhood days. The walls of the room were covered with dark-green flock wallpaper matching the heavy green velvet curtains now faded by the sun, the decor giving the room an almost Georgian appearance. They were the only things in the room that did match, the rest of the room being home to an eclectic mix of ornaments – a Louis XVI clock on the bureau, a 1920s cut glass decanter on the sideboard surrounded by old silverware and a collection of Willow Pattern pottery and other more modern china plates on display. A tall 1940s standard lamp that almost reached the ceiling stood next to the original 1950s tiled fireplace. In the fireplace was a dusty 1970s electric fire standing in front of the old Park Ray solid fuel fire, its glass door broken. In front of the hearth lay a threadbare rug with brown burn marks where sparks had landed years before. His mother's chair was by the fire with her crocheted shawl draped over one arm and her slippers on the floor. To the right of the fireplace was a round pin electric wall socket with numerous adaptors plugged into it. Even the electrical wiring in the house was the original from the 1950s with black rubber cable, round pin plugs and an old fuse box in the cupboard under the stairs that used old-fashioned fuses that one had to wrap fuse wire round when they blew. The ceiling light was lit, casting a dim yellow light around the room. The light had three wooden arms with a lamp containing a dim bulb at the end arm, the bulbs surrounded by cream-coloured lampshades made of what appeared to be thick yellow-coloured paper that had become scorched over the years from the heat of the bulbs. The dark and heavily carved furniture consisted of a large table, a sideboard and a bureau, all of which dated back to the 1930s, no doubt intended to reside in a far grander room in a far more opulent house and, together with the other old furniture in the house, was an encumbrance, an unwanted legacy for the next generation.

On the opposite side of the road were four large detached houses built in what was once a farmer's field, their 1960s construction a contribution to the expansion of urban sprawl – cornfields and meadows replaced with concrete, cul-de-sacs and housing estates. The house on the extreme left of the four had a stone wall that separated it from the large imposing church and graveyard and was occupied by Mrs Beatrice Bassett, recently widowed for the second time at the age of sixty. She was not unattractive and often considered by the opposite sex to be of pleasing proportions, had long flowing grey hair, was always dressed immaculately and not shy to display her generous physical features. She was sitting in her front porch as she often did, observing the comings and goings of the neighbours performing their daily routines: the children next door leaving for their walk to school; Mr Woodruff the bank manager, who lived two doors away, leaving for work a little earlier today and without kissing his wife goodbye as she stood at the open front door, *most unusual, they must have had a tiff,* Beatrice thought. Her attention was drawn to the McAllisters' house immediately opposite. She had been taking great interest in the activities at the McAllister residence that morning, having observed the arrival of Sam, followed later by Duncan emerging from the neighbouring house just after Emma and Kendrick had arrived and parked on his driveway. She watched the activity in the front room of the McAllister's house and saw Sam and Duncan standing near the window looking out when a bus pulled up at the bus stop outside her house, inconveniently blocking her view. It was the number three for the town centre. She looked at her watch – four minutes early. The driver stepped off the bus and lit a cigarette. After lowering her binoculars and refilling her glass from the sherry bottle that stood on the small glass table next to her wicker chair, she picked up her newspaper and resumed the crossword. Two across – a dark fortified wine produced in Jerez – seven letters. O something O something O something O. She looked at the sherry bottle on the table and filled in the blanks – Oloroso, her favourite early morning tipple. The bus driver threw his cigarette end onto the path, trod on it with his right foot, stepped back on the bus and drove away, leaving behind a cloud of black smoke. She raised her binoculars again – Sam and Duncan were still standing in the window.

*

Sam used to stand on that same spot as a schoolboy looking out of the window and watching the world go by. On one occasion he'd looked out into the twilight gloom of a November evening, the tall spire of the church opposite silhouetted against the mist and descending fog like the sails of a great ship appearing through the murk. Occasionally people had walked briskly by, their heads lowered and coat collars turned up against the chill of the autumn air. A Routemaster double-decker bus had appeared through the gloom, its bright-red outline standing out vividly against the grey background as it passed by the house scattering leaves in its wake. Two beams of light from its headlights had attempted to penetrate the thickening fog and its crowded upper deck was brightly lit, showing the outline of anonymous people making their way home. After the bus had passed by and disappeared into the darkness, silence had returned, the silence that often accompanies the gloom and murkiness of a foggy autumn evening. The silence had been broken as the grandfather clock in the hall had struck six. At the time Sam had thought there was something rather comforting looking out on such an evening from the warmth and security of the house, the coal fire glowing in the hearth and the smell of his mother's cooking drifting through from the kitchen. He'd continued to gaze from the window, mesmerised by the fog swirling around the dimly lit street light opposite the house when suddenly his father's Jaguar had turned onto the driveway. Sam had felt a little disappointed as his father walked towards the garage doors, ignoring him as he'd watched from the window. Having opened the garage doors his father had walked back to the car through the misty vapour dancing in the brightness of the headlights. As he'd started to drive the car into the garage Sam had left the room to switch on the porch light for his father.

'He's home, Mother,' he had shouted to his mother in the kitchen. 'I think he's in a bad mood.' He was usually in a bad mood.

His mother had groaned. 'Thank you, dear,' she'd replied.

Sam had returned to the front room and resumed his position standing at the front window, gazing out into the murky evening, when his father had entered the room.

'What are you doing staring out of the window, boy? Daydreaming again I suppose. Have you nothing better to do? Here's a question for you. Which country's name sounds like a type of weather?'

He'd hated his father asking difficult questions. He was always asking difficult questions. His father sat in his chair and lit his pipe and for several minutes Sam had thought of all the country names he knew, starting with the nearest –

France, Belgium, Germany – then with a look of relief Sam had shouted, 'Iceland!'

'No, no, Sam'

'Well ice is a sort of weather.'

'No, Sam, think again. I'll give you a clue. It's a South American country.'

Sam couldn't think of any South American countries so he'd stood in silence, started to quiver nervously as he pretended to think.

'It's obvious, Sam. Think, boy, think!' his father had shouted.

'I don't know. I give up,' Sam had said sheepishly as tears had started to trickle down his cheeks.

'Give up? You won't get far in life if you give up ,boy!' his father had shouted. 'It's Chile! That's the answer! Chile...'

'This is interesting,' Emma said, breaking Sam's dreamy thoughts as she passed him an old crumpled letter across the table. It was a handwritten copy of a letter his father had written to the chief constable of Norfolk regarding his notorious speeding fine in 1974 that had been discussed over the breakfast table all those years ago. Sam started to read the lengthy letter. It was a wonderfully worded account of the events, the events as perceived by his father and well worthy of consideration as a plot for a crime novel or gangster film. It described his work in the wholesale jewellery trade and how, having left his customer's jewellery shop in Great Yarmouth with the boot of his car loaded with valuable samples – gems, rings and watches, he was convinced that he was being pursued by two villains in a Ford Capri intent on forcing him off the road to rob him of his valuable cargo. He had attempted to justify his speeds in excess of 100mph in the ensuing chase over several miles along the Acle straight between Yarmouth and Norwich as his attempt to avoid being robbed. The letter went on to describe his relief that his pursuers were policemen and he'd complimented the chief constable on the pleasant demeanour of his officers and their driving ability. The letter concluded with a plea for leniency, obviously in a desperate attempt to avoid a driving ban, considering he needed his licence for his occupation.

Sam could only imagine the chief constable's reaction to the letter and his father's account of the events as perceived by him. He was unlikely to have been impressed with his officers being portrayed as suspected criminals or modern-day highwaymen and even less impressed with Bernard McAllister's reckless driving that would undoubtedly have been highlighted in his officer's report. The many hours his father must have spent concocting his wonderful work of fiction had been wasted, a six-week driving ban had been imposed in addition to a hefty fine.

'I'd like to keep this, Emma. I remember this.'

'Keep it if you like. It's not important.'

It was important to Sam. He folded it carefully and put it in his jacket pocket. He'd keep it for posterity.

Later, as he sat in his car on the driveway of the old family home, Sam looked at the house, now fading into the gloom of the late October afternoon with dusk fast approaching.

Emma and Kendrick had left for home, Emma with her bag of papers to shred and Kendrick with his notebook. Duncan had locked the house and, after a cursory "goodnight" to Sam, had returned to his house next door, closed the squeaky wrought-iron gate and walked slowly up the gravel path to his front door. As Sam watched his brother he thought he saw the dark outline of a figure turning and moving away from one of the front bedroom windows. He shivered and convinced himself it was the reflection of the tall fir tree in the churchyard opposite moving in the breeze. After Duncan had entered the house a dim light appeared in the front room before the curtains were closed.

Beatrice Bassett watched as Sam drove away, then she locked her porch door and retired to the warmth of her lounge. Unable to satisfy her curiosity regarding the strange activities at the house opposite, she decided to consult her sister Brenda Brierley, the school secretary at the comprehensive school where Sam McAllister worked. She was the fount of all, not so much knowledge as gossip and scandal; the personal confidante of Sam McAllister and other members of staff, a sort of perfect aunt to whom one could discuss trials and tribulations and problems in assumed confidence, a shoulder to cry on in times of need. She had become a useful source of information and intelligence gathering for her inquisitive sister and when quizzed usually responded with "*well, I'm not one to gossip but…*" before freely passing on information that had been given to her in confidence.

Beatrice telephoned her sister and explained the strange goings-on at the McAllister residence that morning.

'Well, as you know, Beatrice, I'm not known for spreading tittle-tattle but apparently Samuel McAllister telephoned Mr Smedley-Barrington the headmaster early this morning to say his mother had passed away and he wouldn't be in school today and I did hear that Mr Smedley-Barrington had given him a few days off. Apparently his brother Duncan, you know the mystery man who lives next door, had taken it particularly bad, what with living next door and looking after her 'n' all. Stands to reason I suppose, don't it, taking it bad.'

CHAPTER 4

The fact that his brother lived in the house next door to the old family home had always puzzled Sam after the previous occupant Reginald Ramsbottom had bequeathed the property to Duncan in his will twenty years earlier. Why he should have done that Sam had never really understood. Even more puzzling was that Duncan, a bachelor as Reginald Ramsbottom had been, should leave the house exactly as it was when Reginald Ramsbottom lived there. All his possessions and furniture had remained where they were, where they had always been. Nothing was moved, nothing discarded.

Reginald Ramsbottom, or Reg as he had been known, had been a tall, skinny man, a strict vegetarian and didn't wear anything made of leather – even his shoes were plastic. He always appeared to wear the same clothes: a dark suit, grubby shirts that were frayed at the collars and cuffs, no socks and always the same plastic shoes. His clothes always looked creased and greasy and smelt filthy. He never washed his straggly black greasy hair and there was always a scattering of dandruff on his jacket collar. He always had a haggard expression and some of his facial features were unsymmetrical, particularly his large bushy black eyebrows, one of which appeared to be higher than the other. They almost joined together above his nose and resembled the bristles of large hand brushes. To say he had large ears would be an understatement, they were enormous, but again one appeared to be higher than the one on the opposite side. Sam, as a youngster, had often studied them with an obsessive interest. Never before had he seen such disproportionally large elephantine human ears and he had often thought if they were both folded forwards they would cover his eyes and meet his nose, not that his nose would want to meet them. When Reg chatted over the garden fence with Sam's mother on windy days his huge dangling earlobes moved in the breeze in a strange rippling motion. Sam's father had small ears in comparison and Sam wondered whether he had inherited his own fascination with ears from his father, who had often pointed at the television when aging politicians were being interviewed, saying "cor, look at his ears, like cabbages" accompanied by prolonged chuckling. The other strange thing with Reg's ears was the amount of hair growing from them, great clumps of black hair protruding from them like a chimney sweep's brush appearing from a chimney pot. Reg had a similar problem with nasal hair, which moved in the breeze when he breathed through his nose; the hair completely disappeared when breathing in quickly or sniffing, only to reappear when exhaling.

Having retired as a jeweller, Reginald Ramsbottom continued to carry out watch and clock repairs in one of the bedrooms of his house he had converted into a workshop, although the room was filthy and dusty and not suitable for precision watch repairs. The walls of the room were fitted with shelving, which housed numerous televisions, old reel-to-reel tape recorders and hundreds of reels of tape. The linoleum floor was covered in thick dust, large cobwebs hung from the ceiling and paint was peeling from the door and cupboards.

As a schoolboy Sam would sit up in the workshop with Reg, watching him carry out his clock and watch repairs, working with tiny springs, cogs and screws with a black magnifying lens clenched tightly to his right eye, his face screwed up to prevent it from falling out. The room was poorly lit, the only light being a rusty Anglepoise lamp on the workbench and the heat from its 60-watt bulb appeared to be Reg's only source of warmth in the room.

'Hey ho, it's cold tonight, I'll have to put a 100-watt bulb in,' he had once said to Sam. As he'd spoken his breath had visibly floated up towards the light bulb in the Anglepoise lamp before disappearing as he'd desperately tried to pick up a small screw with some tweezers, his hand shaking uncontrollably with the cold. His nose was running and a dewdrop clinging to his nasal hair threatened to fall into the delicate watch mechanism below before being wiped away with the back of a shaking hand.

Shortly after his move to Lincolnshire in the 1960s he had traded his old Volkswagen Beetle in for a nearly new Jaguar E-Type, a car which he only used on Saturdays, his Sabbath, when he would drive to his strange church somewhere in Hertfordshire, about 90 miles away. On

Saturday evenings, from the seclusion of his summer house retreat, the schoolboy Sam would often hear the crunch of gravel on the driveway next door as the E-Type returned from the visit to the Church of… whatever it was called in Hertfordshire and he would run round next door and chat with Reg as he washed the car down. In the summer months the remains of flies and moths would be removed from the windscreen and the front of the long bonnet, removing all traces of their brief existence. Steam would rise from the hot bonnet as it was vigorously scrubbed, releasing the lovely hot aroma that only cars of that era seemed to produce. The finale to the washing was to throw several buckets of water over the car as a final rinse. The car, dripping wet, was then immediately driven into the garage where it would remain for another week. Reg, who was always quoting from the Bible would then open his front door, enter his dark hallway and fumble for the light switch, saying, '*Lighten our darkness we beseech thee O Lord.* Goodnight, Sam.'

*

'It'll rust away in no time if he carries on like that,' Bernard McAllister had said when Sam had relayed the method of car washing to his father. 'A car like that needs looking after properly, pampering, caressing like a woman. Still, he wouldn't know about that either. The man's a bloody fool.'

Several things had always puzzled Sam about Reginald Ramsbottom – why had he moved all the way from Northumberland to South Lincolnshire when he retired? Why had he bought the house next door? What was his relationship with his mother? Was it more than neighbourly? Sam's father travelled a lot with his work and from an early age Sam remembered Reg always being around, although he seldom came round when his father was at home. There were visits to the cinema in the school holidays with his mother and Reg – the Battle of Britain film – that was 1969 when Sam was ten. There were other visits to the cinema, other films – *Jungle Book, The Italian Job*, always with his mother and Reg. He was always about, always there. His father's relationship with Reg had deteriorated. They used to be the best of friends, now they rarely spoke and every time his name was mentioned his father seemed to criticise and belittle him.

He also developed his own peculiar smell and as time passed the aroma had become more and more obnoxious. Sam recalled one of Reg's visits to see his mother and she had confronted him on the delicate subject of his personal hygiene:

'I don't know what's become of you', she said in despair. 'Your standards seem to have dropped since you lost your mother. I don't know what she'd say if she could see you now. You used to be so smart, nicely dressed and clean shaven. Now look at you, you look like a tramp and you don't smell much better either. When was the last time you had a bath?'

'I don't have baths and I don't wash with soap and water, it's unnecessary. I use the friction rub method.'

'What on earth are you talking about?' asked Bridget.

'The friction rub method – I use a large towel and rub it over my dry body to remove any dirt and dry skin. It saves water and seems quite effective.'

'Nonsense,' Bridget replied. 'Not from where I'm standing. You can't be serious. Do you never have a bath?'

'Certainly not, it's a waste of water and anyway the taps don't work. Someone does call on me occasionally to wash my feet.'

Bridget looked at Reg in astonishment. 'What on earth are you talking about, man?'

He explained that his religion involved the ritual of the washing of the feet and occasionally other members of the congregation would call and would perform this ablutionary function on each other. Reg's annoying habit of quoting extracts from the Bible was often used in order to justify his strange ways. He explained, 'John Chapter 13: verses 1-17 recounts Jesus's performance of this act. In verses 14-17 He instructs His disciples: If I then your Lord and Teacher have washed your feet, you also ought to wash one another's feet. I have given you an example that you should do as I have done to you.'

'My God, man, and what pray do you wash your pedal extremities in if the bath is out of action?' Bridget asked with a look of astonishment.

'We boil the kettle, go in the front room and use the washing up bowl' was his unashamed reply.

'The man's a bloody nutter!' exclaimed Bridget (who normally never swore) as she relayed this latest revelation to the rest of the family over the dinner table amid requests not to discuss the next-door neighbour's feet whilst they were eating.

'Then he started quoting from the Bible again,' she said. 'He's always quoting from the Bible. I remember in 1969 *before the Apollo 11 mission he said that man would never walk on the moon, claiming it says so in the Bible, something to do with space travel and Man not visiting other worlds.'*

'He got that one wrong as well,' said Bernard. *'I should have had a fifty pound bet with him on that one. That would have shut him up, but then I suppose I'd have got a lecture about the evils of gambling. It's a pity his weird friends didn't give him a good scrub all over. Last time I spoke to him I couldn't get within six feet the smell was so bad. The other morning I got out of bed, opened the bedroom window to take in the morning air, looked next door and he was doing the same with his head and skinny neck sticking out of the window, looked like a blasted tortoise with its head sticking out of its shell. I gave him a quote or two from the Bible last time he came round here talking about his religion – Matthew Chapter 27 Verse 5 "And he went and hanged himself" followed by Luke Chapter 10 Verse 37 "Go and do thou likewise".'*

Oh no, *thought Sam*, he's off. He'll go on like this for hours, once he gets started there'll be no stopping him, moan, moan, moan. *He was right.*

As Bernard poured milk from a small jug into his tea, a dribble of milk landed on the tablecloth.

'Damn the blasted thing! Why can't anybody design anything properly anymore? Why can't someone make a milk jug that pours properly without this happening every time? This country used to make wonderful cars, aircraft and trains, now we can't even make a sodding milk jug that works.'

'Cameras as well,' said Duncan after a few seconds, breaking an awkward silence.

'Eh?'

'We used to make good cameras, good quality, well engineered.'

'Yes, I suppose we did,' replied his father, starting to froth at the mouth.

'Motorcycles as well,' said Duncan 'Nortons and Triumphs.'

'Bridges,' said Emma, 'we used to make excellent bridges, engineers like Isombard Kingdom Brunel. I remember learning about him at school.'

'Yes all right, we get the idea. The point I'm making is we can't make anything now that works properly. Look at the crap British Leyland churns out. No wonder everybody's buying Japanese cars. It's the blasted government and the unions, that's the problem. They spend more time on strike than they do at work.' He had a second attempt to pour the milk with the same result. 'Probably made in China anyway, blasted thing. They'll end up taking over the—'

'Why don't you take your cup of tea into the lounge dear and have a cigar?' said Bridget, hoping he would leave the room and the rest of the family in peace. He stood up, still in a state of rage, slowly making his way to the door with the cup and saucer rattling in his left hand. As the door closed behind him there was a sigh of relief from Bridget followed by, 'My God. That blasted man. Dear oh dear.'

CHAPTER 5

Sam removed a dozen copies of George Orwell's novel *Nineteen Eighty-Four* from the cupboard and placed a copy on each of the empty desks. He paused by a desk, raised a copy of the book to his face, flicked the pages from cover to cover with his thumb and inhaled that lovely aroma of a new book, the scent of virgin pages untouched and unturned by human hands. He loved the aroma of old books as well, that aged musty aroma of an old book that had remained unopened on a bookshelf for years gathering dust, longing to be selected, opened and enjoyed again. To Sam a good novel was a wonderful fulfilling experience, a journey into the imagination. If a worthy book was retained and cherished then that experience could be repeated, the book revisited and enjoyed again later in life, to rekindle the experience, to relive the journey.

He had discovered an old paperback copy of *The Sandcastle* by Iris Murdoch several weeks previously whilst in his attic. The book had been one of his set works he studied for his 'O' level English literature exam forty-four years earlier. This particular book was the edition with the face of a beautiful young woman on the iconic front cover, a blonde with stunning facial features wearing round, black wire-framed tinted spectacles. Having been reunited with the book he had once again gazed in wonder at the beauty of the face on the front cover as he had as a fifteen-year-old, transfixed by its beauty, the perfection of the nose, eyes and lips of the anonymous face on the cover of the book. The face seemed to be almost monochrome apart from the brown tinted spectacles, which seemed to draw one's attention to the beauty of the eyes. When he was first given the book by his English teacher, a Welshman by the name of Evans, Sam as an impressionable youth had become obsessed with what had appeared to him at the time to be the face of a mature woman. He had estimated her age to be about thirty, double his own age at the time. He had fallen in love for the first time, fallen in love with a face on the front cover of a book. As a schoolboy he had probably spent as much time staring lustfully at the front cover as he had actually spent reading the book. Having rediscovered and reread the book again at the age of fifty-nine she now looked youthful, certainly young enough to be his daughter.

He thought of his secondary school English teacher Mr Evans, who, like Sam, had walked round his empty classroom placing copies of a book on the empty desks before his class arrived. What had been Mr Evans' opinion of the anonymous young lady on the front cover? Had he, like Sam, been transfixed by her beauty, or perhaps harboured feelings of lust and desire? Had he gazed into the eyes behind the brown tinted glasses like Sam every time he picked up the book? When all were present and seated Mr Evans had stood at the front of the class with a copy of *The Sandcastle* clutched to his chest with both hands, his head raised and eyes shut as if he'd been seeking divine inspiration from above. Then, as he'd held the book in his left hand he'd caressed the front of the book with his right hand as if caressing the face of the beautiful woman on the cover. He had then raised the book above his head and said his in his deep, loud Welsh voice, 'You will be studying this novel, *The Sandcastle* by Iris Murdoch. It's a wonderful novel. I read it yesterday.'

Yesterday! Sam had thought. *How can he read that in a day?* He had immediately turned to the back of the book to see how many pages there were – three hundred and thirteen pages of fairly small print. How could he read that in a day? Sam had enjoyed reading as a boy but such activities were usually confined to reading in bed having retired for the night. Two or three pages was all he could manage before drifting off to sleep, still clutching his book with the sound of the inevitable piano playing from the room below. Some time afterwards there would be a vague recollection of his father's voice saying "put that light out" as he entered Sam's bedroom rather noisily to turn off the bedside light. When opening his book the following night he was usually unable to remember what he had read about the previous night, so would have to turn back the pages and start again. As a result it took Sam weeks, if not months, to complete a book, so the revelation that Mr Evans had read *The Sandcastle* in one day had left a lasting impression on him.

*

His class began to enter the room as Sam finished distributing copies of *Nineteen Eighty-Four* and he returned to his desk at the front of the class. When the assemblage was complete, and still thinking of Mr Evans, Sam decided to repeat the words of his old English teacher. He raised the book above his head, looked rather nervously at the class seated in front of him and said, 'Good morning, everybody. On your desks you have one of the novels you will be studying for your exams next year –*Nineteen-Eighty-Four* by George Orwell. It's a wonderful novel. I read it yesterday.' (In fact it had taken him three days.) There was silence. No gasps of admiration of his achievement. He scanned the faces of the class in front of him. There was a general look of indifference on the vacant, expressionless, comatose faces that looked back at him. All looked singularly unimpressed.

George Orwell's *Nineteen Eighty-Four* was a particular favourite of Sam's. He had read it several times over the years and on every reading he discovered something new, the use of the strange vocabulary and the futuristic interpretation of the English language, the attempted simplification of the language by erasing and deleting unnecessary words from it. George Orwell's vision of the future of the English language fascinated him, but fortunately it hadn't become reality.

Later, in the staffroom with a free period, Sam sat alone, deep in thought, coming to terms with the loss of his mother and the challenge that lay ahead with the clearing of number fifty-seven Stonebridge Road and ultimately its sale.

He removed an envelope from his jacket pocket, took out the letter his father had written to the chief constable of Norfolk in 1974 and read it again, chuckling at his father's audacious attempt to justify driving at over 100mph for a considerable distance along the Acle straight.

At least the roads will be safer for a few weeks, Sam had thought back then. How wrong he'd been. His father's mother, Granny McAllister, came to stay for the duration of the ban, chauffeuring him around the country in her Mini Traveller so he could continue his work.

Sam had watched in horror as Granny McAllister arrived just before teatime one Sunday afternoon, turning off the road into the driveway too fast and braking heavily to avoid hitting one of the brick gate pillars. He had rushed out to greet her just as she was reversing back out onto the road into the path of a passing car. The driver had blown his horn and shouted some obscenities out of the open passenger window. Unperturbed, she had selected a forward gear and the car had suddenly lurched forwards into the drive, the front wheels locking as she'd stopped abruptly to avoid hitting the garage doors.

'Darling, how lovely to see you. Granny's come to stay for a few weeks while she drives Daddy around in her car and probably round the bend too. Silly Daddy's lost his licence. Still, I expect you know all about that. Be a darling and take my cases in for me' she'd said as she opened the rear doors of the Mini Traveller. Sam had carried two heavy cases through the open front door and put them down in the hall.

'Thank you, dear,' she'd said as she slipped him 10p as if he was a hotel porter being rewarded with a tip. 'Where is your silly daddy?'

His father had emerged from the front room carrying a bottle of wine in one hand and a corkscrew in the other. 'Hello, Mother. I'd prefer you didn't call me that in front of Sam. I get little respect from him as it is without you referring to me as silly.'

'Well you are silly, and a nincompoop too losing your licence like that. What were you thinking of? Being chased by bandits indeed. What a load of tosh. Never mind, Mummy's here to help.'

His father had grunted and disappeared back into the room with his wine bottle and cork screw. Shortly afterwards there was a loud pop followed by 'oh bugger!' as wine had sprayed out of the bottle all over the freshly laid table.

'Bridget! Bridget! Bring a cloth!' he'd exclaimed.

'Silly Daddy,' Granny McAllister had said, with the bangles on her wrists rattling as she'd ruffled Sam's hair.

*

Sam had always looked forward to Granny McAllister's visits. His mother would cook lovely meals, make wonderful blackberry and apple pies, her specialty, and he would sometimes be allowed a small glass of wine with his dinner. The dining table would be perfectly laid with the best tablecloth, starched napkins, silver salt and pepper pots, cut-glass wine glasses and the best silver cutlery monogrammed with an "M" was used. Maybe she'd thought this was how the McAllisters lived all the time but a special effort was made by Sam's mother to impress her, to put on a show as if to prove (not that she needed to) how well she was looking after Bernard "her boy" as Granny often referred to him.

Granny McAllister had been a slim, very elegant and very 'proper' lady with grey permed hair usually with a pink tint and pink spectacles to match. She was born in 1901, the year Queen Victoria died, and was a remnant of the Edwardian period. When Sam was older, after Granny McAllister had passed away, he had often thought of her, what she must have been like as a young lady in the carefree and exciting times of the Roaring Twenties. Despite her elegance and 'correctness' she'd had a wicked sense of humour and would tell stories about her early life and jokes that made his father blush.

The day she had arrived for her six-week visit, when they all sat down at the table for their tea she'd said, 'I watched *The Two Ronnies* last night. It was a scream. Did you see it?'

'Er, yes,' his father had said as he'd poured the wine.

'There was a lovely sketch with them as two old men describing the size of women's bosoms.'

'Yes we saw it,' replied his father, who had appeared anxious for the details not to be repeated at the table in front of Sam. He always seemed to become embarrassed when something slightly rude or suggestive came on the television, as if it was inappropriate for his fifteen-year-old son to witness. When they had watched it the previous evening his father had opened his newspaper and concealed himself behind it, although Sam had noticed it shaking as his father no doubt chuckled, unseen by the others in the room. Sam and his mother had found it moderately entertaining, as no doubt had his father hiding behind the trembling local *Evening Telegraph*. Why hide behind a newspaper and chuckle? Was he embarrassed to show his amusement? Granny McAllister wasn't, she'd thought it was a "scream". Surely he couldn't have had such a strict upbringing with a mother like Granny McAllister, a person so lively, so entertaining, so contemporary and vibrant.

Granny McAllister had ignored his father's intransigence and had continued, 'One of them described a woman he knew as having had breasts the size of melons, another woman's were like oranges and another the size of eggs… fried!'

'Yes. We did see it, Mother. Help yourself to the salad' he'd said, desperate to change the subject.

'It was a scream!' she'd exclaimed as she shrieked with laughter and started waving her arms about in excitement as if she was swiping a wasp.

His father started to pour the wine. 'Yes, we saw it, Mother,' he'd repeated. 'I've got a bottle of your favourite wine for you.'

Granny McAllister raised her glass. 'Thank you, dear. Well here's to the Norfolk Constabulary for allowing me to come and stay with you for six weeks. It'll be a hoot!'

Sam's father had groaned. Then Granny McAllister had bitten heavily into a spring onion.

The noise Granny McAllister made when eating had always intrigued Sam. When he was younger he'd often wondered what the noise was but now as a fifteen-year

-old, with his expanding knowledge of life's mysteries, he'd realised it was the sound of her dentures rattling as she chewed. It was a distinctive sound, rather like that of a car's exhaust system being dragged along the road in the distance. The other fascinating thing was when she drank from her glass of wine the rim of the glass turned a deep red colour. Sam couldn't decide whether it was lipstick or beetroot. Granny McAllister liked beetroot. They only had beetroot when Granny came to stay.

*

'Bernard darling,' Granny McAllister had said after they'd finished their meal.

'Yes, Mother.'

'While I'm staying with you can you arrange for your lovely neighbour Reginald Ramsbottom to bring round his trays of rings one day? I'd like a new sapphire ring.'

'Yes, Mother.'

Sensing that the conversation was about to get all grown-up and boring, Sam had asked if he could leave the table. 'I have to go to the bottom of the garden to check my gentles,' he'd said quite innocently. He remembered Granny McAllister had shrieked with laughter.

'Check your what?' she'd asked, having first adjusted her false teeth, which had been dislodged through strenuous laughter.

'My gentles, my maggots for fishing, they're called gentles,' Sam had said quite innocently. He had learnt the new name for maggots from his *Begin Fishing with Uncle Bill* fishing book and thought the use of the alternative word for maggots would impress his grandmother, not cause hysterical laughter.

'Yes, darling,' she'd said, 'you go down the garden and check your gentles if you need to.'

Sam had left the room, shut the door and walked down the hall to the sound of his grandmother shrieking with laughter.

The following day, Sam and his mother had watched in horror as Granny McAllister, accompanied by his father, set off in her Mini Traveller, the car being steered abruptly, gears crunched and the clutch being slipped. His father had shouted instructions and waved his arms in frustration as the car had disappeared down the road in a cloud of smoke.

That same day, whilst in a school biology lesson, he had discovered the meaning of the word "genitals", which he had concluded must have been the cause of his grandmother's amusement at the dinner table.

His lifelong fascination with words and the complexity of the English language had begun.

CHAPTER 6

Reginald Ramsbottom eagerly anticipated the occasional visits of Bernard McAllister's mother. She had good taste, an eye for a bargain and her requests for him to call next door with his jewellery gave him the opportunity to sell some of his old stock and make a little money. It also gave him the opportunity to indulge in a glass of sherry. He didn't drink, or at least he shouldn't, the total abstinence of alcohol being a requirement of his strange religion. He was frequently quoting Ephesians 5:18: *"And do not get drunk with wine, for that is debauchery, but be filled with the Spirit"*. Granny McAllister liked a sherry and he was invariably offered a glass when he called next door to see her. He didn't want to appear rude and, after all, it would be rude not to accept. Maybe he'd make an exception if he was offered a glass when he called later that day.

He approached his tumbling-down greenhouse, walking through the long grass of his overgrown lawn, fighting his way through the nettles and ivy that had established themselves where the door had once been. He cut a path through into the greenhouse with a pair of garden shears and trod carefully on the broken glass that had fallen from the roof, cursing aloud as a startled blackbird flew out past his face. He lifted a large flower pot and retrieved a key concealed underneath and then pulled up clumps of bindweed to reveal a large safe that had once resided in the stock room of his jeweller's shop in Northumberland, a very heavy safe with a large brass handle on the door. The key was quite rusty and the lock stiff but he eventually opened the door to reveal trays of jewellery, the remainder of his stock from his shop that he had brought with him when he'd retired and moved down to Lincolnshire. He lifted six trays out and put them on top of the safe while he locked the door and returned the key to its hiding place under the flower pot. Having carried the trays back through the long grass into the house, he put them on the table in the front room, opened their lids and pulled back the thick velvet cloth covering the precious contents. Three trays contained ladies' rings with beautiful stones that still gleamed in the sunlight despite having been kept for years in the damp safe in the greenhouse. There were sapphires, rubies, amethysts and emeralds all set into beautiful delicate ladies' gold and silver rings. The other trays contained earrings, brooches and gold and silver necklaces. He removed a dead earwig from one of the trays, closed the lid and blew off the dust.

As he opened the curtains in his front room he heard car tyres crunching on the gravel driveway next door and watched as a blue MGB Roadster pulled slowly onto the driveway of the McAllisters' house. It was 06:35, *a bit early for visitors,* he thought.

Nicolas Postlethwaite had left London at five o'clock that Sunday morning and headed North on a deserted A1 towards South Lincolnshire. He was a little apprehensive about his surprise visit to Emma's home on her birthday, unsure how she would react to his romantic gallantry. He pulled onto the gravel driveway as slowly as possible to avoid making too much noise, unaware that he was being observed by Reginald Ramsbottom from the neighbouring house. He picked up a bunch of red roses from the passenger seat and walked along the gravel path in the front garden, pausing briefly to admire the ornamental wishing well. He stood underneath the small bedroom window that was above the front porch, which he recalled was Emma's room. It had been a warm night, the window was open and the curtains still closed. He picked up a few small stones from the gravel path and gently tossed them up at the window.

Granny McAllister was awoken by a tapping on the window. The tapping noise stopped and she started to doze off again. There it was again, a tapping on the window pane. *Must be a bird,* she thought. She didn't like birds so she got out of bed to close the window in case it came into the bedroom. As she opened the curtains she heard a man's voice as Nicolas Postlethwaite started to sing "Happy Birthday" very softly from below her window. She looked down and saw a stocky young man in his twenties with rosy cheeks holding a large bunch of red roses. He was wearing a tweed jacket, white scarf and cloth cap. 'Looks like Mr Toad from *Wind in the Willows.*' She chuckled. "Happy Birthday" was followed by a louder rendition of "My Love is Like a Red, Red Rose". Singing with his eyes shut and arms outstretched with the bunch of roses in his left hand, he opened his eyes at the end of the first verse to see Granny McAllister leaning out of the window, her greying dishevelled hair and most of her bosom displayed to the world. With a big smile on her face she began to sing *"Don't bring me roses..."* She got the lyrics muddled up and after the first two lines forgot the words.

'That's lovely,' she said in a soft voice. 'No one's ever sung beautifully like that to me before, really lovely of you, but it's not my birthday. Who are you?'

'Er... I'm Nicolas Postlethwaite,' he said, starting to blush profusely. 'I'm a friend of Emma's. I thought I'd surprise her on her birthday. I'm really sorry. I thought that was her bedroom.'

'It is her room but she's in the back bedroom now with her two brothers. I'm her father's mother and chauffeuse, come to stay for a few weeks to drive him around, probably around the bend too. He's lost his licence, silly Billy.'

'You must think I'm an idiot. I'm really sorry, I didn't know you were in there.'

'Not at all, dear, don't apologise. I think you're a charming young man. It was a lovely thought. I'm sure Emma will be pleased to see you.'

Bernard McAllister, who had been awoken by the singing and loud voices, flung open his window in the adjoining bedroom, looked down at the stranger holding a bunch of red roses in conversation with his mother, who was still leaning out of her window.

'Who the bloody hell are you?' he shouted. 'What was all that singing? Are you drunk?'

'He was singing to me, dear,' said Granny McAllister from her window. 'Wasn't that lovely of him?'

'You can bugger off. That's my mother. She's old enough to be your granny.'

'Look, I can explain…'

'Don't bother!' shouted Bernard putting on his dressing gown. 'I'm coming down to sort you out, carrying on like that with my mother, it's disgusting.'

As Bernard opened the front door Nicolas put down the roses and raised his hands saying, 'Mr McAllister it's all a terrible mistake. My name is Nicolas Postlethwaite. I'm a friend of your daughter. I thought I'd surprise her on her birthday. I thought that was her room. How was I supposed to know your mother was in there?'

'Any normal person would phone to say they were calling or better still ask if it was convenient to call instead of just turning up at some unearthly hour on a Sunday morning unannounced and waking everybody up. That's what a normal person would do.'

'Well it's a lovely morning for a drive up here, Mr McAllister, top down, wind in your hair and flies in your teeth. It's the only way to travel,' said Nicolas Postlethwaite in a futile attempt to humour Emma's father.

Woken by the commotion, Emma had come downstairs and stood behind her father at the front door with a bewildered look on her face.

'Nicolas!' she exclaimed. 'What are you doing here?'

Bernard turned to face his daughter. 'Do you know this Nicolas Postle… what's it… person?'

'Well, yes. He's a friend of mine. We were at college in London together – he's a singer.'

'Yes, we've heard him, so has half the neighbourhood. He seems more interested in your grandmother than he is in you, singing sweet nothings under her window, holding roses. It was like the balcony scene from *Romeo and Juliet*.'

'I've explained, Mr McAllister, just a simple mistake. I'm very sorry.'

'The only simple thing round here is you. Why don't you bugger off back to where you came from?'

Bridget McAllister, who had also appeared at the bottom of the stairs behind Emma, immediately recognised the unfortunate Nicolas Postlethwaite.

'Nicolas, how lovely to see you again.'

'You've met this specimen before?' asked Bernard.

'Yes, dear. He called once with Emma when you were away on business. Don't be so rude, Bernard, and don't call him that, his name's Nicolas. Do come in, dear,' she said, holding out her hand. 'I'll put the kettle on.'

He reluctantly entered, squeezing past Bernard McAllister, who was growling on the door step at the unwelcome intrusion, muttering, 'Oh, what's the use?'

Over a cup of tea at the kitchen table Granny McAllister, still in her dressing gown and still revealing more than was appropriate, looked Nicolas Postlethwaite up and down approvingly. Having been widowed at an early age her only escape into romance was the occasional Mills and Boon novel. As she studied the unfortunate Nicolas with lecherous eyes, he became aware of her apparent fascination in him and started to blush.

'I think you're a charming young man. Such a lovely thought to surprise Emma on her birthday. How romantic.

It's the sort of romance I read about in my books. I didn't think it happened to people in real life. Never happens to me anyway. Oh, how lucky you are, Emma.'

'Would you like to stop for some lunch, dear?' asked Bridget. 'I've made one of my blackberry and apple pies.'

'I call them hedgehog pies,' said the young Sam as he joined the others at the table. 'When you stick your spoon in they go all red and gooey like a hedgehog that's been run over. Do you know why the hedgehog crossed the road…?'

'Shut up, Sam,' whispered Emma as she kicked him under the table.

'That's very kind of you, Mrs McAllister, but I think I'll be going soon,' he replied, not wanting to wear out his welcome or endure more of Emma's father's wrath or eat something that resembled a hedgehog pie. Before he left he used the bathroom facilities and managed to block the toilet, resulting in the toilet overflowing and soaking the floor. In apology, his excuse was to mention to Bridget McAllister that he had a large stool.

'Large stool indeed,' she had said to Sam later that day. 'More likely flushed too much paper down there.' The naive young Sam had thought for a moment and asked his mother what the size of a chair had got to do with blocking the toilet. She had sighed in frustration and gave her usual reply whenever an embarrassing or delicate question was asked, 'I'll explain when you're older, dear.'

As Nicolas Postlethwaite emerged from the front door and walked up to his car on the driveway, Sam and Duncan were both walking round his MGB enthusiastically.

'It's teal blue, isn't it?' asked Duncan.

'Er... I'm not really sure.'

'Have you got a tonneau cover for it?'

'I don't really know,' replied Nicolas, unsure what a tonneau cover was.

'Has it got overdrive?'

'Yes,' replied Nicolas confidently, certain that it had.

Duncan looked up towards the sky as if for inspiration, then started reciting a series of facts about the car. 'They were first launched in 1962 as a Roadster, followed in 1965 by the MGBGT coupe and powered by a 1.8-litre 'B' series engine. The suspension was a bit agricultural though. Yours is quite a nice example in teal blue with the Rostyle wheels, but personally I prefer them in British racing green with the painted wire wheels...'

'Yes, well I really must be going' Nicolas said as he got in his car and looked in the mirror to adjust his cloth cap.

'I know – I'm boring,' said Duncan.

The MGB disappeared into the distance as the McAllisters waved farewell, Bernard muttering 'idiot' under his breath. None of them would see or hear from Nicolas Postelthwaite again. He was rather dejected and depressed as he drove away on his return to the comparative sanity of the metropolis. He reflected on his plan to impress Emma. Everything seemed to have gone disastrously wrong, singing to the grandmother under the window by mistake and incurring the wrath of Emma's father. Emma's mother was nice and Granny McAllister too, although at times he'd thought she was trying to seduce him. He was unimpressed by Emma's little brother Sam and his reference to the hedgehog pie. Duncan he had found rather boring, a little odd, like a walking talking reference book.

Oh well. Pity really, he thought.

*

Later that day the front doorbell rang. Bernard opened the door to reveal Reginald Ramsbottom holding six jewellery trays, the top tray wedged under his pointed stubbly chin.

'Oh it's you,' said Bernard. 'I forgot you were coming round. Come in. We've just got rid of one and then another one arrives.'

'One what?'

'Oh, nothing. Never mind.'

Bernard showed Reg through to the front room where his mother was seated at the table in excited anticipation of his arrival and was pouring herself a glass of sherry.

'Reg, how lovely to see you,' she said. 'Thank you for calling, you *are* a darling. Would you like a glass of sherry, dear?'

'Thank you. I shouldn't really, but maybe just the one.'

Bernard grunted, left the room muttering "hypocrite" and disappeared into what he considered the sanity of his piano room, not to emerge until summoned by Bridget for his tea.

Liberal and frequent dispensing of sherry was used as a negotiating tool by Granny McAllister, a means of "softening the prices" as she called it. Two hours and five glasses of sherry later Reginald Ramsbottom bid her good day and staggered back round next door carrying his trays, now six rings lighter, and returned them to the safe in the greenhouse, together with an envelope bulging with crisp twenty-pound notes. He locked the safe door, replaced the key under the flower pot and went indoors, unaware that he had been observed by the fifteen-year-old Sam, who had been spying through a knot hole in the wooden fence.

CHAPTER 7

With Bernard McAllister's driving ban served and licence restored, Granny McAllister's six-week stay came to an end one fine Sunday morning in July. She would be departing the following day and the house, without her presence, her sparkle, her laughter and charisma, would revert to its normal state, for Sam as a teenager, more monotonous, more gloomy, more… as it had always been.

Being a pleasant morning Reginald Ramsbottom had decided to sunbathe in his derelict conservatory while he listened to Alistair Cooke's weekly broadcasts of 'Letter from America'. Most of the glass in the conservatory was missing, the wooden frame rotten, and what little glass that remained in the roof was covered in thick moss. He turned on the radio that was always tuned to Radio 4, removed his clothes, sat on his old rusty sunlounger with dirty and split cushions and reclined, waiting in anticipation for his programme to begin.

His weekly visits to the Church of… whatever it was called in Hertfordshire had come to an end after losing control of his precious E-Type one wet Saturday morning on his journey there. He'd been driving rather exuberantly, had exited a roundabout on the A1 a little too enthusiastically and the car had lost traction on the wet road and had eventually come to a stop facing in the wrong direction. The only thing dented was his confidence but the occurrence, together with his concerns with the reliability of the aging car, persuaded him to call it a day. If his confidence in driving had been shattered, so too was the peace and tranquillity enjoyed by his neighbours as his visits to his strange church had been substituted with listening to Alistair Cooke's broadcast, usually at a loud volume so all the neighbours were able to listen whether they wanted to or not.

His rear garden was quite secluded and not overlooked but his tumbledown conservatory could be seen quite clearly from the McAllisters' garden through a broken section of the wooden fence.

Bernard McAllister was in the habit of mowing the lawn with his motor mower at about the same time as the broadcasts in an attempt to drown out the "racket" as he called it. As he passed the broken section of fence he paused, looked through the gap in the fence, then continued with the mower, shaking his head in disgust.

'He's at it again, lying there stark naked,' he said to Bridget when he went indoors for his morning coffee. 'Bloody disgusting if you ask me, exposing himself like that. He wouldn't do that if his mother was still alive.'

'Well his mother isn't alive anymore,' replied Bridget, 'which is probably why he's doing it. Some people like to do that sort of thing, for the freedom. Being at one with nature they call it.'

'Bloody disgusting, that's what I call it,' said Bernard.
'He probably thinks he can't be seen.'

'*I* can see him.'

'Well then don't look.'

'Anyway why are you always sticking up for him?' asked Bernard.

An impending argument was avoided and the situation defused by the ending of the Alistair Cooke broadcast next door. Peace and quiet had been restored, but not for long.

Bernard returned to the garden and was about to resume his grass cutting when the same 'Letter from America' broadcast started again. He looked through the gap in the fence and shuddered at the full-frontal nakedness of Reginald Ramsbottom returning to his sunlounger from a visit to the reel-to-reel tape recorder on the shelf.

Bridget, who had brought Bernard's forgotten coffee out to him, peered over Bernard's shoulder.

'Oh, I see what you mean dear, nice and tanned, isn't he?'

'Skinny little bugger, looks like a shrivelled up stick insect,' said Bernard sniggering.

Bridget moved a little closer to the gap in the fence for a better view before turning away. 'He told me the other day he'd bought a new reel-to-reel tape recorder. He must have started recording his programmes so he can play them back and listen to them again.'

'He needn't start doing that every week. It's bad enough having to listen to it once without him repeating it, not just for us either, the other neighbours must be able to hear it too.'

'Do come away from the fence, dear,' said Bridget. 'If the other neighbours see you they'll think you're a peeping Tom.'

'A peeping Tom! What about him? Exposing himself like that. You could call him a flasher.'

Bernard then marched across the lawn towards the summer house, the source of loud music. He flung open the door to be confronted by Sam reading an LP record sleeve he was holding in his left hand. His right hand was hanging out of the back window of the summer house holding one of his brother's dog-ends that he'd lit just before the door had opened.

'Turn that blasted music down! Don't you start, it's bad enough with the racket coming from next door!' shouted Bernard.

'It's not a racket. It's "Black Dog" by Led Zeppelin. It's on their new album.' Sam shouted back.

'Well it sounds like a racket to me. Turn it down!'

A little later normality was restored. The rerun of 'Letter from America' had finished as had the grass cutting. Sam looked out of the summer house window at the house. His father appeared in the lounge window and sat down at his piano, his mother was in the kitchen preparing the lunch and Granny McAllister was sitting by the lounge window with her Sunday paper. Sam moved away from the window, lifted the stylus on the record player, turned up the volume and played "Black Dog" again, this time undisturbed.

*

Sam had often been described as a daydreamer by his parents. In later life he preferred to think of himself as nostalgic or as an 'obsessive reminiscer'. He often wondered why he reminisced so much about his childhood and was able to relive in his mind the events and conversations that had taken place in his younger days, events that nearly fifty years later were so vivid, so real, as if they had occurred only a few days earlier.

From an early age he'd started to write poetry, or at least he tried to, and one of his first attempts was inspired by the old neighbour Reginald Ramsbottom:

The man next door was a strange one,
A peculiar man was he,
His name was Reg,
He ate fruit and veg
And drove a Jaguar 'E'.

He never got around to writing the second verse of his poem. He considered the first one summed up the neighbour perfectly. It was rather sad that someone's character and disposition could be described so briefly in five lines of a verse, but there really wasn't much else he could think of to say about him – certainly not much else that rhymed easily.

CHAPTER 8

Several weeks after his English literature class had been introduced *to Nineteen Eighty-Four* and had had the opportunity to read and digest George Orwell's wonderful book, Sam turned the blackboard round to face the class to reveal a list of words he'd written earlier.

　　Cool = great
　　Chill = relax
　　Epic = grand
　　Hot = attractive
　　Far out = cool or great
　　Sweet = fantastic
　　Wicked = perfect or excellent
　　Pants = bad or awful

Sam had always been a stickler for correct use of English and detested modern colloquialism and what he liked to refer to as the bastardization of the English language. He would cringe when he entered a pub with Morag and was asked by someone behind the bar 'What can I get you guys?' He was similarly irritated by what he considered was the incorrect use of the words he'd written on the blackboard.

'What's wrong with these definitions on the board?' Sam asked the class.

'Nothing,' replied Blenkinsop, who was sitting at the rear of the class. 'We use those words all the time.'

Blenkinsop was a chubby, spotty faced youth who wore round glasses that made him look studious. He was. In fact he was probably the most intelligent person in the room. He revelled in debate and discussion and always seemed to come out on top of any verbal exchange he entered into, much to the annoyance of the teaching staff. Sam had discovered a way of avoiding answering Blenkinsop's difficult questions by saying, 'That's a very good question, Blenkinsop. I'm glad you asked that and I shall be covering that a little later on.' Of course he never did, which enabled him to refer to the dictionary or a reference book to establish the answer, which he returned to at a later date, usually the next lesson when he would say, 'I'm sorry, Blenkinsop, last time you asked me a question I didn't have time to answer.' He would then confidently answer the difficult question which seemed to keep Blenkinsop happy.

Today was different. Today Blenkinsop was on form. 'We use those words in those contexts all the time. It's slang yes, but it's the modern way of talking,' he said.

'Well it's not correct!' replied Sam sternly, banging his fist on his desk. 'Cool means moderately cold or not too warm, chill means a sensation of cold or an illness, epic means a long film or book, hot is the opposite to cold, far out means a long way away, sweet is the opposite of bitter or having a charming character, wicked means evil or extremely bad and pants are an undergarment. Why do we have to reinvent our wonderful language?'

'It's modern rhetoric,' said Blenkinsop. 'It's just like in George Orwell's *Nineteen Eighty-Four*. I've read it and it's no different to what he describes as Oldspeak and Newspeak in the book, the modern interpretation of language and the ditching of old words we no longer use. In the book a new dictionary is written with modern language included. The old words that are no longer used are deleted. That's what we need to do, bring our language up to date.'

'Well it's lazy, modern colloquialism, Americanisms and it's not correct and I don't like it,' said Sam, who had the uneasy feeling that he was being backed into a corner.

Blenkinsop continued with his arguement. 'It's like Chaucer or Shakespeare. They used different words. We don't say things like thou or thyne anymore. Words like that have been ditched in everyday language. They're obsolete. Surely the English language has developed as time has passed. It's still evolving. I don't see what's wrong with it.'

The rest of the class looked indifferent. This was between Sam and Blenkinsop.

'You make an interesting point, Blenkinsop. Does anyone else have any views on this?'

Nobody had, so Sam moved on and started to discuss more peculiarities of the English language. 'Why do we have so many words that mean the same thing?' Nobody seemed to understand.

'I'm referring to what are known as synonyms. For example take the word beautiful – we could equally use words like pretty, nice or attractive that have the same meaning. It makes our language very complex.'

Blenkinsop had more points to make and raised his hand. 'In George Orwell's book he describes the Newspeak dictionary, a revised dictionary that erases words like the synonyms you mentioned. They deleted words like beautiful, pretty and attractive and just used one word, like nice.'

'English is a stupid language with stupid spellings,' said a boy at the front of the class. 'Why do we spell quay with a "Q" and yacht with a "C" and an "H" in it? Why is there a "G" in phlegm? It must be a nightmare for foreigners to learn. Other languages like German seem to have one word for one meaning, makes it easier to learn.'

'Yes, a good point,' said Sam. 'It does have its peculiarities and yet the English language has been adopted internationally for communication in maritime and aviation. Pilots all use English to speak to air traffic control wherever they are in the world.'

Maisie Fergusson sitting at the front of the class raised her hand rather timidly and said, 'Sir, music is an international language as well, Miss Stein said so.'

Sam cringed a little at the mention of Miss Stein, the music teacher who Sam secretly called Phyllis.

'Yes that's right, Maisie. I suppose you could put a sheet of music in front of two musicians who don't speak the same language and they'd both be able to play it even though they couldn't communicate with each other verbally. That's a very good point.'

Blenkinsop started to shuffle in his seat, a sure sign he was about to deliver more words of wisdom. Either that or ask an awkward question. Sam continued before he had the opportunity. 'The other thing I find extremely annoying in our modern world is what George Orwell would probably describe as Textspeak if he was around today. I'm referring to the ridiculous abbreviation of words used in text messages just because we're in so much of a hurry all the time, with no time to spell them correctly. When I was your age, oh my Lord I sound like my father, we had to write letters, things like "thank you" letters to relatives who had sent a birthday or Christmas present. We wrote a letter, put it in an envelope, stuck a stamp on it and posted it. When was the last time any of you lot did that? Soon people won't even know how to write properly, let alone spell.' Sam turned towards the blackboard, picked up some chalk and started to write. 'I suppose now you'd send a text message something like this,' he said, as he wrote *Thks 4 the pres u sent for Bday.*

'Something like that yeah,' shouted Geraldine Brierley from the back of the class, 'but we'd probably spell thanks as THX.'

'Oh you would, would you?' replied Sam, 'Well I don't get it. I just don't get it.'

'That's slang, sir. Slang for I don't understand,' said Blenkinsop. 'Even you're doing it now.'

Everyone laughed.

'Alright then,' Sam said, smirking as he looked sternly at Blenkinsop. 'It's an informal use of vocabulary, the concept and use of which I do not comprehend.'

It was getting near the end of the lesson and Sam changed the subject before Blenkinsop became difficult.

'Next time we'll be continuing to talk about our changing language and discussing words in the English language that are being used more frequently – words like crypto and polemicist.' He spoke the word polemicist with a piercing stare directed at Blenkinsop. 'We'll also discuss words that are used less frequently, words such as egregious and unguent.' They all looked confused. Even Blenkinsop looked confused. Sam felt in control again.

The bell rang for the end of the academic day, the end of the week.

Thank God that's over, thought Sam after he'd dismissed the class.

After they'd scraped their chairs back on the floor, collected their books and hurriedly made their way towards the door like a herd of stampeding wildebeest Sam walked round the classroom straightening chairs under the desks. He noticed a strange smell in the vicinity where Geraldine Brierley had been sitting. He couldn't decide whether it was the aroma of her family pig farm, something nasty she'd trodden in, or BO. Yes, it was definitely body odour…

'Go and change your shirt, boy!' his father had shouted to him as he'd walked by him in the kitchen. Sam, aged fifteen, had cycled vigorously back home from school on a particularly hot day and was sweating profusely. Unknown to Sam (because it had never been explained) he had reached that age when one's body changes. No one had ever mentioned the possible beneficial use of antiperspirant or

deodorant but he eventually worked out the significance of "go and change your shirt, boy". A visit to the nearby corner shop with pocket money had proved confusing. What was the difference between antiperspirant and deodorant? Which did he need? Aerosol or roll-on – which was best? Conscious that he was being watched by the shopkeeper, he had panicked and picked up the first thing that came to hand, which having left the shop he realised was ladies' perfume in a squirty bottle. Nothing in life was ever explained. He'd always had to work things out for himself. Things like that leave you scarred for life – psychologically.

A few minutes later Sam looked down from the third-floor window as students streamed towards the gates and parked cars, all, without exception, on their mobile phones, all looking down texting or whatever it was they were doing but still managing to walk without colliding with anyone else, all seeming to arrive at their intended destinations as if guided by some built-in navigational system. Those who were using their phones for their intended purpose, actually talking to someone, were walking hither and thither, all engrossed in conversation, unaware of travelling considerable distances in huge figure-of-eight patterns in the car park.

Sam had what he liked to refer to as his daily two-minute moaning session, and as he looked down from the window he decided that today the subject would be mobile phones. He hated mobile phones but had come to look on them as a modern-day necessity. He'd often thought if we were invaded by aliens they could be forgiven for thinking cell phones were the master race as they seemed to control humans. How did we ever manage without them? Nowadays if someone went out without their mobile phone, having realised, they would panic as if they'd forgotten something really important like their glasses or their underwear. He thought back to his first mobile phone in the late nineteen eighties. Called a transportable it had resembled an army field telephone. It was carried in a large bag over the shoulder, had a huge heavy battery, almost like a car battery. In time they had got smaller, pocket-size, and then they started getting bigger again. As he continued to gaze down from the window it occurred to him that apart from a few people talking on their phones, people weren't actually talking to each other in a physical way. The art of conversation was gone, now replaced with a cell phone. Now couples sit together in silence in pubs and restaurants looking at their phones. He'd often noticed diners taking pictures of their food as soon as it was brought to the table, then as a prelude to eating the meal they would send the image to so-called friends. Why? What are they trying to say? Were their so-called friends really that interested in what they were about to consume? He knew what he would think if someone sent him a picture of a plate of food – he'd think they were deranged. He'd have to ask Kendrick for his view on the matter. It probably signified some sort of insecurity complex. He'd ask him.

He was also intrigued and irritated in supermarkets by people who manoeuvre their shopping trolleys whilst bent over and leaning on the handle with both arms folded with their arses stuck up in the air whilst looking down at their phones. They usually took small steps with their feet spread apart walking like Charlie Chaplin. Surprisingly, they appeared able to navigate the isles without colliding with anyone or anything whilst completely engrossed in whatever it was they were looking at on their phones. On several occasions in supermarkets he had been convinced that an approaching trolley-leaning person had been talking to him, when in fact they were having a phone conversation using some sort of unseen earpiece or microphone, or even worse with a loudspeaker activated so everyone could hear. *Strange people*, he thought, *still, there's nowt as queer as folk.*

With his daily moan concluded and the classroom empty he walked from the window and sat at his desk still deep in thought, again thinking fondly of his old teacher Mr Evans. He had always put Mr Evans on a pedestal, respected him, looked up to him, idolised him and in a way he had almost become him. Would he be remembered by his students in the same way, or as a miserable old-fashioned git who didn't embrace modern technology, a man to whom words like "streaming" and "trending" were part of a different language he didn't understand and didn't want to understand? Would he be remembered as a stickler for the old ways and the old values? Would he be remembered at all? Perhaps he'd be forgotten, the memory of him and his existence erased, as some were in George Orwell's wonderful book.

CHAPTER 9

Although content with life and his teaching career Sam McAllister still had what he called his "Walter Mitty" moments when he would daydream and imagine himself doing something else, being someone else, someone important like a surgeon or a politician or an astrophysicist. He often reflected on what life would have been like if he'd taken a different path. If he had joined the police to the dismay of his father, what could he have become? Would he have remained a constable or maybe worked in traffic and booked his father for a traffic offence, or could he have progressed through the ranks and become a chief constable? Could he have become a dentist and sadistically worked on his father's teeth? If he had joined the RAF what would that path have led to? Maybe a Harrier pilot in the Falklands conflict, a Tornado pilot or navigator in the Gulf War, or could he have become Air Chief Marshal Sir Samuel Bartholomew McAllister? Maybe if he'd taken more interest in Reginald Ramsbottom's clock and watch repairs in his younger days he could have become a leading horologist. Or if he wasn't a person of such a secular disposition maybe he could have joined the clergy and become the Archbishop of Canterbury. One never knows, do one? as the great Thomas 'Fats' Waller would have said.

Sam often thought back to his father's "words of wisdom" lecture, the advice given to him when he was faced with the decision of a career opportunity:

'Life is like a journey along a road, son. When you come to a fork in the road, or a junction, you might ask yourself, which way do I turn? What lies ahead if I take this turn or the other turn? If I decide to go one way and don't like what lies around the corner can I go back and have another go? Usually that's not an option, you're stuck with the decisions you make and you have to stand by them. I remember saying to you when you were younger that you looked at life through rose-tinted spectacles. You probably didn't know what I meant by that but teenagers look at life too casually. It's not until you get to your age that you realise the big wide world is out there waiting for you and you have to fend for yourself and pay your own way.'

Sam had waited for the inevitable. Then it came.

'When I was your age there was a war on. I was in Holland and France with the Royal Tank Corps. I hadn't been home or seen my family for months. Even after the war finished thousands like me came out of the army and had to do any work we could get, we were grateful for anything. Things were scarce, there was still rationing. You youngsters don't know you're born. You've never had it so good.'

His father had paused to light his pipe, then after wafting the smoke away from his face the monologue continued relentlessly as they always did, digressing from its initial purpose of useful career advice being imparted, to recollections of *his* own past using the usual stock phrases like – "times were hard back then" or "when I was your age".

He pointed the stem of his pipe at Sam as he continued his monologue, reminding him of Alf Garnet. Apart from the pipe, several things about his father reminded Sam of Alf Garnet – his constant moaning, his political views and his bigoted outlook on life.

'The other thing with life, Sam, it's also about events and coincidences. For example if I hadn't been stationed near your mother's village in Kent during the war, or if I hadn't walked into her post office and bought a postage stamp that day, we would never have met. If I'd been blown up in my tank, or your mother's house had been bombed one night in an air raid we'd never have married and you wouldn't be here now listening to these words of wisdom.'

As he listened to his father ranting on, he rather wished he wasn't.

He remembered a similar conversation that had taken place at the dinner table when he was a schoolboy. Duncan had returned home from university where he'd been studying entomology among other things, intending a career in forensics, to announce he'd left and taken a job with the local funeral directors Graves and Day.

Coming as something of a shock to his father he'd raised his arms in frustration. 'You spend all those years at university studying entomology, all those bugs and creepy crawly things with the prospect of a good career in forensics, then you end up digging graves. What's all that about? I suppose you call that putting your qualifications to good use, do you?'

'I can't do that for a living, pulling maggots out of some dead person's nasal cavity and ears with a pair of tweezers and trying to establish how long the poor bugger's been dead. It's all about metamorphosis, that's the transformation of a larva into its adult form. By calculating the incubation period they can discover how long the victim's been dead. It's all very interesting but it's not for me.'

His father had pushed his plate away having suddenly lost his appetite. 'It's like that friend of yours you were at school with, Walter, whatever his name was, spending years studying law and then became an interior decorator.'

'No, that was Stanley,' said Duncan. 'Walter qualified as an accountant, thought it sounded dull so started working for British Rail as a porter. He might end up as a train driver one day. He thought it would be a bit more exciting than accountancy.'

'Well you're all nuts. In my day you chose a career, got some qualifications and off you went – job for life, boy, job for life.'

Duncan had always been a macabre sort of character and he considered himself well suited to working for an undertaker. Some did consider him to be a little odd at times. He had a tendency to bore people with facts, figures and minutiae that he memorised from textbooks and workshop manuals. He was an obsessive thinker and had developed an encyclopaedic knowledge, appearing to be an expert on most subjects that arose in conversations, conversations that were often brought to an abrupt end when he started to regurgitate detailed facts, which tended to baffle the listener resulting in them walking away in frustration, boredom or lack of interest. His latest obsession was learning and using unusual words, usually long, rarely used words, which he used in otherwise normal conversations. This often resulted in frustration for the listener, or as Duncan preferred to think, highlighted their own inadequacies and ignorance of the English language.

He enjoyed his work with Graves and Day, soon progressing to a pall-bearer and driving the hearses. He loved the Daimler hearses and took pride in keeping them clean and polished and also undertook minor mechanical repairs and servicing, which gave him the excuse to memorise the maintenance manuals, which were his usual reading material when he retired to his bed at night. For several weeks he studied lubrication charts, wiring diagrams, servicing schedules and torque wrench settings and became an expert on all things Daimler, adding them to his extensive encyclopaedic knowledge.

Douglas Graves had little to do with the running of the business but Duncan's other boss Agnus Day was impressed with Duncan's enthusiasm and mechanical abilities and she put him in charge of the small fleet of vehicles. Things ran smoothly for a few years until one day in 1984 Duncan was working on the specification for a new Daimler hearse and ordered it with the registration number B1 BYE.

'You can't put that registration on a hearse, what were you thinking of?' exclaimed Agnus.

'I thought it was rather nice, rather appropriate,' replied Duncan.

'Well it's not. It's offensive. It's distasteful. It'll have to be changed.'

Duncan McAllister's days with Graves and Day came to an end a few years later when he became a librarian at a college in Lincoln. There he could study technical manuals to his heart's content, expand his knowledge of all things irrelevant and learn more rarely used long words to use in future conversations; or disquisitions and dissertations as he preferred to call them.

CHAPTER 10

The conversation in the kitchen between Duncan and his mother was not unlike that which you could expect to hear between two elderly ladies in a post office as they queued at the counter for their pensions, or stamps, or whatever else elderly ladies queued at post office counters for.

They were giving their account of the day's activities to Sam, who had called to collect Alistair McAllister (always referred to in that way as the two names had a pleasant poetic flow), who had spent the day with his grandparents on the first day of the school summer holidays. Duncan and his mother continued enthusiastically with their detailed report of the day's activities and the assumption that he'd really enjoyed his day out, although the vacant expression on his son's face, a sort of comatose numbness, suggested to Sam that he'd probably been rather bored all day and hated every minute. It transpired they'd taken him on a trip to Skegness accompanied by the neighbour Reginald Ramsbottom. Everything they did always seemed to involve Reg from next door. Sam's father rarely went out and never took his grandson anywhere, just as he'd never taken Sam anywhere when he was a boy. It was puzzling. It was always his mother, Duncan and Reg. When Sam was ten years old in 1969 Reg had always been around, now in 1996 with his son ten years old, Reg was still there, still around.

'Go and say hello to your father before you go,' his mother said.

Having plucked up courage, he reluctantly entered the lounge to see his father seated at the Steinway grand piano just as he was thumping out the final few bars of some Brahms. Or was it Liszt? Or was it both? There was a whisky bottle and an empty glass on top of the piano. Sam had timed his entry to the room perfectly as his father reached the end of the piece. The early evening sunlight streamed in through the open curtains highlighting layers of cigar smoke and dust particles in the air. He coughed to announce his arrival so he wouldn't startle his father as he approached him from behind. His father suddenly span round on his seat, his dark outline silhouetted against the bright sunlight. There was something strange about him. Sam screwed up his face and raised his left hand above his eyes to shield the glare of the sun as he tried to focus on his father's face. He was looking at Sam sternly – a penetrating, almost menacing stare. Then he asked loudly, 'Why have you never called me Dad?'

The directness of the question took Sam by surprise for a few seconds but no, he was right, he couldn't recall ever calling him Dad. As a small boy he remembered calling him Daddy when he'd asked him for his pocket money, but later, never Dad, possibly due to a lack of affection in childhood and adolescence and a mutual lack of respect thereafter.

'Well, I suppose it's because you've… well … you've never really been much of one,' Sam said in reply to the unexpected question.

'What do you mean!' shouted his father.

Sam, wishing he'd gone straight home without entering the room, thought again.

'I don't really have any recollections of much affection, or as a child of sharing any activities with you.'

'Times were different then, there was a war on!' shouted his father.

'No there wasn't, unless you were in Vietnam. It was the 1960s,' replied Sam, who was starting to think his father was losing his marbles.

'No, quite correct, the war was over. Anyway, things were different then, I was away a lot with my work, trying to earn a living to keep a roof over your ungrateful head and food on the table. Nowadays you lot seem to want everything for nothing.'

'It's no different now,' said Sam, wondering what he had done to incur his father's wrath. 'I've always worked and paid the bloody mortgage and the bills. I've never had to come to you cap in hand to ask for anything. The difference is I'm not selfish, I don't lock myself away in a room like you have for years since you retired. I'm always there for my family. We still find the time to do things together, all the things most normal families do. Now you have a wonderful second opportunity to get involved, this time with your grandson. You're retired and have all the time in the world, but oh no, you'd rather sit at that bloody piano all day, every day and let Mum and Duncan, or Duncan and Reg or all three of them take Alistair McAllister for days out. It's all very strange. He's going to grow up with as few memories of you as I have. Does that answer your question?'

Sam turned towards the door, noticed he'd left it open and was sure his mother and Duncan must have overheard the row. He gathered Alistair McAllister and his belongings together and stormed off, slamming the front door.

As he drove home Sam looked at his son and wondered how he had viewed his day out with his grandparents, or rather one of them, accompanied by his uncle and the strange man from next door.

He thought back to his own childhood and visits to *his* grandparents in the late 1960s during the school summer holidays. Each year a two-week stay with his mother's parents in the Kent village where she was born was relished. Living such a long distance from Lincolnshire it was the only opportunity during the year to see them. They had lived a simple but contented life, uncomplicated by such things as owning a car, holidays or many of the appliances and gizmos that we have all come to depend on nowadays. Entering the front door of their house was like stepping back in time. Nothing had replaced the Aga solid fuel range, the mangle, the carpet sweeper, the hand mincing machine and the cool box with a wire mesh door that served as a fridge and probably had since the 1940s. In fact the whole house was reminiscent of the 1940s with its dated decor, its green and cream painted sash windows and its green front door. The house also had a distinct aroma, the wonderful combination of TCP, Wright's coal tar soap, his grandfather's pipe smoke and on cooler days the smell of the coal fire. They had a large pantry which had white tiled walls and a flagstone floor that kept it cool on even the hottest of summer days. Sam had fond memories of descending the twisty wooden staircase in the mornings to be greeted with the smell of bread being toasted on a long toasting fork as his grandfather sat in front of the Aga with the fire door open, the glowing embers casting a warm flickering red light around the kitchen. During his stay, Sam would help his grandfather dig up potatoes and break up huge lumps of coal in the coal shed before it was brought into the house to feed the Aga. He would help his grandmother prepare the evening meals, cutting up runner beans, peeling potatoes and shelling peas, all from the garden. As they had no fridge or freezer he would walk the short distance to the shop to buy a small block of Wall's ice cream for their tea, which would be wrapped in newspaper to keep it cold while he carried it home. Their house was not unique. The entire village was something of a time capsule with most of the houses retaining their 1940s appearance.

Sam's grandfather was a cobbler and had his shop adjoining the house. There was always a wonderful aroma of leather, glue and his grandfather's pipe smoke in the shop, a smell that would remain ingrained in Sam's memory forever. He also had wonderful memories of fine summer evenings when he would accompany his grandfather to the village bowling green to watch him play, the gentle clunk of the bowls interrupted only by the screeching of swallows, swifts and house martins as they flew low overhead, occasionally settling on the telephone lines above the green. His visits to his grandparents' house in Kent seemed to last forever but after two weeks with the new school term approaching his parents would arrive to collect him. The following day as they drove away from the house he would look back from the car's rear window, waving to his grandparents until they disappeared from view. It would be another year before he would return.

He had such vivid, happy and cherished memories of his childhood visits to his grandparents. What memories would his son Alistair McAllister have of his? He would probably have more fond recollections of his other grandparents, Morag's mother and father. He spent more time with them at their lovely old stone cottage in the nearby village of Yarling-on-the-Hill, always seeming to return home happy and content, not numb, bored and desensitized as he had appeared that day.

As he continued to drive home Sam thought again about his strange conversation with his father and started to compose a new poem:

'Why have you never called me Dad?'
Asked the father of the son.
Having thought for a while the son replied,
'Well, you've never been much of one.

'Little affection or love do I remember
'Certainly none that I recall,
'It's obvious to me that I'm a mistake
And shouldn't be here at all.'

Satisfied with the first two verses, he'd try to remember them and write them down when he got home. He looked at Alistair McAllister asleep in the passenger seat and chuckled to himself thinking he was probably exhausted after his action-packed day with the "Crankies" – a term he and Morag had come to use to describe the combination of his mother, brother and Reginald Ramsbottom.

In the town centre they were held at a red traffic light. Waiting at the lights, Sam looked into an electrical shop window on the opposite side of the road and became mesmerized by the television sets in the window all displaying the same picture, looking from one set to another as the picture changed. He contemplated the hundreds of channels that were now available and the fact that there was still hardly anything on that he considered worth watching.

The old antiquated television sets he remembered from his childhood could only receive BBC1 and BBC2. One old TV had been encased in a wooden cabinet with doors and looked more like a cocktail cabinet than a television. A knob on the front panel had to be frequently adjusted to control the "horizontal hold" as the picture annoyingly kept rolling and as much time seemed to be spent adjusting the set as watching it. When it eventually packed up someone had called to take it away to turn into an aquarium.

His father had never bought a new television, usually acquiring second-hand sets that didn't work for very long or old sets that were passed down by his mother, Granny McAllister. Sam's school friends would often discuss television programmes that were on ITV, like *Batman* and

Thunderbirds, programmes that were unknown to Sam and they even sang advertisement jingles like the one for Esso Blue paraffin that Sam had never heard before. The one modern item his grandparents in Kent had was their television and his stays during the summer holidays gave him the opportunity to sample this other world, the world of commercial television that he was denied at home.

Now, most people on the television annoyed him. He considered that if one wanted to succeed in television it seemed to be a requirement to be excessively camp or a pillock, or preferably both as that combination of questionable qualities seemed to proliferate the entertainment industry – if "industry" is the right word, or indeed if "entertainment" is the right word.

His thoughts were interrupted by the car behind tooting its horn. The lights had changed. Moan over.

Later that evening he thought about the conversation he'd had with his father earlier in the day. He felt a slight sense of guilt about what he'd said but it was all true. His childhood relationship with his father *had* been strained and awkward most of the time with little affection shown in his younger years, just the constant criticism and interminable moaning and petulance, not the basis of a good relationship. Sam had surprised himself with the fortitude he had shown when answering the question "Why have you never called me Dad?" Maybe it was a latent feeling that had been bottled up for years and the cork had suddenly popped.

It was several weeks before he visited his parents again. During his absence a local solicitor was promoting a discounted will writing service and Bridget McAllister mentioned this to Reginald Ramsbottom next door. 'You really ought to think about making a will, Reg. You've no family and if you die intestate the government will take it all. I'm doing mine and so is Duncan.'

CHAPTER 11

Later that evening, after Sam's heated discussion with his father and his hasty departure, the McAllisters' front doorbell rang. After a short delay while she adjusted her hair in the hall mirror Bridget opened the front door to be greeted by a strange sight – the Brierley family.

Mrs Brierley, the school secretary, had mentioned to Sam that her husband Gerald, the local pig farmer, needed a new watch, so arrangements had been made to call that evening when Bernard was at home.

'Good evening, Mrs McAllister,' said Mrs Brierley. 'I hope you don't mind us all coming. We've been to see my sister Beatrice who lives just over the road. It's her birthday. Not such a happy occasion this year unfortunately. I suppose you've heard her husband died last week.'

It was rumoured that Beatrice Bassett had an insatiable sexual appetite and her dearly departed husband had succumbed to heart failure in the bedroom after giving her his best and sustained attention.

'Yes. He was such a nice man,' replied Bridget. 'I heard it was a heart attack – a terrible shame at his age.'

'Yes, but I don't suppose it'll take her long to find a replacement. You know what she's like with men,' said Mrs Brierley raising an eyebrow.

'No I'm afraid I don't. Anyway, do come in,' Bridget said, looking disapprovingly at the Brierley trio as they filed past her.

Mr Gerald Brierley was a large, stocky man about forty-five, wearing highly magnified round glasses, the lenses of which were badly scratched and virtually opaque. He was always dressed in the same attire regardless of the occasion or time of year – blue denim dungarees, large brown boots and a cloth cap, which covered a very round bald head that appeared to be attached directly to his broad shoulders with the absence of anything resembling a neck.

In contrast his wife of similar age was a short, petite lady with a small mouth, large front teeth, big eyes that were too close together, large ears mostly concealed by her shoulder-length brown, hair and she had the beginnings of a moustache, all strange features, which gave her the appearance of a rodent. She was always smartly dressed and used strong perfume in a futile attempt to disguise the piggy smell of her husband. For some reason they had brought their daughter Geraldine – a strange, scruffy creature about 16 years of age, slim, with long bright-red coloured hair tied up on top of her head. She wore a long cream-coloured woollen jumper that almost reached the tops of her large black laced-up boots. Bridget looked her up and down and smiled, thinking she resembled a Swan Vesta match.

'This is Geraldine, our daughter. Geraldine's in

your Sam's English class at school,' said Mrs Brierley proudly.

'Good evening, Geraldine,' replied Bridget McAllister putting on her posh voice.

''Ow do, bloomin' cold, innit? I got a sister at school 'n' all. She be a bit younger than me. She's the littler one' came the reply as Geraldine stepped into the house confidently, her black leather boots squeaking annoyingly on the parquet flooring.

'Yes. Well, er... I see,' Bridget said wondering why this scruffy specimen had accompanied her parents on what must have seemed to her a boring and mundane outing. Maybe there was a reluctance by Mrs Brierley to leave her not unattractive daughter at home at the pig farm alone and vulnerable, at the mercy of young male admirers intent on broadening their knowledge of the rudiments of life, particularly concerning the fairer sex. It was rumoured at the school that young Geraldine could at times be quite accommodating in that regard and had once been caught behind the bike shed with a boy known as "Acne Alan" in the process of loosening her clothing for explorative purposes.

Entering the hallway, they reacted as most other visitors did – they stood and stared at the strange surroundings. The eclectic mix of furniture and incongruous ornaments was indeed striking. Most of them were old family heirlooms given to Bernard McAllister by his mother over the years. Old Persian tapestries hung on the walls of the hallway next to a grandfather clock that dated from the early 1900s. Pictures faded by strong sunlight hung on the walls with the remains of a large number of small flies trapped behind the glass. What was known as the hall seat, a large, heavily carved dark wooden piece of furniture, dominated the hall. It was out of proportion with the rest of the furniture, inconveniently positioned opposite the staircase, and had to be walked around carefully as one passed by.

'Bernard's in the lounge, that's the room at the back, do go through.'

They walked slowly along the parquet-floored hallway, stopping to admire the grandfather clock as it struck 7pm.

Three more contrasting people from the same family were difficult to imagine. Mr Brierley was a rough and ready character, rather scruffy, a constant embarrassment to his wife and rather "common" as Bridget later described him, not that she was a snob. His wife appeared to be the opposite, smartly dressed and well spoken but it soon became obvious she was a woman trying to be posh, imagining herself to be of a higher echelon of society, no easy task when saddled with Mr Brierley and a delinquent daughter. When Mrs Brierley spoke she employed a strange rhetoric, an annoying habit of inserting an "R" in certain words in a poor attempt to sound a bit hoity-toity.

'Beautiful tarpestries,' she remarked as she paused to admire the Persian tapestries on the wall.

Mr Brierley had an equally annoying habit of dispensing with the first letters of some words and mispronouncing other words. As he passed the tapestries on the wall he also looked up at them in admiration. 'Yes, very 'tractive, very 'andsome. They give your 'allway a nice ambulance they does,' he said.

Mrs Brierley quickly corrected her husband 'I think

you mean *ambience* dear, the word is *ambience*. My husband has lost his watch. He thinks he lost it in the pig sty when he was feeding them the other day.'

'Looked everywhere for it 'n'all. I can't find it nowhere. Even Geraldine couldn't find it neither, not even with her 'tector.'

'Her what?' asked Mrs. McAllister.

'Her 'tector. She's a 'tectorist. She's got a metal 'tector. Goes all over 'tectoring, don't you, girl? Couldn't find my watch though. I reckons a pig ate it. Still, suppose it'll come out of t'other end sometime soon. Stands to reason, don't it? Coming out t'other end.'

'Yes – well do go through to the lounge,' said Mrs McAllister pointing the way.

They entered the room as Bernard was finishing laying out a selection of different styles of his wrist watches on the closed lid of the Steinway grand piano.

'Oh what a beautiful piarno!' exclaimed Mrs Brierley. 'I used to play the piarnoforte when I was a girl. I've never seen one this big. Is it a concert grarnd?'

'Er, yes, a concert grand,' replied Bernard, a little taken aback by the woman's strange pronunciation.

Bridget, anticipating some rude comment from her husband, changed the subject and quickly asked, 'Would anyone like a cup of tea?'

'Not for me, m'duck,' said Mr Brierley. 'How about you, cupcake?' he asked his wife.

'No tharnk you, Mrs McAllister. I usually only drink crarnberry green tea.'

Bernard, who was in the process of lighting a cigar

coughed violently at Mrs Brierley's pronunciation of "cranberry" and said, 'I don't think we've got any *crarnberry* tea, have we, Bridget?'

Bernard, viewing the Brierleys as imposters disturbing his peace and tranquillity, seemed determined to get rid of them as soon as he could and came straight to the point. 'What type of watch are you looking for, Mr Brierley? I have several end-of-line models that have been discontinued and they are very reasonably priced compared to what you'd pay in a jeweller's. The wholesale price really. All good quality, Swiss made.'

Mr Brierley's eyes gleamed as he looked at the selection laid out before him.

'Them's bootiful, ain't they? I'd quite like one of them there dignals.'

'Dignal?' queried Bernard.

'Yer, dignal. One of them', he said, pointing at a watch.

'Oh, you mean *digital*,' chuckled Bernard.

Mrs Brierley picked up the watch her husband had selected. 'That is a nice watch, dear, very *farncy*. Nice leather strap too, so much nicer than *plarstic*.'

She handed the watch to her husband, 'Yeah, one o' them'll do nicely ta,' he said.

He examined it closely, turned it over to inspect the back and looked puzzled.

'How do you wind it up?'

'Don't be silly, dear,' said Mrs Brierley. 'You don't wind it up, it has a barttery. Everyone knows *thart.*'

Having agreed a price Mr Brierley produced a wad of money from his trouser pocket and placed some dirty notes on top of the grand piano lid. The notes were filthy and looked as though they had passed through the digestive system of one of his pigs, probably together with his missing watch. Bernard McAllister carefully picked them up, put them in his pocket, then wiped the piano lid and his hands with his handkerchief.

With the transaction completed and Gerald Brierley proudly wearing his new watch, they followed Bridget McAllister back through the hall, again pausing to admire the tapestries on the wall as they passed. Geraldine seemed to be interested in a particular tapestry.

'They're Persian tapestries, dear,' explained Bridget. 'They were Bernard's father's. He was in Persia after the First World War and brought these back with him.'

Geraldine gazed up at the ceiling in deep thought, 'Persia, that's near Evesham, ain't it, Mum? Where Aunt Esmeralda lives – ain't it between Evesham and Worcester?'

'No, Geraldine dear, that's Pershore. Mrs McAllister is talking about Persia.'

'It's called Iran now,' explained Bernard. 'It used to be called Persia.'

Geraldine appeared to be totally confused and continued gazing up at the tapestry.

'That's a funny lookin' 'orse ain't it? It's got a long neck and a big lump on its back.'

'It's a camel, dear,' said Bridget. 'I suppose you've got a busy year at school, have you Geraldine?'

'Yer, lots of exams.'

'What's your favourite subject?'

'Obviously not geography or zoology,' muttered Bernard to himself.

'Dunno really. Not much good at English. I ain't the goodest at English, are I, Mum?'

Bridget smiled, trying to conceal her amusement and asked, 'What do you want to do when you leave school, dear, are you going to work on the pig farm with your father?'

'I'd like to, but I've thought of being one of them there vetin… verterninny… a vet.'

'It'd be reet handy with a veterinny… veterinarian in the family. Some of them's bills is 'normous, ain't they, m'duck'? said Gerald Brierley looking at his wife, who tried to avoid the pig subject whenever she could.

'Well good luck with that then, dear,' said Bridget McAllister as she opened the front door.

Bernard and Bridget McAllister looked out of the front room window as the Brierleys crossed the road and entered the driveway of Beatrice Bassett where Gerald had parked their old Austin Westminster.

'Nice old Austin he's got, or should I say Orstin?' said Bernard chuckling. 'If Sam's her English teacher we'd better have a word with him, he's certainly got his work cut out with that one. I wouldn't want her looking at my pet either if she ever becomes a vet if she can't tell the difference between a horse and a camel.'

'My God what a rabble,' said Bridget. 'Sam said they were a bit odd. I'll go and get the air freshener.'

'*Mein Gott* indeed,' agreed Bernard.

CHAPTER 12

Another Monday morning had predictably arrived and Sam closed the door of the school secretary's office having collected a revised timetable for the week ahead. Mrs Brierley had gone into great detail about her recent visit to the McAllisters' home, recalling enthusiastically the incongruous items in the hallway, the pictures, tapestries, furniture and grandfather clock, not to mention the beautiful Steinway "grarnd piarno" in the lounge.

'Your parents are quite charming, dear, quite charming, and Gerald is so pleased with his new watch.'

As he walked to his classroom along the corridors bustling with students he sarcastically repeated Mrs Brierley's words in a silly voice – *Gerald is so pleased with his new watch.* 'Lucky old Gerald,' he muttered to himself.

Sam had wanted a new watch when he was thirteen years old. He'd entered the front room and his father had been sitting at the table, which was covered in black display boxes with red linings, each box containing a glistening new watch. There were ladies' and gents' watches, a few pocket watches and some upside down watches, the sort worn by nurses on their uniforms. They were all part of his father's new stock that had arrived and he was making notes of the stock numbers and entering them in his records. All were glittering and sparkling in the sunlight. Sam loved the sight and sound of new watches, the sparkling, the gentle ticking and the aroma of newness emanating from the open boxes. For a long time he had wanted a chronograph and his attention was immediately drawn to one with a shiny black face with gold roman numerals, a gold bezel with three gold buttons and a black leather strap. He picked up the box to admire it.

'Don't get your sticky finger marks all over it please,' his father had said as he'd snatched the box from Sam and returned it to the table.

'I like that one,' Sam had said.

'It's a new model.'

'How much is it?'

His father had tutted, showing his annoyance at being disturbed. He picked up his price list. 'It retails at nearly thirty pounds. The wholesale price is thirteen pounds.'

'Can I have one?'

'Have you got thirteen pounds?'

'No,'

'Well you can't have one then can you. Anyway what's wrong with the watch you've got?'

'I've had that since I was about five. It's a bit small and I've always fancied a chronograph. I've got a birthday coming up and I still have five pounds left from my Christmas money that Granny McAllister gave me.'

'Oh well. We'll have to see then, won't we?'

A few weeks later Sam had been presented with the new black chronograph for his fourteenth birthday but still had to hand over Granny McAllister's five pounds.

As he arrived at his classroom door he checked the time on his wristwatch, his dependable black chronograph, still on his wrist after all those years, still ticking away. It had served him well. He entered the classroom, raised the blinds on the large windows and the classroom was suddenly brilliantly lit by the morning sunshine. He glanced at the clock on the wall – eight forty-five. Then, looking at his wristwatch he tilted his hand in the sunlight so that the dial of his watch caught the sun, the gold numerals and sweeping second hand became highlighted in the bright sunlight. He watched the numerals disappear as the second hand swept across their path, only to reappear almost immediately. There was something comforting about that watch, the watch he'd looked at longingly thirty-six years ago on the front room table, the watch he had wanted so badly, the watch his father said he couldn't have, the watch he'd cherished for so many years, the watch that was now telling him it was eight forty-eight. He'd better get on. The rabble would be arriving soon.

*

Later that morning, with a free period, Sam McAllister sat alone in the school staffroom gazing out of the window, mesmerized by the trees swaying in the breeze and the dark clouds of an approaching storm. It was at quiet moments like this that his mind wandered and he would drift off into his dream world, the exciting alternative world of his imagination. He had often imagined the school being somewhere else, not in the busy built-up area of the town but out in the wilds of the Lincolnshire countryside, remote and isolated. It was a mirror image of his old secondary school he'd attended as a boy, the buildings, classrooms and corridors all familiar to him. He'd called it the South Lincolnshire Academy for Practical Studies (SLAPS for short), the students being affectionately referred to as "Slappers" by members of staff. It was a further education college where the brightest and best from a wide area attended prior to moving on to university. Being an agricultural area many of the students moved on to agricultural colleges so they could pursue a career on the family farms. There were practical courses such as mechanical engineering, welding and fabrication, hairdressing, bricklaying and more traditional courses such as English language and literature.

The Lincolnshire Fen landscape surrounding the college was flat, featureless and desolate, even a nearby village proudly displayed a sign "Twinned with the Moon". Agricultural tractors seemed to be the main form of conveyance in the area. No ghastly "Chelsea Tractors" here, these were real tractors, old Massey Fergusons and David Browns running on red diesel or chip fat oil. Most of the daily school runs were made by tractor or tatty old pickup trucks, not cars or shiny new 4x4s driven by city types who never got their tyres dirty. On arrival at the car park the wellington-booted offspring would jump down from the tractors and wander reluctantly into college.

Some of the students, having acquired their tractor licences at sixteen, drove themselves to college in their own aging tractors, the car park resembling a display of vintage tractors at an agricultural show. At break times small groups would gather round the tractors in mutual admiration of each other's vintage machinery discussing amongst themselves the advantages of the three-point linkage and the attachment of ploughs and harrows. At the end of the academic day there would be a cacophony of noisy diesel engines accompanied by clouds of black smoke as the tractors were started. What followed resembled the start of a Grand Prix as the tractors rushed to get to the college gates first before disappearing in clouds of smoke across the fields back to their isolated homesteads.

In the autumn and winter months shortcuts were taken across fields of sugar beet and freshly ploughed fields, resulting in great clods of earth being deposited in the car park. In the spring and early summer the landscape changed dramatically for a few weeks, the fields becoming a mass of colour with the bright yellow of oil seed rape, and red from acres of tulips being grown. On warm summer mornings the horizon shimmered in a heat haze and those who chose to walk to the college would arrive with a yellow tint to their clothes and skin from walking across fields of the oil seed rape in full flower, the air filled with its pungent aroma. In the dry summer months the approach and arrival of the tractors would be accompanied by great clouds of choking dust. What must have appeared to the city dweller as a dysfunctional, chaotic lifestyle was perfectly normal in these parts.

Sam's dreamy thoughts were interrupted by the entrance of Edmund Floyd the psychology lecturer.

'Morning Sam, have you got a free period?'

'Er… yes. Sorry, I was miles away, deep in thought.'

'Daydreaming again, Sam? You must come and chat with me about your fantasies sometime.' He laughed, took a notebook out of his jacket pocket, looked at Sam, made some notes, picked up some books and left the room chuckling.

Sam gazed out from the staffroom window and shivered as the wind picked up and raindrops appeared on the glass. His mind started wandering again, thinking what life would be like at his imaginary South Lincolnshire Academy for Practical Studies. The rain was falling heavily now and rattling on the windows. He started to doze…

It was a fine sunny June morning in the Lincolnshire Fens, a blue sky and not a cloud in sight. It was 08:15 and Sam looked out of his third-floor classroom window at the open countryside at the front of the college, enjoying his coffee before the start of the day. All was right with the world. A gentle breeze blew through the open windows carrying with it the scent of fertilizer and the unpleasant aroma from Gerald Brierley's nearby pig farm. The only noise was the sound of skylarks on high. Sam considered that life as a skylark would have its attractions, floating and fluttering on the warm summer air currents above the yellow fields of oil seed rape, singing on the wing all day then returning to the ground, back to the nest. No bills or mortgage, just the nest, the missus and a few eggs to look after. Knowing his luck, if he built his nest on the ground as skylarks do, some bugger would come along in a tractor and flatten it or spray it with insecticide. Either that or he'd get eaten by a fox or a weasel.

There was a loud noise, the sound of a car backfiring. He looked down at the car park below to see Rod Steele, the metalwork lecturer, coaxing his 1935 3½-litre Bentley the final few yards into a parking space next to Sam's MGB. Why is this place full of extraverts? thought Sam as he looked down at Rod lifting his 1940s leather case from the back seat and walking away from the steaming and smoking Bentley. Then Phyllis Stein the music teacher arrived and parked her Morris Minor Traveller next to the Bentley. The door dropped a couple of inches as she opened it and it started to swing shut as she attempted to extricate her bulging, well-nourished figure from the car. As she did so her dress caught in the window winder handle accompanied by the sound of tearing material. She lifted the car door, slammed it shut, then examined her torn dress. 'Oh bollocks, not again,' she said in a loud voice, which could be clearly heard by Sam from his vantage point at the third-floor window. The rear doors of the Morris Traveller creaked as she opened them to remove her cello case from the car. Having shut the doors with difficulty she walked away carrying her cello and exposing a large portion of left buttock through her torn dress.

Charming, *thought Sam.*

He had an ardent dislike of cellists, who all seemed deprived of a sense of humour and indulged in displays of excessive histrionics when playing the dreadful instrument. He had written a poem, which he recited as he watched the unfortunate music teacher struggling across the car park:

The cellist is a strange breed
What strange people they are,
They sit with their legs apart
It really is quite bizarre.

A girl was playing her cello
She was told it sounded sublime,
To others it sounded atrocious,
She couldn't play in time.

She was told she had such a talent,
A gift between her legs,
But all she could do was scratch it
And adjust the tuning pegs.

All cellists seem to move about,
They move in a ridiculous way,
Heads rolling, swaying and groaning
In a wild histrionic display.

"Such a gift and a talent"
I've heard some people say,
But what a din and a racket
They do make when they play.

Yes, the cellist is a strange breed,
What strange people they are,
They sit with their legs apart,
Why not learn the guitar?

Sam continued to gaze from the window and his attention was drawn away from the car park below to a slight rise in the ground far away on the horizon. You couldn't really call it a hill. There weren't any hills around here, just bumps in the landscape. Puffs of black smoke and the silhouette of agricultural tractors appeared on the skyline resembling the impending attack of menacing Indians in a cowboy film or General Custer's last stand.

Oh Lord, here they come. Such a lovely day in prospect and I'm going to be stuck in here with a load of reprobates who don't want to be here anymore than I do, *he thought.*

Sam looked down into the car park again as other members of staff arrived. Jenny Taylor, or Jenny Taylia as Sam had secretly named her, the young, attractive blonde biology teacher, was parking her car next to Phyllis Stein's Morris Traveller followed by the Ford Capri of Bernie Bunson the science teacher.

Sam returned to his desk to plan the morning lesson. He was going to talk about the sound and 'shape' of different words and started to think about what he was going to say although he hadn't a clue where to begin. He tried to think of words that sounded nasty and vulgar, words that when spoken, conjured up a vision of unpleasantness. He thought for some time before writing down the first word – Scrotum. Yes, scrotum was a horrible word, the very utterance of which created a vision of nastiness and something that was of little use other than to contain the testicles. Testicle, that was another horrible, nasty-sounding word, not a nice word to say and even less pleasant to think about. Was it a coincidence that all the nasty-sounding words he'd thought of so far related to the male reproductive region?

In contrast, the lady bits had nice-sounding names like Mons Pubis and Labia Majora, which he thought sounded like a star system in some far-off galaxy. Oh dear, maybe his students would think he was some sort of pervert. That was another nasty word – pervert. If someone called you a pervert, even if you didn't know what one was, one would be offended as it sounded offensive. By contrast, if someone called you a pillock you'd probably laugh it off as the word sounded funny.

His thoughts then moved onto the pronunciation of words in different dialects. If "scrotum" was spoken with a Birmingham accent with the letters "r" and "o" being accented it sounded even worse. If a Glaswegian accent was used the effect was horrible, particularly if the R's were rolled. Sam couldn't roll his R's too well so he started to practise, saying "scrrrotum" aloud several times, unaware that Jenny Taylor had entered the classroom.

'Miss Taylia, sorry I mean Miss Taylor. I do apologise, I didn't know you were there.'

'That's alright, Sam,' she said, looking a little puzzled. 'I was just passing. What on earth are you talking about?'

'I was just practising rolling my R's.'

'Oh, I see. That's not a nice word to use ,Sam.'

'That's exactly my point, Miss Taylor, not a nice word at all.'

'Why don't you use a different word – like rowlocks? You could roll the 'R' with that word.'

'Yes. That's a good word. Thank you.' Sam referred to his notes on his desk and wrote it down. Then he scrubbed it out and wrote "bollocks" instead, considering that to be an even better nasty-sounding word worthy of consideration.

'In your biology curriculum do you cover reproduction and all the associated naughty bits?' Sam inquired.

'Yes, of course. Why do you ask?'

'It's just that this morning I want to talk about the sound of different words, nasty-sounding words that, when spoken, create an equally nasty picture in the mind of the reader and nice-sounding words that create a nice image – words like daffodil or fluffy. So far the only nasty-sounding words I've come up with relate to the male genital area,' he said, handing Miss Taylor his list of words.

Miss Taylor looked down the list disapprovingly. 'Oh I see what you mean. It's quite normal to use some of these words in a biology lesson but surely a bit odd in an English class. Your students might think you're a bit odd.'

'Yes, I take your point, Miss Taylor. It's interesting though – words are strange. Take Devil for instance. Most people would agree not a nice word, but call him by another name, Old Nick or Beelzebub, and he sounds quite a jolly sort of fellow.'

Miss Taylor gave Sam a strange look. 'Yes. I see what you mean. Well good luck with that one,' she said and left the room.

Sam looked at his list of nasty words – scrotum, testicle, pervert, pillock and bollocks. She's right, this won't do at all, he thought and tore up the list.

He hadn't time to compose a new list of nasty and nice words as his class were reluctantly starting to enter the room and take their seats so he decided to return to that subject at a future date after he could give the matter more thought and with better preparation. He walked to the back of the classroom and closed the door.

'Morning all,' he said as he walked back to his desk

'Morning, Mr McAllister, sir,' was the unenthusiastic reply.

Sam shuffled around in his desk drawers looking for another interesting lesson he had planned.

'Ah, here we are,' he said as he picked up some papers. 'Can anyone remember what a synonym is? We discussed them the other day.'

No one could remember so he refreshed their memories.

'They are words that have the same, or nearly the same meaning as other words. For example bad, awful, terrible can mean the same, and by a strange coincidence best describe you lot. Good, fine and excellent are also synonyms which could describe you lot if you paid attention and worked harder.

'Oh yes,' someone mumbled from the back of the class.

Sam couldn't decide if the mumbling in the affirmative was in vague recollection of what a synonym was, or in agreement of his assessment of their ability.

'Today we're going to be discussing homonyms – words that are sometimes spelt the same that have more than one meaning. Can anyone think of an example?'

Nobody could.

'What have I just been doing whilst I was looking for my papers? I was fiddling around and looking in my drawers.'

There was hysterical laughter from the class.

'That doesn't mean to say I've had my head in my underpants. I've been fiddling around looking in my desk drawers, the word drawers having two meanings, in fact several meanings. Sam picked up his large dictionary and fumbled for the correct page. 'Drawer – "a lidless sliding

container that fits into a framework", like my desk drawer, in plural form it's an undergarment or a chest of drawers. If it's pronounced slightly differently the same word can mean someone drawing a cheque or money order or someone drawing out drinks, like pulling a pint in the pub.'

A faint murmur of understanding went round the room.

'Can anyone think of any more words that are homonyms?'

'Chest,' shouted Geraldine Brierley. 'Chest as in chest of drawers like what you just mentioned or one of these', she said lifting both her breasts up in a slightly suggestive sort of way.

'Well... er yes, Geraldine, or it could be a large box as well, like a money chest. You get the idea then. Now let's discuss the way the English language has changed with the passing of time. Has anyone seen the 1933 film Going Gay?'

Laughter filled the room once more.

'Or maybe you've heard of the 1934 musical The Gay Divorcee *starring Ginger Rogers and Fred Astaire? Gay used to be a word widely used in the '20s and '30s. A lovely old word that has now been hijacked by a certain section of society to mean something completely different from its original meaning.' Sam consulted his dictionary again while sniggering continued to circulate the room. 'Definition of Gay – lively, cheerful, merry, bright in colour, showy, nothing to do with what first came into your minds. It's like "cool", that's another word that's been taken over by you lot, the younger generation.' Sam pointed at a boy at the front of the class. 'When Maisie Fergusson arrived at college yesterday on her Massey Fergusson tractor I*

heard you describe it as "cool". How can a tractor be cool? The definition of "cool" in my dictionary is moderately or pleasantly cold or not too warm. Why do we have to reinvent the English language? There's nothing wrong with it.'

'I wasn't referring to the tractor,' the boy responded meekly. 'It's an awful tractor, it was just the fact that Maisie Fergusson was driving a Massey Fergusson, rather cool, ain't it? It's a bit like having a personal number plate.'

Sam drew a deep breath in frustration and continued, 'Another word we no longer use in its original meaning is ejaculate.' Hysterical laughter filled the room once more. 'The definition in the dictionary is to "utter suddenly, to shout or to exclaim". Has anyone ever read the wonderful books by Sir Arthur Conan Doyle? He wrote the Sherlock Holmes novels.'

Nobody had.

'At that time, we're talking late 1800s and early 1900s it was a word widely used in literature. There was a lot of ejaculating going on in literature in those times. Whereas now it might be written "'Stop!" shouted the policeman", in those days it could have been written "'Stop!' ejaculated the policeman". Anyway, that's enough of ejaculating policeman, we'll move on. There is of course a physiological meaning to the word but I'm sure Miss Taylia will cover that in her biology class.'

'Do you mean Miss Taylor, sir?' interjected a boy at the front.

'Yes, quite correct, of course I meant Miss Taylor.'

Geraldine Brierley raised her hand at the back of the

room. 'Does that mean them two words, cool, gay and ejaculate are them there homononymums 'n' all, sir?'

'Yes, Geraldine, but that was three words – obviously your maths is as bad as your English.' Light hearted chuckling circulated the room. 'And it's homonyms, not homononymums or whatever it was you said.' Sam drew a deep breath and continued, 'I have a brother called Duncan Gylchrist McAllister. He's older than me but I remember whenever he used to read a book if he came across a word he'd not seen before or didn't know the meaning of he would write it down. He would look the word up in his dictionary to discover the meaning of the word in the context that it had been used. When he'd finished reading the book he would always have a list of dozens of words, new words that he'd discovered, new words that he could use in his future social intercourse.'

A roar of hysterical laughter filled the classroom again. Sam raised his hands for silence.

'There you go again,' said Sam. He picked up his dictionary from his desk. After a few moments he found the page, looked around the room and continued.' "Intercourse – dealings of people with each other, communication, social interaction, fellowship, copulation". I should imagine it's the last meaning of the word that immediately sprang to your minds, but that's another example of a word that we seldom use for its other meanings. Returning to my brother Duncan Gylchrist McAllister, by compiling his list of "new" words he expanded his vocabulary, acquiring an extensive vocabulary of long, unusual words, most of which his listeners didn't know the meaning of. This had a tendency to baffle the listener, who either dismissed the conversation *thinking he was boring, or a smart-arse, or they lost interest due to their own inadequacies and ignorance of the English language. What's the point of reading words on a page if you don't know their meaning? So when you're reading if you come across a word that you don't recognise, or don't know the meaning of, don't just gloss over it and read on, take a leaf out of Duncan Gylchrist McAllister's book, write it down, look it up, remember it and use it.*

'Here endeth today's lesson.'

He suddenly woke up with a start and was returned to reality with the sound of loud voices approaching and the staffroom door being flung open. Lunchtime had brought his dreamy thoughts to an abrupt end. Maybe he could use some of them in one of his real-life lessons, or perhaps not.

CHAPTER 13

As the years passed little changed, or if it did Sam McAllister didn't notice, apart that is from the annual influx of new students – different names and different faces but the same challenges. Nevertheless, life for him was comfortable, though predictable. He'd never been particularly adventurous, had no great desire to travel or to further his career, being content to remain in the area he knew, with the people he knew. The prospect of everything remaining much the same until retirement depressed him somewhat. *Retirement – can't wait,* he thought, *I can start doing the things in life I've always wanted to but never had the time.* He wondered if his father had had the same thoughts. His long retirement had begun at fifty-five and he'd followed the same daily routine ever since, shutting himself away with his blasted piano all day, only emerging for a visit to the bathroom or when summoned by Bridget for his meals, a routine only broken at certain times of the year to watch Wimbledon or the indoor bowls tournaments on television.

Much had changed in Beatrice Bassett's world. She had found brief excitement in the acquisition of husband number two, Eustace, the bachelor younger brother of her first husband, a convenient marriage in a way as a change of surname was not required, saving Beatrice considerable time in correspondence. She did however briefly consider adopting the double-barrelled surname of Bassett-Bassett in keeping with her Bassett husband tally. This idea was soon rejected however as she considered Beatrice Bassett-Bassett would sound rather ostentatious.

Eustace, or "useless" as she was soon to refer to him, was rather a disappointment in a physical sense compared to his late older brother, displaying poor stamina and endurance as he struggled to meet her demanding physical requirements. Oh how she tried to encourage and train him, but for him the novelty of married life soon wore off and the lure of *Coronation Street* or a football match on television was too great and he continued to dissatisfy.

Eustace was a keen horticulturist and worked for a large local garden centre. On Tuesday evenings he tended the garden of a local artist and on Thursday evenings the garden of the nearby vicarage. The artist and vicar were both openly gay and Eustace would often return home apparently stimulated and enlightened by conversations on theology he'd had with the vicar and enthusing on his homemade elderberry wine. When not occupied at the vicarage or the artist's gardens, his evenings were spent on his allotment or in his greenhouse tending his seedlings and engrossed with stem cuttings and propagation of orchids. Beatrice, having become more frustrated, sought solace with the sherry bottle and reading cheap erotic literature as a substitute for her husband's lack of interest in her and his apparent preference of propagation in the greenhouse to copulation in the bedroom.

Each morning Beatrice would sit in her porch awaiting the arrival of the postman, a pleasant-looking young man who wore a T-shirt and shorts whatever the weather, displaying what she considered to be tanned physical perfection. So too it seemed to Beatrice did Eustace, particularly when waiting with great anticipation for the delivery of his monthly gardening magazine. This had given her cause for concern – was she married to a closeted homosexual horticulturist? she wondered, sighed in despair then reached for the sherry bottle.

One evening Eustace returned home from his allotment after a particularly strenuous evening of weeding and digging, had his bath and emerged from the bathroom to be confronted by Beatrice standing suggestively in the bedroom doorway modelling her latest red lingerie in an attempt to arouse 'useless' Eustace. It seemed to have the desired effect. She turned and walked into the bedroom. He followed, then stood behind her, facing the window with the bright evening sunshine glistening on her long flowing greying hair. Eustace kissed her shoulders gently and inhaled the scent of her perfume. He unclasped the fastening of her bra, slid the straps off her shoulders and let the garment fall to the floor. Still standing behind her his hands gently caressed her breasts. Beatrice groaned, broke away from his embrace, walked slowly towards the window and raised her arms to close the curtains. At that precise moment Mr Dennison's double decker bus was passing on its return journey from the town centre and all eyes on the upper deck were turned to the right in appreciation of the full frontal nakedness of Beatrice Bassett as she began to close her curtains. She heard Eustace utter a deep groan followed the sound of him falling onto the bed, no doubt she thought in anticipation of what he was about to receive, no doubt thinking whatever it was he was about to receive may he be truly thankful and grateful to be married to a vibrant and stimulating woman like herself.

She walked slowly to the bed and sat astride Eustace's recumbent body, untied the belt of his tartan dressing gown and leant forwards to kiss him, recoiling immediately at the sight of his fixed idiotic smile and wide open eyes. She slapped his face. No response.

'Oh bugger!' she screamed. 'Not another one! Not again!'

Beatrice Bassett's curtains remained closed.

Duncan McAllister, although still working as librarian at the college in Lincoln, had become as part-time as part-time could be and spent increasing amounts of time at home with his parents, to the frustration of his father and the delight of his mother. For years Bridget McAllister's existence had been mundane and lonely but had become enriched by the constant presence of Duncan and *his* world seemed to revolve around his mother. He had become her constant companion whilst his father continued to shut himself away. This strange relationship resulted in Duncan becoming mollycoddled and cosseted by his mother, at times almost as if she was protecting a small child from all the nastiness in the world and all the nasty people. He seemed unable to go anywhere without her and would probably have asked her permission in the unlikely event that he wanted to. He seemed willing to remain a bachelor, willing to be deprived of a 'normal' independent life. Perhaps unintentionally, or maybe not, what appeared to be his mother's long process of control and manipulation had begun.

Sam often sat alone with his thoughts, contemplating life, and one evening was in a sombre mood as he reflected on his brother and men throughout history who'd had a maternal obsession and been controlled, even dominated, by their mothers. Adolf Hitler as a child is known to have had a dislike of his father but a close and obsessive relationship with his mother. On the big screen this strange phenomenon had also been portrayed by characters like Norman Bates in *Psycho* and James Cagney in *White Heat* – "*Made it Ma! Top of the World!*" the memorable closing line in the film.

'You look serious,' said Morag.

'Oh, just thinking,' replied Sam. 'Everyone seems to be living the life of Riley except us. I seem to be the only bugger in my family who has to work for a living anymore, who has to work to pay the bills and the blasted mortgage. That's another thing, I'm the only one in the family who's needed a blasted mortgage. We've been paying it for twenty-five years, still, only a few more to go.'

'Well you are the youngest, Sam. We're still only in our fifties. The others have done their bit.'

'Done their bit! If Duncan had to do a day's work he'd need a week off to get over it, poor darling.

'I remember Dad patting me on the back after I'd been

in my first job for a year and saying, "Well done, son, you've proved to me you can hold a job down." It was like something out of a 1930's film, strutting round the room with his pipe in his mouth – proper stiff upper lip stuff.'

'Do try to calm down. You'll make yourself ill,' said Morag.

Ignoring Morag, he continued. 'Where does time go Morag? We were married at twenty-two and our lives have passed by at an alarming rate as if the fast forward button had been pressed. From the start of our working lives we seem to wish time away. Why do we do that? Why are we obsessed with time? Every week it's, "*I* must buy next week's television programmes." Every month I seem to say to myself, "It's only two weeks until the next pay cheque." Every year, "It's only five weeks until Christmas. I must get a diary and calendar for next year, another year gone." We spend so much of our lives wishing time away that when we approach retirement age we wonder where it's all gone. Can I have another go please? "No that's your lot, sonny. You only get one go, so make the most of it," my father once told me. He'd been right as usual of course.'

Morag, sensing Sam would continue into one of his tedious, extended monologues, picked up a magazine and started to flick through the pages.

'But what is time, Morag? Perhaps merely a convenient division of people's lives – days, weeks, months and years, the divisions conveniently split into recognisable periods. It makes you wonder if previous civilisations had similar problems with the passing of time, or for them maybe time didn't exist other than night and day and the seasons. For someone living in a cave or an Iron Age roundhouse with none of the modern-day distractions that dominate *our* lives – careers, mortgages, the internet, clocks, social media and television – for them, with time calculated by the sun, the moon and the seasons, had time seemed to pass slower? Every day I look at the clock on the classroom wall and think, *it'll soon be time to go home, the end of another day. Tomorrow is the end of another week. Next week is the end of another month. Next month will be the end of another year.* The passing of another year is something to be regretted, Morag, something to be mourned, not something to be celebrated. As you well know I hate New Year's Eve and the fact that it's your birthday makes it worse.'

'I don't much like it either, but I can't help when I was born,' said Morag putting down the magazine thinking Sam had finished his moaning.

'What a terrible day to have a birthday, Morag, the most depressing day of the year. If we want to go out for a nice quiet lunch somewhere, we can't. Most places are shut in preparation for the arrival of the expected hoards of revellers, those who overindulge, those who are convinced rather naively that things in general, the world and their lives, will be so much better tomorrow, the start of a new year, a new beginning. It's almost as if they think that from midnight they'll be passing through some sort of gateway to a different world, a better world. It's all bollocks. The next day and the next year will be the same as the previous one, or even worse – the same old shit, just a different date.'

*

The passing of time had resulted in the old neighbour Reginald Ramsbottom's behaviour becoming more strange and eccentric. The E-Type, still in the garage rusting away as Bernard had predicted, had become unloved and unused and had been replaced as a general conveyance by a mobility scooter, a sporty little model with a detachable hood, indicators and lights.

'Marvellous machine,' he said enthusiastically to Bernard one day over the garden hedge. 'It goes for miles on a full battery, just like a little car, much cheaper to run though, no road tax or insurance. It's a bit slow though. I got pulled up by the police on the ring road yesterday. Damned fool said I wasn't allowed on the dual carriageway, cheeky bugger. I said I'd got as much right as anybody else to be on the dual carriageway. He started getting shirty with me. Said he'd give me a police escort to get off the dual carriageway. I told him I didn't want a blasted Ford Escort, got a Jaguar E-Type in the garage. He didn't believe me though. He didn't look old enough to be a policeman, looked like a blasted schoolboy. Do you remember when all policemen had moustaches and drove around in Wolseleys and Morris Minors? Wouldn't have caught me in a Morris Minor, I'd have had the legs on him.'

He'd now developed an annoying habit of trying to convert others to his strange religious beliefs and what he considered to be his high moral standards, resulting in the few people he came into contact with to consider him a bigot. His vegetarian diet had become stricter and on a rare visit next door to see the McAllisters he started to lecture Bridget on the importance of a healthy diet.

'Don't you stand there and tell me what to eat!'

exclaimed Bridget. 'Look at you, all skin and bones. You haven't eaten a proper wholesome meal in years. You look like a garden rake. You don't drink milk or have any dairy products. Your body needs calcium to keep your teeth and bones healthy and strong.'

'Milk and cheese? I don't think so, they're full of fat. Bad for you,' replied Reg.

'You don't even eat vegetables anymore.'

'They're all poisoned with sprays and insecticides,' he said.

'Rubbish, man.'

Bridget put the kettle on. 'It's time for Bernard's morning cup of coffee. I won't bother to offer you one. I know you don't drink tea or coffee either. All you seem to eat is fruit.'

'I get my fluid intake from my fruit diet. I don't even buy fruit juice now, it's full of sugar.'

'You should drink water then,' said Bridget.

'Tap water's full of impurities and chemicals.'

'Rubbish!' exclaimed Bridget.

'I bought a water purifier but don't use it anymore, uses too much electricity. No, I get all the fluids I need from my fruit diet thank you.'

'Nonsense,' said Bridget. 'You'll make yourself ill.'

Reg shrugged his shoulders and moved onto the subject of how food should be chewed correctly, going into some detail on the subject of good mastication.

'Mastication is so important, each mouthful should be chewed twenty times before swallowing to aid proper digestion,' he said.

'Don't you tell me what to eat and how to eat it!' exclaimed Bridget.

Her advice fell on deaf ears, extremely large deaf ears with black hair protruding from them. It came as no surprise when a few weeks later Mr Reginald Ramsbottom was admitted to hospital with kidney failure.

He never returned home.

*

The funeral was a quiet affair attended by the McAllisters and a few of the congregation from the Church of… whatever it was called – the "Happy Clappy brigade" as Bridget McAllister referred to them. There was a lot of incoherent mumbling at the graveside by the odd church 'friends' after which they all dispersed without saying a word to anyone else.

'Strange people,' remarked Bridget McAllister as she watched them walk slowly away in a long line towards their minibus, clutching their Bibles. 'Very strange. Call themselves Christians? I've never seen such an odd bunch.'

A few days later Bridget McAllister and Duncan were back at the solicitor's office. It was fortunate she had mentioned the discounted will writing service to Reginald Ramsbottom a few weeks previously. He had left his entire estate to Duncan, apart from a considerable £25,000 donation to the Church of… whatever it was called.

Whether as a result of Bridget McAllister's influence, or just Reg's goodwill, Duncan McAllister inherited a considerable estate, Reginald Ramsbottom's house and the Jaguar E-Type that was still languishing in the garage.

CHAPTER 14

Duncan's good fortune enabled him to move out of the depressing house he had resided in for several years. The property with the strange name of "Rock Mead" was owned by his father and was a large Victorian semi-detached house divided up into several bedsits and had remained unchanged for the twenty years his father had enjoyed an income from the rent. As the years passed he had been reluctant to modernise the property or to update it to meet the changing fire regulations, so when the five tenants left one by one over time, they weren't replaced and the property eventually became empty. Duncan had moved in, confining himself to living in one room that had previously been one of the bedsits. The house was dismal, drab, dark and damp. The only toilet was downstairs and would originally have been located outside but had been incorporated into the main house by a rickety lean-to structure with crumbling plaster walls and a leaking tiled roof. The WC resembled something from the 1940s, having a dark-green wooden door, the bottom of which was about nine inches from the ground. Inside, it had cream-painted brick walls and an uneven brick floor. The toilet itself was an original Thomas Crapper "pull and clank" model. The cistern was located near the ceiling and was connected to the toilet below by a vertical metal pipe covered with peeling brown paint. A white rubber handle dangled at the end of a long rusty chain that swung in the draught from the small high window that was permanently open. The toilet door opened onto a red-brick-floored corridor which led to the main house in one direction and in the other direction what can only be described as a lean-to kitchen with damp mould-covered walls, rotten window frames and an ancient rusty and stained gas cooker.

Each of the five rooms, which had previously been used as bedsits (the three bedrooms and two large rooms downstairs), were furnished with cheap furniture – a wardrobe, an iron framed bed, a bedside cupboard, a small table with a single chair, and each room had a two-bar electric fire built into the old fireplace.

*

A few weeks after Reginald Ramsbottom's funeral Sam called on his parents, managing to avoid his father, and sat talking with his mother.

'Your father and I have been at Rock Mead with Duncan today, poor dear,' she said. 'We met someone from a charity shop there who wanted to look at the furniture in the house. We were hoping they'd take it all but they don't want any of it, bloomin' cheek, it's all lovely quality furniture. We've got to empty the house. Your father's putting it on the market so everything will have to go to the tip, such a shame.'

'Best place for it. Mother, I wouldn't want any of it in our house. All that stuff was bought in the 1970s, it's awful, wanted chucking out years ago. Things have to comply with fire regulations so they wouldn't be able to sell it anyway.'

'That's the trouble with people today, they want everything new. When we were young we were grateful for anything we could get, there was a war on. Duncan's next door. He's been busy moving in all week, poor darling. Why don't you pop round and see him?'

As Sam walked down the hallway to leave he paused at the open door of the front room and looked in to see his father sitting at the table counting money and putting coins into neat piles before entering figures into his records with grunts of satisfaction. He'd returned from Rock Mead with bags full of money having emptied the electric pay meters that the tenants had used to pay for their electric. Thinking the spectacle resembled a scene from *Scrooge*, Sam sniggered and left the house.

*

The front door of Reginald Ramsbottom's old house next door was ajar and creaked loudly as Sam slowly pushed it open. He walked slowly through the hallway, its tiled floor covered with thick dust and the leaves that had blown in with the wind over the years. As he entered the large kitchen he saw Duncan sitting at the table, looking a little agitated with his head leaning on his left arm and a pen in his right hand. 'It grieves me, but I do it – I have to do it,' he wailed.

'That sounds a bit melodramatic. Is that Shakespeare?'

Duncan, being startled, turned suddenly in his chair. 'Oh, it's you,' he said.

'Yes, it's only me. Sorry to disappoint you.'

Sam glanced around the room. The kitchen table was littered with letters, bills, bank statements and empty beer bottles. There was nowhere to sit, the chairs around the table being piled high with car workshop manuals, car parts and general clutter.

'You don't want a drink, do you?' Duncan asked.

Sam, having decided that the assumption had already been made that he didn't want a drink by the way the question had been asked, replied in the negative.

'That's alright then,' said Duncan.

Duncan had written a cheque and his hand was quivering as he tried to sign it. Sam had often admired his brother's neat handwriting and wonderful flowing signature, but before he signed his name his hand always shook and his fingers twitched, rather like the teleprinter that used to give the football results on Grandstand on BBC1 in the 1960s when the teleprinter had always appeared to hesitate before it got going.

'I've got to send a cheque to that ghastly church in America. I've been putting it off but they've written to me asking where their money is, the bastards.'

Duncan had been dealing with the probate on the late Reginald Ramsbottom's estate and he thought if he forgot about the church donation in the will, then so would they, or were they even aware of their imminent windfall? They were very much aware. They hadn't forgotten.

As Duncan's hand continued to shake violently before signing the cheque, Sam walked from the kitchen and briefly entered the lounge. A more eclectic combination of items was hard to imagine. He recognised some of his brother's things and items of furniture that had belonged to their grandparents that he'd acquired. There were car parts everywhere; cylinder heads, an old gearbox and a Jaguar bonnet sat in one corner of the spacious lounge. There were carburettors, wiring looms, steering wheels scattered around and even an old Alfa Romeo engine. Duncan's possessions had been interspersed with Reg's furniture and meagre possessions, resulting in a strangely incongruous combination of items.

'This could be a lovely home, have you got any plans? Maybe a skip?' asked Sam sarcastically.

Ignoring the sarcasm Duncan poured some whisky into his cup of black tea, just a cheap blend of a nondescript brand. He stood up from the table and started stirring his tea vigorously as he looked out of the kitchen window with his back turned, his usual posture on the rare occasions he had visitors.

Sam moved to the kitchen window and stood by his brother's side looking out at the overgrown garden, the trees and bushes that had been left to grow unchecked. What was once a lovely garden was now a vision of abandonment and neglect. The wooden conservatory where Reginald Ramsbottom had sunbathed naked all those years before whilst being observed through the gap in the fence by their father had tumbled down long ago, as had most of the fence. The floor of the derelict conservatory was covered with what appeared to be scrap metal – old car engines, gearboxes and axles together with old car wheels and tyres, probably things that Duncan thought would be useful one day, but that day had not yet arrived and probably never would. The vigorous stirring of the tea continued. Sam looked out of the window where the greenhouse had once stood. Only its brick base remained with a mass of ivy above it. The ivy had once covered the derelict greenhouse, which had then collapsed beneath it and strangely the ivy had retained a vague greenhouse shape.

At last the teaspoon was returned to the saucer.

'Why didn't you clear out all Reg's crap before you moved in?' asked Sam. 'I'd have helped you. You only had to ask.'

'It's not crap. They're Reg's possessions. He was a wonderful man…'

'He was a crackpot with a weird diet and a strange religion. All you've done is move in and keep all his old stuff and add yours to it.'

Duncan picked up the teaspoon and resumed stirring his tea, even more vigorously now as he became agitated. He continued to stare out of the kitchen window, still with his back turned. 'You can have a look upstairs if you like.'

Sam climbed the bare wooden staircase with Duncan following. The bathroom door was open and from the landing, Sam, with no desire to enter, looked inside at the chipped and badly stained ceramic bath. The washbasin was in a similar condition with one of the taps pointing ninety degrees from where it should be and above it was a cracked mirror on the wall. Wallpaper was hanging down revealing large cracks in the plaster and the ceiling light, like a large glass bowl, contained a multitude of dead insects. As Sam looked in despair at the antiquated toilet with its broken seat, Duncan seemed to read his thoughts. 'I do miss my Thomas Crapper pull and clank toilet,' he said as he turned his gaze skyward as if seeking divine inspiration, a sure sign he was about to regurgitate some facts that had been retained in his memory for years. Then, inevitably he started... 'Thomas Crapper was born in eighteen thirty-six and started his plumbing and sanitary business in eighteen sixty-one, opening his first bathroom showroom, in fact the world's first bathroom showroom, and he went on to patent the floating ball cock...'

Sam, anticipating a long monologue on Thomas Crapper's life story, started to walk from the bathroom onto the landing, leaving Duncan in the bathroom mumbling something about earth closets and the introduction of the water flushing system. From the landing he entered the bedroom that had once been Reg's workshop, where Sam as a young boy had sat with him as he carried out his watch repairs. It was just as he remembered. His old workbench still dominated the room with its rusty Anglepoise lamp and small tools scattered about on it. Even his small black eyeglass, now grey with thick dust, lay on the workbench, everything left as if he was expected to enter the room at any moment to continue his work. Also on the workbench was a box of Reg's old photographs, photographs of people, no one knew who, maybe old relatives long since dead, or so-called friends from the Church of... whatever it was called in Hertfordshire. The old television sets and tape recorders were still there and had been joined by video recorders and cassette players from the 1980s. Dozens of videotapes now shared the shelves with cassette tapes and spools of audio tape. Sam swept aside cobwebs that were dangling from the ceiling as he moved about the room and approached the window. One of the curtains was closed, the other hanging down from a broken curtain rail revealing a windowsill with its paint peeling, covered with dead flies, wasps and spiders, all brown and shrivelled up from years of exposure to the sun. Underneath the window was an old bicycle, Sam's green Puch racing cycle. Just before his sixteenth birthday his grandmother on his mother's side had moved to the area from her Kent village shortly after his grandfather had died and she had bought it for Sam. Most of his friends had progressed to mopeds, yellow Puch Maxi mopeds. Sam wasn't allowed a yellow Puch moped, he had a green Puch racing bike. He'd never had a new bike before. He'd never had a new *anything* before apart from his school uniform, a Smiths watch for his fifth birthday and the chronograph for his fourteenth birthday that he'd even had to put some of his own money towards. He had lived in a world of hand-me-downs, other people's cast-offs; his cousin's old jeans he'd grown out of and his brother's jumpers and old bikes that had to be fitted with wooden blocks on the pedals so his feet reached them. Two years after his grandmother treated him to his new Puch racing bike Sam had sold it to his father for forty pounds. Four wheels were about to become his preferred mode of transport and he needed one hundred and fifty pounds to buy his mother's old Wolseley Hornet from his father. Why couldn't he simply just give it to him or sell it to him at a lower price? He never gave him anything although he was always spending money on himself, his pianos and his cars. When he'd managed to eventually pay for the car thanks to his part-time job as a cashier at a petrol station his father had said, 'Don't forget to buy some "L" plates before you have lessons.' He even had to buy his bloody 'L' plates. At the time Sam thought if he ever had children he would buy them things. It would be nice to give them things, to treat them if they deserved it. Maybe *he* didn't deserve it. Maybe it was his father's revenge for Sam going to sleep at night leaving the light on, having too much marmalade on his toast, being rebellious, taking up the banjo or playing Led Zeppelin too loudly in the summer house when he was younger.

His mother had taught him to drive. She was patient and good-natured. His father couldn't teach him anything. He couldn't teach him how to play the piano or drive a car. He was bad-tempered. It would have to be done his way or not at all. He was always right.

Sam pulled the bike away from the window, wiped the dust from the saddle and sat on it thinking it would be nice to have it back, to ride it again after all those years. Duncan had never used it and probably never would. He wondered if Duncan had bought it from their father or had been given it. He'd probably been given it. *He* was given everything. The tyres were flat but it still looked good under all the dust. One day he'd ask for it back. Duncan was generous. Duncan would give it back to him if he asked him.

Sam heard Duncan's voice on the landing. He left the room and followed Duncan into one of the other bedrooms. It had been Reg's mother's bedroom. Sam remembered when he was about eleven years old Reg had called round one morning and said that he couldn't wake his mother. Sam's mother had gone next door with Reg to discover she had passed away in her sleep. That was in 1970. The bed was still there, it hadn't even been stripped, her clothes were still lying on a chair at the bottom of the bed and others still hung in the wardrobe, moth eaten and dusty. A scent bottle and a hairbrush with strands of her white hair were still on the dusty dressing table. A shiver went down Sam's spine and a feeling of uneasiness, a strange feeling that there was someone else in the room apart from himself and Duncan. *I've got to get out of here*, he thought. *This is just awful. It's weird.*

Sam rushed down the bare wooden staircase to the front door, flung it open and breathed in the fresh air.

'Don't let me detain you,' Duncan shouted from the top of the stairs. 'I'm sure you must have more pressing business to attend to. Shut the door on your way out.'

Sam walked briskly along the gravel path towards the front gate. If he could have run he would have but his feet were slipping in the deep gravel. He had a strange sensation as he approached the gate that it was getting further away from him, as if he was being prevented from reaching the gate by something that was restraining him and trying to pull him back towards the house. With relief he reached the gate, got in his car and locked the door. Before he drove away he looked up at the house. Duncan was standing in the bedroom window, his outline highlighted by the dim light of the naked bulb hanging from the ceiling.

Having arrived home, Sam poured a large whisky, sat down at the kitchen table and shook his head.

'Whatever is the matter?' Morag asked.

'It's Duncan. I've just been round to see him. He's moved all his things into Reg's old house. Most normal people would clear all the old crap out of a house before they move in. Not him, he just puts everything on top of what was there already. Now all his stuff is mixed up with Reg's. Most of it wants chucking out. Reg must have been as bad. His mother died in 1970, that's forty years ago. Her bedroom is the same as the day she died. I half expected to see her spin round in her old chair with the light swinging from the ceiling like that scene from *Psycho*.'

'It's not normal,' said Morag.

'No,' replied Sam, 'but what is normal? If being normal means conforming to a usual standard or being conventional and not being eccentric, strange or idiosyncratic then you're quite correct, it's not normal; but then you can't describe anyone who's lived in that house as being normal.'

*

A lot of bachelors – either through destiny or circumstances, who live a solitary existence in a large house without the guiding influence of a woman, be they wife or mother – would in many cases succumb to a decline in domestic standards of cleanliness and tidiness and perhaps eventually even personal hygiene.

In Reginald Ramsbottom's case all three had applied. It was concerning to Sam that the first two of those questionable qualities were already apparent in his brother's demeanour and he had been living in the house for only a few days.

What was it about that house? Was the house somehow saying, "'Will you walk into my parlour?' said the spider to the fly".

CHAPTER 15

'Cor, look at this one, she's double-fronted. A vulgar display of protuberance,' remarked Duncan as he observed a particularly large-chested woman walking by the camper van wearing a T-shirt with what lay beneath unrestrained, leaving little to the imagination. The windows of the camper van had privacy glass, ideal for what Mrs McAllister called "people watching" and together they would sit and observe people in the car park with Duncan making sarcastic comments about people passing by, safe in the knowledge that he could neither be seen nor heard.

Emma and Kendrick's camper van had led a cloistered life, only being used for occasional meet-ups with the rest of the family at a motorway services halfway between their home in London and the McAllisters' in South Lincolnshire. Bernard McAllister never joined them, preferring to spend the time alone at home with his piano. The quarterly meetings were usually arranged for a Saturday morning and about a week before Sam would receive a phone call from his mother asking the usual question: 'Are you available to drive next Saturday as usual, dear?' Sam always drove.

The camper van saved Bridget McAllister, now in her late eighties, the arduous walk from the car park to the cafe and it provided more privacy for their conversations and Duncan more entertainment with his observations. 'This is much nicer sitting in here, isn't it?' he said. 'We don't have to sit in that awful cafe with all those other ghastly people – nasty common specimens.'

Kendrick looked at Sam and raised an eyebrow before taking out his notebook, no doubt to record Duncan's strange behaviour.

Sam had a sudden rush of inspiration for a poem and also took out a notebook and pen from his jacket pocket and started to write a few lines before his brief period of creativity deserted him:

Behind the privacy glass of a camper van
Sat a sinister, bitter and twisted man,
Dressed like a tramp and with dishevelled hair
He would sit and moan and laugh and stare
At passers-by, the unfortunate few
Who happened to walk by within his view.

A woman approached with a radiant glow,
Wearing a T-shirt with all on show,
What lay beneath unrestrained and free,
Proudly shown for all to see,
'Look at this one coming,' said he in the van,
That sinister, bitter and twisted man.

Sam looked at Duncan, who was still peering from the window waiting for his next victim to approach. Sam then looked at his mother. His mother was looking at him, a penetrating stare, almost as if she knew what he was thinking, as if she knew what he'd just written. He was almost expecting her to say, "Don't be rude to Duncan dear." With his brief period of inspiration over he returned his notebook and pen to his jacket pocket. He'd finish it later. He recalled the embarrassment of a previous visit to the cafe before the acquisition of the camper van. As they had walked to the cafe from the car park progress had been slow as Mrs McAllister was a little unsteady on her feet even with Emma clutching her arm.

'Do you want your stick, Mummy?' Duncan had asked.

'No I don't and do stop calling me Mummy, call me Mother. You're over sixty for heaven's sake, you're not a child,' she had replied sternly.

In the absence of the walking stick Duncan had started to circumnavigate his mother in a bizarre sideways skipping motion, first clockwise, then anticlockwise, with his arms outstretched ready to support the lady if she stumbled. Sam had looked on in astonishment at this bizarre sight, thinking his brother's strange actions resembled a deranged morris dancer performing some sort of ritual folk dance. His strange antics had started to attract the attention of others passing by, so Sam had followed some way behind to distance himself from the group to save any personal embarrassment.

'What on earth are you doing, boy?' Mrs McAllister

had remarked. 'Why don't you walk properly? People will think there's something wrong with you.'

Undeterred, the sideways skipping motion and circling of his mother had continued until reaching the safety of the cafe. The next two hours would be spent drinking coffee, just one cup being consumed by Duncan and Mrs McAllister, as an excessive fluid intake would undoubtedly result in a visit to the public toilets, which was something Mrs McAllister and Duncan avoided at all cost; the reason in Mrs McAllister's case being the physical difficulty unless accompanied and in Duncan's case to avoid possible embarrassment – there would probably be other people in the latrines. Sam often pondered on his brother's ability to avoid visits to the toilets. How did he do that? Did he have an unusually large bladder or just superhuman control? After all, a two-hour car journey, a large black coffee followed by two hours seated in the cafe and a two-hour return journey home, that was six hours without relief, an incredible feat of self control and in the middle of winter too.

At least we won't have to go through all that again, thought Sam as he finished his coffee in the camper van waiting for Duncan's next delivery of insults to be directed at a man walking towards them. He suddenly thought of the beginning of another verse:

> *Next came a man with a straw hat and sandals,*
> *A large moustache complete with handles*
> *Approached unaware he was being observed*
> *With a barrage of abuse duly served...*

His mother was looking strangely at him again, as if she was reading his thoughts. He'd memorise the four new lines and write them down when he got home.

Kendrick sighed. 'I think I'll just pop out for a smoke. I won't be long,' he said.

'I'll come with you,' said Sam wanting to escape the confines of the camper van and the rudeness of Duncan's observations.

As they walked slowly around the car park Sam said 'If *I* talked about other people like that, Mum would tell me to grow up and not to be so rude, but *he* seems to get away with it. She even finds it amusing and seems to almost encourage it. It's very strange.'

'I know,' said Kendrick. 'They're like two peas in a pod.'

'How's the world of psychiatry, Kendrick?'

'I'm thinking of retiring soon and writing a book on the subject.'

'You'd have enough material there for several books if you used him as subject matter,' said Sam chuckling as he glanced back at the camper van.

They sat down on an empty bench.

'How's the teaching going?' asked Kendrick as he lit a cigarette.

'Same place, same students, not much changes really. I still sometimes imagine myself doing the same job at the other place though.'

'Oh yes, you mentioned that before, the South Lincolnshire Academy for Practical Studies, wasn't it? It's probably in your imagination as a sort of escapism, to free yourself from the bonds and confines of your proper job.

It's not unusual to sometimes live in an imaginary world, a sort of parallel life.'

'The problem is, Kendrick, I sometimes get the two worlds mixed up. I forget which one I'm supposed to be at. I call my colleagues different names at SLAPS, just for amusement, but I have to think sometimes before I talk to them at the secondary school.'

'What sort of names?'

'Well, when I imagine myself to be at SLAPS I call the music teacher Phyllis Stein. At the secondary school she *is* Miss Stein but her first name's not Phyllis, it's Doreen, but I'm always accidentally calling her Phyllis. At SLAPS I call the assistant music teacher Amanda Lynn but at the secondary school her surname is… I can't even remember her real name now I've been calling her Amanda Lynn for so long. I think it's Lynley or something like that. You see my problem, Kendrick?'

'Yes, I see what you mean. Maybe you should stop imagining yourself at SLAPS so much and concentrate on the real world at the secondary school before it becomes embarrassing for you.'

'It's a bit late for that, Kendrick. At SLAPS I call the gorgeous new biology teacher Jenny Taylia, but her real name is Taylor.'

'Jenny Taylia. Yes that makes sense. I suppose it's a sort of word association and understandable if she's attractive. She possibly arouses sexual desires in you.'

'That's right, Kendrick, I've started dreaming about her, always the same dream. We're in a dimly lit room with red table lamps and blue velvet curtains blowing gently in the breeze from the open window. I'm sitting in a big leather chair, reading a book, smoking a cigar and drinking red wine. The room is full of hazy smoke. She's lying naked on a dark-blue chaise-longue looking at me suggestively and smiling with her arms outstretched. I put my glass down on the table and my cigar in the ashtray. I approach her slowly and just before I reach her I suddenly wake up.'

'What wakes you up, Sam?' asked Kendrick as he took his notebook from his pocket.

'Usually a strange noise, often it's the milkman but last night it was the cat being sick.'

'Oh dear, the cat was sick in the bedroom?'

'Yes, in my slippers, Kendrick. It's so unfair. Why couldn't the cat have waited a few minutes? Why do I always wake up as it's starting to get interesting? It's almost as if someone has decided at what point I'm going to wake up and plans the events in the dream around it.'

'Well it might be worth reading that book I lent you, *The Interpretation of Dreams* by Sigmund Freud.'

'I started to but couldn't understand a word of it, Kendrick. I gave up on page fifty-four. I have written a poem about it though.'

Sam recited his poem as they started to walk slowly back to the camper van:

There's a young man sitting in a chair,
Rings of smoke hang in the air,
He's thinking thoughts, dreaming dreams,
Nothing is quite what it seems.

A girl walks by with long fair hair,
The young man just sits and stares,

Thinking of bygone days,
Staring through the smoky haze.

Blue velvet curtains, a bottle of red,
A book on the table partly read,
Some things best thought, never spoken,
Thoughts and dreams, always broken.

'That's as far as I've got with that one, it needs another verse.'

'That's very, good Sam, very striking, very revealing,' said Kendrick as he turned a page in his notebook and started to write.

'Maybe you could write a book about us all, Kendrick, the whole family's crackers.'

As they settled themselves back in the camper van, Duncan was still peering from the window making rude observations about passers-by, who were unaware of the barrage of insults directed at them or even of the presence of the disagreeable person concealed within.

'Cor look at this one coming. I'm glad I don't have to wake up next to her in the mornings,' he said.

'I'm sure she'd say the same about you, Duncan, if she could see you.' said Sam.

Emma changed the subject in an attempt to stop Duncan's rudeness. 'We're putting the house on the market, Mother, after Kendrick's retired. We're thinking of moving to Lincolnshire to be nearer to you and Dad.'

'That will be nice but I don't think your father will be around much longer,' said Bridget. 'He's going funny,

funny in the head. He's behaving very strangely and finds it difficult to write and spell certain words and perform normal tasks. He's lost his coordination. It takes him ten minutes to open a bottle of wine with a corkscrew so I've started buying him bottles with screw tops. He's stopped driving. He used to take his car out until recently and admitted he often got lost and struggled to find his way home.'

Sam chuckled to himself.

'What's so amusing about that?' asked Emma.

'It's just that I read recently that in some countries they take elderly relatives who've gone funny for a long ride in the car and leave them sitting on a park bench somewhere with some sandwiches and then just drive away, leaving them there. They don't know who they are, where they are or where they've come from. It saves a fortune on care home fees. I could do that if you like?'

'That's a horrible, cruel thing to say,' said Emma.

'Sorry, it's only a suggestion. He doesn't have enough to occupy his mind, that's the problem. He retired at fifty-five, now he's eighty-eight and he's had the same daily routine all that time. He gets up late, rarely goes out, never has normal conversations with people and spends all day sitting at that blasted piano unless he's watching television. It's no good for him. He's not using his brain. There's nothing to stimulate his mind.'

'He's watching the snooker all this week,' said their mother. 'The television's been on the blink for weeks and now everything on the screen is purple. How can you watch snooker when the balls and the table are all the same colour? When he watches the motor racing all the cars look the same. Still, he doesn't spend much time watching anything, after about half an hour he falls asleep and only wakes up when I take him something to drink, or his meals in on a tray. He sometimes spends all day sitting in that blasted chair and then goes to bed.'

Having spent a couple of hours chatting and drinking the usual limited quantity of coffee they bid their farewells to go their separate ways. Sam waited for the predictable sarcasm as his brother settled himself in the back seat of the Volvo estate, his tatty 1980s leather jacket squeaking irritatingly on the leather upholstery.

'Bloody Volvos, it's like a hearse,' said Duncan. 'What were you thinking of when you bought it? All you need now is a cloth cap and a couple of Labradors in the back.'

'It's comfortable, roomy and reliable and it'll get you home, which is more than can be said of either of your relics,' said Sam. Anyway it's got style; something you wouldn't understand.'

'Don't be rude to Duncan, dear,' said their mother from the front seat.

The rest of the journey was made in silence, no conversation, just occasional grunts when accepting the mints frequently offered by their mother.

'Nice cup of tea, Mummy?' Duncan asked as the car pulled onto the driveway of the old family home.

'Oh yes please, dear, and do stop calling me Mummy,' she replied. She looked at Sam. 'Oh, he is a darling, would you like to come in for a drink, pet?'

'No thanks, I'll be getting off,' said Sam, even though

he was desperate to use the bathroom. His bladder control was pathetic in comparison to his brother's but he was determined to avoid visiting the bathroom. He had several recollections of flushing the toilet and watching the water rise to an alarming level before it retreated at the last moment. *That bathroom, never again*, he thought.

'I'll pop in tomorrow,' he said, and drove off.

*

The following morning, being Sunday, Sam paid his usual visit and walked into the kitchen of fifty-seven Stonebridge Road to be greeted by the aroma of coffee and, unusually, a general air of joviality.

'Come and sit down, dear,' his mother said 'and I'll make you a coffee.'

'I'll just pop in the lounge and say hello to Mr Misery,' replied Sam.

'Your father's not here,' his mother said.

'Oh, where is he then?'

'Hospital.'

'Hospital?' said Sam.

'Hospital,' repeated his mother and Duncan in unison.

'When we arrived back yesterday he was playing his piano as usual and I took him a cup of tea in. I went in the room and said "we're home, dear" and put the tray on the table. There was a terrible noise and I thought he'd thumped the piano keys like he does when he's disturbed but he'd slumped forwards onto the piano making a groaning noise. We called for an ambulance straight away. Turns out he'd had a heart attack, so he's in hospital.'

'Did you cough?' asked Sam.

'What you mean, did I cough?'

'When you went in the room – did you cough? You know he doesn't like being startled when you go in the room and walk up behind him.'

'Well I suppose I must have done, I've been doing it for long enough. At least I think I did.'

Later, when Sam left the house, he was struck by the strange demeanour, the almost cheerful nature of his mother and Duncan. As he walked up to his car on the driveway the bells from the church opposite began to ring, summoning the small but bigoted congregation to the Sunday morning service, the tolling of the bells scattering rooks and pigeons from the trees in the graveyard. His mother had been organist there for many years and despite his protestations as a small child he'd been forced to attend and endure the drudgery of Sunday morning services. As he'd sat amongst the elderly congregation as a boy, he had always been intrigued by the abundance of "Sunday Best" garments and the wide variety of ladies' hats and furs that seemed to proliferate that generation. Elderly ladies who'd sat in nearby pews had reeked of cheap perfume and mothballs and would mumble loudly, their mouths in constant motion as they'd chewed peppermints and adjusted their dentures in preparation for the singing of the next hymn. Later, the inevitable and tediously long sermon was delivered by the vicar preaching his Victorian values, using his terrifying rhetoric, threatening the congregation with eternal damnation should they not change their ways, repent as sinners and follow the ways of the Lord. At the end of the service the congregation were left quivering in the pews and later, terrifying old ladies, still quivering, wearing thick stockings with their ankles bulging over their tight shoes, their mouths still mumbling and chewing, would solemnly make their way towards the door in single file. Every week one very tall old lady with bright lipstick that had somehow got onto her rotten and stained teeth would approach Sam's mother and compliment her on her playing. She always appeared to blink very slowly, opening one eye momentarily before the other and after her commendation was given she would look down at Sam approvingly and always say the same thing: 'Oh I say, hasn't he grown.' Every week, the same menacing old lady, who Sam was convinced was a man, would say the same.

'I can't have grown that much in a week, Mother – she said that last week,' he'd said as they crossed the road on the way home.

'She's just being polite, dear,' she'd replied.

He became increasingly bored with his compulsory church attendance and considered the whole Sunday spectacle to be farcical, almost resembling a fashion show with people admiring each other's coats, hats and general dowdy attire, although the same distasteful garments seemed to be worn each week regardless of the weather or time of year. Sam's mother usually wore her best Ocelot coat and furs, grey fur gloves made from the skin of some poor rabbit probably bred for the purpose and a fur stole around her neck, all items of clothing that had probably once belonged to Granny McAllister, who had no doubt worn them in the 1940s when they were acceptable and fashionable items of clothing and had handed them down to Bridget. Excuses were made on Sunday mornings to avoid what seemed to him to be a gathering of obnoxious bigots and a complete waste of his time. Headaches, nausea, bad hay fever were the usual imaginary, though convincing, ailments and his church attendance dwindled and finally stopped altogether. From an early age he had formed his own opinion of religion and what he considered the hypocrisy of many of the congregation. Some would happily sing "All Things Bright and Beautiful, All Creatures Great and Small" in the Sunday morning service and later could be observed in the countryside with shotguns blasting away at anything with fur or feathers that dared to move, no doubt singing "the Lord God made them all" as they squeezed the trigger.

With the ending of his association with the church came a suggestion from his father that his Sunday mornings should be spent practising the piano in the summer house, but much to his father's dismay he lost interest and took up the banjo instead. It seemed to Sam that everyone was against him, the rightful opinion of every teenager. Even Reginald Ramsbottom had described the banjo as "the instrument of the Devil" and when he'd heard Sam playing it in the summer house he'd referred to the building as a "den of wickedness". Unperturbed, Sam had persevered and before long the summer house had reverberated to the strains of "Blackberry Blossom" and "Salt Creek."

The church bells stopped ringing, the rooks and pigeons returned to their roosts and Sam drove away. Grief-stricken, he called at the hospital on his way home. His father seemed confused at times, at other times perfectly coherent. As Sam sat by his side his father lifted the oxygen mask from his face and managed to say "I'm done for" as he shook his head. Then a nurse entered the room to check him and replaced his oxygen mask. He was trying to tell Sam something but he was rambling and incoherent and there was a look of panic, a look of fear in his eyes. Sam stupidly just nodded and smiled as people sometimes do when someone says something you can't hear or can't understand properly.

The next day Sam telephoned his mother to say he would be calling to see his father at the hospital on his way home from school.

'I shouldn't bother, dear – he's dead.'

He had passed away that morning. Sam was struck with grief and the insensitive, almost callous way the sad news had been broken to him. Sam put the phone down. What had his father been trying to say to him the previous day? What had he been trying to tell him? He would never know. He arrived home and relayed the sad news to Morag.

'I told her I was going to visit Dad today and she said don't bother, he's dead. What an awful thing to say. She almost sounded pleased. How can you spend sixty-six years married to someone and detest them so much?'

*

After the funeral, which was a quiet family gathering, Bridget seemed to almost relish the fact that he was no longer around, no longer in her life. He had left the house and its contents to her in his will as sole beneficiary and now she could do what she liked. For some reason, possibly a trait of their generation, the house had always been in Bernard's name only, not in joint names as is the preference for most couples nowadays. Now, for the first time in her life, she had control.

'Things are going to change,' she proclaimed. 'I'm going to enjoy myself and start to live a little. I'll spend some money on the house. Yes, I'll make some improvements, starting with a rewire to replace all the sixty-year-old wiring, some proper central heating and a modern kitchen and bathroom. I'll spend some money on myself starting with a perm and a new upper set of dentures.'

In reality, nothing would change. The house would remain the same and become neglected, dusty, dirty and damp.

Nothing changed, not even the dentures.

CHAPTER 16

Emma dragged a large cardboard box out from under the grand piano and blew the dust off. As she opened the box a small moth flew out and headed towards the velvet curtains. Duncan sprang up out of his chair chasing after it, dodging the boxes and clutter strewn across the floor shouting, 'Clothes moth, damned thing!' The moth appeared to realise it was being pursued and put on a spurt of speed, reaching the safety of the curtains before Duncan was able to get within striking distance. Duncan turned back, looked at his mother and raised his arms in despair. 'Common clothes moth mum, Tineola bisselliella its technical name. We don't want any of those in the house. They'll ruin the curtains, not to mention the carpets.'

Kendrick looked over the top of his glasses at the strange antics of Duncan, took his notebook and silver pen out of his jacket pocket and started to write, probably noting Duncan's strange behaviour and spontaneous recall of the technical details of the common clothes moth.

'Oh for heaven's sake sit down, it's only a blasted moth!' exclaimed Emma as she pulled out another box from under the piano.

Kendrick's recent retirement enabled the move to South Lincolnshire as planned so he could begin writing his book in the peace and solitude of the countryside. Several boxes had been stored at the old family home before she and Kendrick had moved, some of them brought back by Sam from their meet-ups at the motorway services.

Duncan, having spent several minutes attempting to locate the creature without success, reluctantly returned to his chair. Everyone watched in fascination as his head swivelled from side to side, up and down and rotating in what appeared to be impossible angles, resembling an owl, his head in constant motion scanning the room for any signs of moth movement.

'You look like a Battle of Britain pilot scanning the sky for the enemy. It's not going to sneak up behind you and open fire, it's only a moth,' said Sam sarcastically.

Duncan stood up to leave the room and walked towards the door with cries from Sam of 'Red Leader here, bandits vector two seven zero!'

Duncan paused at the door, turned round with a blank expression on his face that Sam recognised. He was about to enter encyclopaedia mode and begin one of his factual monologues.

'It's strange you should mention the Battle of Britain. A lot of fine aircraft made by De-Havilland carried the Moth name, the DH-60 Tiger Moth used as a trainer for Second World War fighter pilots. Then there were less well known ones like the Puss Moth, Gypsy Moth and Hornet Moth from the inter war years—'

'That's really interesting,' interrupted Sam, 'and you say we've got the common clothes moth, the tineola bissy thingumybob moth…'

'Yes, Tineola bisselliella, that's its scientific name, a nocturnal insect that—'

'Oh for heaven's sake,' interrupted Sam again, 'we're not really that interested. How do you remember all this garbage? Why do you remember it?'

'Because it's interesting,' mumbled Duncan as he left the room.

'Don't be rude to Duncan, dear,' said Mother. 'He's very sensitive and just got a thing about clothes moths in the house. Your father was the same with woodlice.'

'Yes, I do remember, Mother,' said Sam.

'We had regular infestations of those,' she continued. 'They seemed to come in through the gap in the French doors. Your father would spend hours waiting for them to emerge from behind the furniture with his dustpan and brush. He always said they must have been attracted by the warmth of the house.'

'Hardly,' said Sam chuckling. 'They like rotting wood and damp conditions… Oh God I sound like Duncan, now I'm an expert on woodlice. That's why they came in through what was left of the rotten French doors. They probably thought it was nice and cold, damp and mouldy in here, so they moved in.'

'Your father didn't like putting the storage heaters on. He said it would dry out the wood in the pianos.'

Emma and Sam had been discussing the state of the

house with each other a few days earlier and Emma seized the opportunity to bring up the matter. 'Mum, when Dad died you said you'd have the house rewired, have proper central heating put in, have the bathroom modernised and make the house more comfortable. That was a year ago and it's still just the same, the same sixty-year-old wiring and the same cold, damp walls with mouldy wallpaper. Nothing's changed. Please think about it, the house would be a lot more comfortable for you and you can afford to have the work done.'

Duncan had returned to the room during the conversation. 'I don't think we want the upheaval, do we, Mummy? Think of the noise, the inconvenience and workmen coming in, not to mention the mess everywhere.'

'You'll have a lot more mess if the place catches fire with all that dodgy wiring up in the roof,' said Sam.

'Stop it! All of you!' exclaimed Bridget. 'I'm quite happy as I am.'

Emma and Sam looked at each other. Sam shrugged his shoulders. Duncan had a look of triumph on his face.

Some weeks later there appeared to be an infestation of clothes moths in the house.

Strange, Emma thought, they had been there for years and gone about their moth business unnoticed, doing the sort of things clothes moths do. It was only after the escape of the moth in the box that came from London that her mother and Duncan seemed drawn to the presence of the others. Evidence of their long-term existence in the house was everywhere; the moth-eaten carpets and curtains, the white remains of moths' eggs lying around the edges of the carpets, together with the mothballs used over the years in a futile attempt to eradicate them. The sale of mothballs had been banned for many years and Bridget McAllister, being a prolific user, had bought a considerable quantity for future use while they were still available. Over years of storage, the mothballs had lost their potency and the colony continued to thrive.

For Duncan, the annihilation of the moths became an obsession and a vast arsenal of weaponry was acquired consisting of fly swats, sticky insect traps, insect-repelling sprays and a small rechargeable handheld vacuum cleaner.

'I shall be removing all my boxes you've kindly stored for me, Mum,' said Emma on her next visit to the old family home. 'We've brought the camper van today so we can take them home and get them out of your way.'

'Good,' replied her mother. 'Just don't open any more here. We've been infested with moths ever since that blasted insect flew out of the box. Take them home and open them there.' As she spoke two clothes moths flew past her face. 'You see, they're everywhere, we can't get rid of them.'

Duncan sprang into action with his latest weapon that resembled a tennis racquet. As he pursued the moths he explained its operation in detail. 'These wires are electrically charged by operating a button on the handle. This kills the moths on contact,' he said as he took wild sweeps at one of the moths, the scene resembling a furious rally at a tennis match. Despite several attempts he missed but, unperturbed, continued swiping accompanied by curses of 'blasted thing', 'little bugger', 'come back here, you swine' and 'damned nuisance'.

'They are all descendants of that one you brought in the box from London,' continued Bridget. 'Poor Duncan's even got them next door. They must have followed him round there or got into his woolly jumper.'

Emma, usually a person of a relaxed disposition, started to become agitated and lose her temper. 'You mean the jumper that was already full of holes, the one that's been moth-eaten for years. He probably brought the little buggers round here in the first place. When was the last time you went round next door? It's as filthy and moth-infested as this house. You can't blame me for all this and one solitary clothes moth that came from London in a cardboard box,' said Emma.

'Well I do, and don't be so rude about Duncan.'

Emma left the room, closed the door quietly, then screamed.

*

Bridget McAllister appeared to enjoy her new lifestyle as a widow, although she had become a victim of routine and inactivity just as her husband had before her. Duncan called on her regularly, preferring to traverse the gap in the fence in the back garden from his house next door rather than use the more conventional form of entry through the front door. He and his mother seemed content in their strange symbiotic world, she benefiting from his constant companionship and Duncan the devoted son benefiting from the same companionship and living next door, which allowed him to exist in his sheltered, reclusive and secure world.

Medical appointments and occasional visits to Emma and Kendrick's nearby house were the only reasons Bridget McAllister left the house. Having returned home with Duncan she would often criticise their extravagant lifestyle, as she did Sam and Morag's, although extravagant they were most certainly not, quite normal people really, living fairly ordinary, comfortable lives no differently to most other people. It was the "comfortable" element of their lives that Bridget McAllister seemed to take issue with, echoed of course by Duncan, they agreed on everything. They both seemed willing to exist without any of life's little comforts, not so much luxuries but basic things that make other people's lives more pleasant and bearable. In Mrs McAllister's case, despite her proclamation that things would change, she seemed content to retain her sixty-year-old bathroom with worn out taps, her grubby old kitchen and to continue residing in a house with no proper heating although now she could well afford to make her life more comfortable if she so desired. The same dated features applied to Duncan's house next door and he also seemed content to live without a proper cooker or even a television. They both disapproved of gas central heating boilers and modern appliances such as microwave ovens, both of which they considered unnecessary and dangerous.

Bridget McAllister had once been very house proud, the house always reasonably clean and tidy, but with the passing years, and noticeably since the death of Bernard, her standards had dropped, standards which were mirrored in Duncan's house next door. They lived in their own little world, cocooned, sheltered from reality, and both seemed to take pleasure in criticising and passing judgement on others who lived normally and comfortably, but they both seemed unaware of how their own standards were declining, both houses becoming cluttered and filthy.

On Sam's Sunday morning visits he would sit talking with his mother in the front room. There was often a tense atmosphere when he visited, a feeling that he was encroaching into her and Duncan's world, interrupting their routine, a feeling sometimes that his presence was almost resented. If Duncan wasn't at his mother's house he soon arrived from next door having seen Sam's car on the driveway, taking his usual garden route to the back door. Before Duncan entered the room Sam often had the feeling that he'd been listening at the door as it would suddenly open with no prior sound of approaching footsteps on the parquet flooring in the hall. Conversations were often difficult, they weren't really interested in other people or what was going on in the world, and after long periods of silence his mother would sigh and say "right…" followed by a long pause, as if it was a request or an instruction to leave, as if what she really wanted to say was, "Right, nice to see you, but now leave us in peace. Off you go."

CHAPTER 17

'Where are you, Duncan?' asked his mother sternly after he'd retrieved his ancient mobile phone from his grubby raincoat pocket.

'I'm with Sam. We've just popped out for a while.'

'You're not looking at another car, are you? You've already got two that don't work.'

'No, Mother. We're just having a quick pint at the Nobody Inn. It's a pub in the town.'

'Well don't drink too much. You know how it upsets your tummy – and don't be long, I was starting to get worried. When you came round at ten o'clock you didn't say you were going out. I was wondering where you were,' she said before hanging up abruptly.

Sam gave his brother a look of disbelief. 'You're getting on for seventy and can't even go out for a couple of hours without telling Mother where you are or what you're doing. It's pathetic.'

'You know how she worries. I'd better not be too long,' said Duncan.

Her three adult offspring were indeed a constant source

of worry to Bridget McAllister. When there was nothing for her to worry about, she still looked worried, as if she was trying to think of something to worry about, but couldn't.

Duncan started to reach forwards to pick up his beer glass and suddenly started clapping his hands loudly and quickly, first directly in front of him, then over his left shoulder, then over his right shoulder, the strange spectacle resembling the movements of a Spanish flamenco dancer. People sitting at nearby tables suddenly stopped their conversations and looked on in astonishment. Duncan then looked at the palms of his hands, smiled at everybody and said triumphantly, 'Got the bugger. Drosophila melanogaster – commonly known as the fruit fly or vinegar fly. They're attracted to fruit and fermenting beverages. Little blighter was in my beer glass.'

Duncan finished his beer and looked at his watch.

'Do you fancy another?' offered Sam, hoping he wouldn't.

'No. I'd better be getting back. It's nearly lunchtime. Can you take me home now please?'

As Sam pulled up on the driveway of the old family home he noticed the outline of his mother standing in the front room window.

'Are you coming in?' Duncan asked.

'No thanks, I'll get off,' he replied as he watched his mother move slowly backwards into the darkness of the room. 'Tell Mum I'll be round on Sunday morning as usual.'

Having arrived home, Sam began to relay the events of the morning to Morag.

'He didn't enjoy it then?'

'Not really. You'd think he would have, a rare opportunity for a break from Mother for a few hours. I give up. As soon as he's been gone for half an hour he's worrying about Mum and wants to get back. She's as bad. If she doesn't know where he is, she's ringing him. "Are you all right, dear? Where are you?" She treats him like a child, worse than a child. At least a child is allowed to go out and play with friends. She's ruined him. He's nearly seventy for heaven's sake. She's been treating him like this for over thirty years. She's ruined his life. God only knows what she'd say if he found a good woman.'

'Well he's leaving it a bit late.'

That evening the phone rang. Morag answered it and was surprised to hear Duncan's voice. He rarely telephoned them.

'Is Sam there?' he asked.

'Yes I'm very well thank you, Duncan, how are you?' replied Morag sarcastically.

'Is Sam there?' he repeated.

'Oh what's the use?' she mumbled as she passed the telephone to Sam. 'It's Duncan. He's so rude. He sounds a bit agitated.'

'Hello. Is everything alright? It's unlike you to use your telephonic instrument to communicate, it costs money you know.'

'No, everything's not alright,' Duncan replied. 'I've come round to get Mummy upstairs to bed. She's halfway up, sitting on the bend in the stairs. She can't move. I can't get her up or down. She's stuck. I need a hand.'

'Do you want me to phone the fire brigade?' asked Sam sarcastically.

'Don't be stupid. Can you come round and give me a hand?'

Fifteen minutes later Sam arrived and was greeted at the front door by an agitated and stressed Duncan.

'I feel so silly,' said their mother as they joined her on the stairs. 'My legs have gone all funny. I can't go up or down.'

'You're a bit like the Grand Old Duke of York,' said Sam chuckling.

'What do you mean?'

'The Grand Old Duke of York,' repeated Sam. 'He marched his soldiers to the top of the hill.

'And when they were up they were up,
'And when they were down they were down,
'And when they were only halfway up,
They were neither up nor down.'

'Don't make me laugh. You'll never be able to move me if I start laughing.'

Together they lifted, pushed and shoved Bridget McAllister in a rather undignified manner to the top of the stairs where she sat for a while regaining her strength.

For a few moments Sam stood on the landing staring at the bathroom door, the glass bathroom door. It was one of the few so-called improvements made to the house in the 1970s when the wooden bathroom door was replaced with a glass one. It had a subtle floral pattern that was supposed to make the glass obscure but was totally ineffective. It didn't really matter if the door was closed or open, there was little privacy. As a schoolboy Sam recalled the occasion the salesman called to discuss the door with his father and the look of astonishment on the salesman's face when he received the order. Maybe there was the promise of a fat bonus to the first person to sell a virtually see-through bathroom door to some mug. Surely no one has transparent glass bathroom doors Sam had thought at the time. None of his school friends' bathrooms had got one. Theirs had.

Duncan walked by on the landing, entered the bathroom and turned on the light using the grubby pull cord with a large knot tied on the end. There was a dreadful metallic squeak as he turned on the cold tap in the washbasin to fill a glass with water for their mother, a fast dribble the best the antiquated tap could offer. With the light on the horrors of the old bathroom were exposed. It was the original, dating back to the mid-1950s, and now, over sixty years later, had taken on a ghastly, depressing appearance with its black wall tiles and lime-green ceramic bath and basin, both chipped and stained.

During Sam's childhood only two baths a week were permitted, on Wednesdays and Sundays. Everybody in the house had baths on Wednesdays and Sundays. So that the antiquated emersion heater in the airing cupboard could keep up with the demand for hot water, bath times were staggered and only a limited quantity of hot water was permitted, resulting in only a few inches of water. If the hot tap had been running for too long the blurred outline of his father would appear on the other side of the glass door as he shouted, "Leave some hot water for somebody else, will you!"

Before the arrival of the glass bathroom door, for several weeks during the particularly hard winter of 1962/63, no baths were permitted at all unless you wanted to share a cold bath with several large goldfish and two tench. Bernard McAllister, being concerned for the welfare of the fish, had removed them from the garden pond before the thick ice formed and brought them into the house to reside in the bath until the weather improved. Although only three or four years old at the time, it was yet another childhood memory engrained on Sam's mind.

The bathroom was exactly how Sam had remembered it, unchanged like everything else. There wasn't a blind or any curtains in the window. It was a draughty louvered window, which used to be impossible to open in the cold winter weather if the condensation on the inside froze. The toilet was situated immediately by the glass door and Sam recalled the considerable embarrassment that was endured when seated on the toilet if someone should walk by on the landing. At night with the bathroom light on, using the toilet or the bath, or undressing, was best avoided due to the lack of privacy, and some visitors had even claimed the person responsible for the glass door had voyeuristic tendencies.

After she had rested for a few minutes Duncan and Sam managed to stand their mother up and walk her to her bedroom.

'I feel so silly,' she repeated as she dropped onto the bed. 'I am a funny old girl.'

'Thank you,' said Duncan to Sam. 'I can manage now.'

Sam left, deep in thought as he drove home. *How can he manage? He's still got to get her into the bathroom, get her undressed and into bed. How can he manage that on his own? Then tomorrow he's got to get her back downstairs again. Still, if he needs a hand he can call me again.*

When Sam arrived home he poured himself a whisky and contemplated the current state of affairs, his mother's decline in health and refusal for any kind of help, medical help or social care. Whenever any kind of assistance was suggested it was rebuffed with the usual reply: "We can manage." "We" being herself and Duncan, who was starting to struggle both physically and mentally with the constant attention she needed. It was starting to wear him down.

*

Sam recalled how his father and grandmother Granny McAllister both used to say, "It's no fun getting old." How right they'd been. As a small child he had often listened to the older generation going on and on about their health problems and ailments in their later years; conversations he'd overheard about arthritis, rheumatism, cataracts, glaucoma, varicose veins and hearing loss. Things he didn't understand as a child, words that meant nothing to him. Now, nearly sixty, he understood. He was even starting to suffer from some of the ailments himself. *Well,* he thought, *the future's grim for all of us. They were right. It's no fun getting old.*

His mother appeared to be on the same slippery slope of reduced physical activity and mental stimulation that his father had succumbed to six years earlier. He had retreated into a world of denial, refusing practical or medical help, now history was repeating itself with his mother.

When Sam visited, the house was always smelly and stuffy, the windows were never opened and on warm summer days when he suggested she sit outside in the garden to enjoy some fresh air she always replied, 'I'm fine where I am, leave me alone.'

On several occasions suggestions were made by Sam, Emma and Kendrick to install a stairlift and convert the large cupboard under the stairs into a downstairs toilet to save her using the stairs so frequently, but at the point of her agreeing that they should contact a builder the plans were thwarted by the intervention of Duncan with his usual comment 'I don't think we want builders in, do we, Mummy? All that noise and upheaval, think of the dust, think of the cost.'

'No, you're right, dear, I'm quite happy as I am,' was her usual response.

For years she had controlled him. Now he was a controlling influence on her and nothing anybody said or suggested seemed to alter the situation.

CHAPTER 18

Sam unlocked the front door of fifty-seven Stonebridge Road and walked into the hallway to be greeted by the stuffy, musty smell he had become accustomed to. Today there was another smell, rather like molasses. He'd just started to think what it could be when his mother called out, 'Hello, Duncan dear, is that you?'

'No, it's me, Mother.' The front room door was open. Sam entered to see his mother sitting in her chair clutching an empty sherry glass.

'Oh, it's you,' she replied, sounding almost disappointed.

'I finished school early. I'm having a haircut later so I thought I'd call and see you on the way.'

'Why are you wearing your shorts, dear?'

'It's a warm day so I changed into them before I left school. Why don't you open a window or go outside and sit in the garden and enjoy the fresh air and the sunshine?'

'I'm perfectly happy where I am thank you,' replied his mother, said in such a way that she probably meant *mind your own business*.

'You used to make such a fuss when you went to your secondary school in short trousers. Now look at you, every time the sun shines you wear them.'

'Yes, funny thing life, isn't it. Mind you, Mother, at nearly sixty my legs are generally admired and considered to be one of my better physical features. Someone half my age would be proud of these.'

She laughed and handed Sam her empty glass. 'Pour me another sherry, pet. The bottle's on the table. I don't know why you're going to the hairdresser. Your hair doesn't need cutting. Let it grow. Duncan's got lovely hair and he hasn't been to the barber for years. He cuts it himself.'

'That's obvious, Mother. He only cuts the bits at the front he can see, it always looks a right proper mess. He looks a right Herbert, as Dad would have said.'

He started to pour some sherry into her glass as she made a circular movement with the extended index finger of her left hand, as an instruction to continue filling it to the brim.

He carefully passed her the glass wondering how many she had consumed during the afternoon. 'Thank you, dear. I've noticed you've started using a lot of words your father used. I don't like it,' she said sternly.

'I know, I think I'm turning into him.'

'What do you mean?'

'I'm becoming a cantankerous old git like he used to be, a belligerent old bugger. I sometimes look at myself in the mirror and see him, the same mannerisms and expressions. I've started smoking his favourite brand of cigars and drinking his favourite malt whisky. I've even bought a baby grand piano off Phyllis Stein. It's been years since I stopped playing but I've decided to take it up again. I've even started learning some of the pieces he played that I hated so much, can't play them like he did though. I often say things and then I think, *Dad would have said that.* I've started correcting people about their poor use of English. Bad use of grammar winds me up so much, just like it did him. I've even joined the Misplaced Apostrophe Society. People on the radio and TV annoy me who start every sentence with "so". I shout abuse at them. Everyone's starting to think I'm a pain in the arse. Isn't it strange?'

'Not really,' said his mother laughing. 'Not if you're turning into your father, he was a pain in that area of the anatomy.'

'Do you remember when Dad was watching the TV, moaning and groaning about whatever he was watching? He used to make a strange sibilant sound, a hissing noise when singers started vocalising or someone he disapproved of came on the telly. I've started to do that as well, not the hissing sound, I just curse and swear. Sibilance replaced with anger.'

'Oh yes. I used to think, *why doesn't he clear off into the other room and leave me in peace*?'

'I've started doing the same as he did, always moaning about people on the television, especially all the obscure moronic people I've never seen or heard of before but who have somehow acquired celebrity status. Offensive entertainers categorized as comedians who aren't remotely funny. Then there are all the footballers behaving like a load of half wits when they score, hugging and kissing each other, then running round the pitch spitting everywhere. Goalies who raise their arms in astonishment when they let goals in and point at other players as if it's their fault and football managers who can hardly string a sentence together in proper English. When they're interviewed on television they have an annoying habit of stating the bleedin' obvious – "If vee score more goals dan de udder side then vee vill vin". What a load of overpaid tossers.'

'Do try to keep calm, dear, your father used to work himself up into a rage, just like this.'

'That's exactly my point, Mum, I'm becoming him.'

'God help us,' she said.

His ranting continued. 'Then there are people who call themselves musicians. If you put a piece of sheet music in front of them half of them wouldn't know what it was, let alone be able to read it or play it. It would be like calling yourself a writer, unable to read or write a word of English. People idolise them and put them on a pedestal. Then you've got singers, or so-called singers. Most of them can't sing, all they can do is wail and scream.'

'Well, don't be late for your hair appointment, dear,' said his mother, thinking he'd finished his ranting and raving.

He hadn't.

'Then there are those so-called talent competition programmes on the television. Talent my arse – even the "Phyllis Stein Four" string quartet at the school has got more talent in their little fingers than that lot put together. The judges are no better, how can you have talentless judges judging a talent competition? They're all impostors and charlatans.' Sam drew a deep breath and continued, 'Stupid politicians who prevaricate all the time, unable or unwilling to answer simple questions. When they're interviewed and use irritating "buzz" words all the time – like "transparent", that's the latest one. One starts to use the word and the next thing you know they're all at it.'

'Do stop, dear, you'll make yourself ill.'

Sam sighed deeply. 'Where's Duncan?'

'He's next door having a rest. He's very tired, been working in the garden all day.'

Sam knew what was coming next and they both said "poor darling" simultaneously.

'Don't be rude,' she said. 'I wanted a word while he's not here. Will you promise me something, dear?'

'What's that, Mother?'

'When I'm dead and gone, will you promise me you'll look after him?'

Sam was a little shocked by the question. 'Why can't he look after himself? Anyway, the way I feel sometimes it'll be me who wants looking after.'

'You've got Morag. He hasn't got anyone. He'll be round in a minute, it's four o'clock. He always comes round at four to pour me a sherry and make my tea, bless him.'

As she spoke, Duncan walked by the window towards the front door.

His mother gulped down her sherry, emptying the glass.

'I'll talk to you again about that sometime soon,' she said.

*

Sam arrived at the hairdressers and was beckoned immediately to an empty chair. His hairdresser, Monika, known as Mo, started to raise the chair whilst looking in the opposite direction, talking to a lady with her head under a drier on the opposite side of the salon. The lady gesticulated that she couldn't hear what Mo was saying so Mo turned up her vocal volume a few more decibels. Her normal speaking voice was loud, but when she was competing against the hairdriers, the noise of other conversations and the racket coming from the radio, her shouting was unbearable for anyone within a two-metre radius of her.

Sam was only usually in there for five minutes but always left with a headache due to a combination of the noise and the cranial beating given by the heavy clippers. Mo turned back to look at Sam in the mirror.

'Number four all over, isn't it?' she said as she picked up the clippers.

'Yes please, same as usual.'

Mo turned round again to speak to the lady under the drier while the clippers made heavy contact with the front of Sam's head. He winced with pain. 'For Christ's sake look what you're doing,' he muttered to himself as a second painful blow was struck. Mo turned to face the mirror and started to speak to Sam. She had an annoying habit of speaking whilst looking at her reflection in the mirror, never making eye contact with the poor sod sitting in the chair, always looking at herself in the mirror. Sam often had conversations with himself in the bathroom mirror, but these were in the privacy of the bathroom, behind a locked door, but Mo seemed to enjoy this strange behaviour quite openly. Another blow was struck with the clippers to the side of the head.

'On the way home, are we?' asked Mo.

'I am,' replied Sam. 'Don't know about your movements.'

'Eh?'

'You said, "On the way home, are *we?*" We, being the plural of I. I replied saying, "I am", meaning on my way home, don't know about you.'

'Oh never mind,' said Mo tutting, choosing to start a loud conversation with Vera, her partner in the business who was doing a lady's highlights in the next chair. 'Good night in the pub last night, weren't, it Vera?'

Sam looked in the mirror at Mo. She was still looking at herself in the mirror whilst talking to Vera, not paying attention to where the heavy clippers were going to land next on Sam's head. Then it came, a heavy blow behind his right ear.

'Yeah, I had a few too many gins,' said Vera equally loudly whilst she also looked at herself in the mirror in front of her client, a lady in her seventies with grey hair and the beginnings of a black moustache.

'I could do with a trip to the pub myself. I've had a crap day,' said Sam, who got the impression his attempt at conversation was being ignored. He was right.

'You certainly did, girl, thought I'd have to carry you home,' said Mo.

'And to top my crappy day off I had to come here and listen to you lot cackling away,' said Sam, safe in the knowledge that they weren't listening to a word he was saying.

'Yeah. Nigel weren't too pleased when I walked through the door at half eleven last night.'

Mo always wore a low-cut top displaying her ample cleavage. When she stood in front of Sam he attempted to divert his gaze by looking down, only for Mo to yank his head up again so she could continue with her work, leaving him no choice but to gaze in admiration at her bosom. A few seconds was all he could manage before becoming embarrassed so he looked down again at his legs.

'You could do my legs when you've finished beating me about the head, maybe a number two?' She seemed oblivious to his comment, abruptly pulled his head up again with both hands and continued talking to Vera.

'Did you see Mrs Blewitt from number twenty-two in the pub? Her old man's only been dead two weeks and that young bloke she was with was all over her.'

Now convinced that his comments were being ignored or not even heard, Sam put his theory to the test again. 'When you've done my legs, if you've got time maybe you could do my bikini line with the cut-throat razor, it gets awfully itchy down there in the summer.'

'Shocking, ain't it?' said Vera.

'Too right,' said Sam. 'It's a nightmare in this hot weather.'

'Makes you wonder if they were carrying on before,' said Mo.

'Before what?' asked Vera.

'Before her husband died, silly.'

Sam looked at Mo in the mirror again. She obviously hadn't got a bloody clue what he'd been talking about – too busy cackling.

The lady in the seat to his right with the grey hair and the moustache appeared to have overheard Sam's one-sided conversation and threw him a strange look. Sam couldn't decide whether it was a look of amusement, disgust or one of intrigue. Still, it didn't really matter.

Beatrice Bassett was sitting in the seat to his left under the hairdryer. Their eyes met as Sam looked in the mirror. She smiled and raised an eyebrow. She seemed familiar but Sam couldn't place her. Beatrice Bassett knew very well who Sam was. She'd observed him many times visiting the old family home as she sat in her porch. Next time she saw Brenda her sister she would have to advise her of the strange behaviour of the head of the English department.

'That's you all done then, Sam,' said Mo.

'Well and truly,' said Sam as he stood up and handed over ten pounds. Ten pounds for sitting in the chair for four minutes being beaten about the head and having his ears tortured. *Still*, he thought, *there's the entertainment value I suppose.*

When Sam arrived home he poured himself a scotch, lit a cigar and sat down in a chair at the table and put his head in his hands, sighing deeply.

'Whatever is the matter?' asked Morag.

'I had a haircut on the way home. I finished work early so I called on Mum to pass some time so I wouldn't have to sit and listen to those dreadful women at the hairdressers cackling away like a load of chickens. I got a lecture from Mother. "Your hair doesn't need cutting, let it grow. Duncan's got lovely hair and he hasn't been to the barber for years. He cuts it himself," she said.'

Sam went on to describe the rest of the conversation he'd had with his mother.

'She did say something strange. She said, "When I'm dead and gone will you promise me you'll look after him." What's all that about?'

'She's probably realised that he could end up a lonely and vulnerable old man,' said Morag. 'Apart from your mother he's only got you and Emma, no friends.'

'Whose fault is that? She's denied him a normal life for years. She's manipulated and controlled him. For the last thirty-five years his life has revolved around her. Now she's worried what will happen to him when she's not around. If she brings the subject up again I'll have to say we'll all keep an eye on him and not to worry.'

Unfortunately, Sam McAllister never had the opportunity. A week later she passed away. (Which is where this story began, but I have digressed and reminisced – author).

Sam had visited his mother in hospital the day before she died. She had also tried to say something to him, just as his father had, but whatever she was trying to say was just a meaningless mumble. Again, Sam had just smiled and nodded as she'd tried to communicate, just as he had done with his father. What was it she had been trying to say?

CHAPTER 19

'I've found these,' said Emma as she removed three envelopes from the wooden bureau in the front room of the old family home. She passed one to Sam. 'This is for you. We've each got one.'

The envelopes contained a note from their mother with her wishes regarding particular items from the house she wanted each of her three children to have.

'I've spoken to Emma,' his mother had told Sam several years earlier. 'I'm leaving her all my jewellery and there's some furniture she would like, oh, and a mirror. I've spoken to Duncan, but he doesn't want to discuss it. Silly boy, I told him I won't be here forever. When I'm dead and gone I just want to leave all my affairs in order, so there are no arguments between the three of you. I know you've always liked the grandfather clock and the old French clock, it's Louis XVI, would you like those?'

'Well, I...'

'Good. I'll put them down for you then. What about the Persian tapestries?'

'Well, I...'

'Good. You can have those as well. That was easy wasn't it?'

The conversation had been so brief and to the point that Sam wondered if she had already decided which items he should have, or maybe they were the items his two older siblings had no desire for. He'd always been fond of the old clocks but other than those there really wasn't much in the house that he particularly liked or had got room for. He'd never really given the matter any thought but it was obvious that it was a subject that had troubled his mother. Her other "when I'm dead and gone" request was that fifty-seven Stonebridge Road should be sold and the proceeds equally divided.

'I've found these as well,' continued Emma as she emptied a bag of black-and-white photographs onto the front room table. There were some old family photographs, the usual things that people keep but rarely look at – old wedding photographs, school photographs and photographs of distant long-forgotten relatives. Sam picked up a large photograph, which had drawn his attention. His father had never spoken much of his war years. All Sam knew was that he had driven a Churchill tank. This photograph was a revelation. His father was seated at a grand piano on a stage with a group of other musicians, what looked like a seven-piece dance band – a saxophone, trumpet, double bass, a drummer, a fiddle player and a vocalist standing in front of an old fashioned microphone on a tall tripod – all dressed in army uniform and trying to force a smile as they posed for the camera. Across the back of the stage was a large banner with "Stars in Battledress" written in large letters. They all looked uncomfortable, as if they didn't want to be there. Maybe they were thinking they shouldn't be there. Maybe his father was thinking he should be somewhere else driving a tank, not driving a grand piano. Maybe they were thinking they were the lucky ones, away from the horrors of war for a while, entertaining the troops. Sam stared at the photograph wondering who the other band members were. What were their names? What tunes had they played? Where had they played? He turned the photograph over – "Holland June 1944" written in his father's handwriting. He wanted to know more about his father and his past, but all he had was a photograph, a photograph and his childhood memories of a father quite strict and difficult to approach, but the photograph revealed a different person in a different time. He wanted to know more of the life he had led. He should have asked. He wished he'd asked. It was too late now. He was gone. His mother was gone; both gone forever.

CHAPTER 20

'We need a valuation of the house for probate,' announced Kendrick. 'I've arranged for a couple of estate agents to call tomorrow to take a look. I told them we'll be putting it on the market straight away. One of them knows a builder who might be interested in buying it for complete renovation. That might be our best option for a quick sale, then we can get your mother's will finalised.'

Duncan started shaking his head and making a strange wailing noise.

'It would make a lovely family home again,' said Emma. 'Don't you think it would be good to see it improved and a family moving in, making it a nice home?'

Duncan banged his fist on the table. 'No I don't! Think of the noise, the hammering and bashing, things being pulled apart and dumped in a skip on the drive. I couldn't stand looking out of my window next door and watching all that going on. Hairy-arsed builders marching in through the front door with sledge hammers and wheelbarrows…'

'Well keep the curtains closed then and don't look out of the window,' said Sam.

'Then there would be arguments about the fence, whose boundary it was, I couldn't stand it.'

'Well that's what Mum wanted so you'll have to get used to it,' said Sam. 'While I'm here I'll take the French clock away and take it to the clock shop to get it overhauled and working again.'

The grief-stricken Duncan had not been able to read the instructions left by their mother about which items she wanted each of her three children to have so he stood up and looked out of the front window with his back turned to everyone.

Sam walked over to the carved wooden bureau where the clock had resided for years. As he lifted it, clear footprints were revealed where the clock's four feet had stood undisturbed for years, the rest of the surface of the bureau covered in dust. He took the clock over to the window for closer inspection. It used to be a deep red colour with elaborate gilt decorative work but now all its former beauty was covered in thick grey dust and cobwebs that had accumulated from years of neglect. Sam shook his head in disgust at its condition then placed it gently on the table and walked through to the hallway to look at the grandfather clock. He paused as he passed the old Persian tapestries hanging on the wall. Their beautiful carved wooden frames were covered in dust and the tapestries, once a vibrant orangey-red colour, had faded from years of exposure to the sun and were now an insipid, bland yellow.

The grandfather clock, which had once stood tall and proud, was in a similar state of neglect. It hadn't worked for many years and the veneer on the front of the clock case was cracked and chipped, the once shiny polished wood now faded. He carefully pulled the clock away from the wall and inspected the back. The rear panel was full of worm holes and piles of yellow dust lay on the floor below, evidence of recent woodworm activity. He opened the door at the front of the clock and peered in. One of the heavy lead weights had dropped down into the bottom of the case where there were mouse droppings and the remains of a nest.

Sam became enraged at its condition and, turning to Duncan, shouted, 'This is a disgrace! How can you let these lovely old clocks become so neglected and end up in this state? They haven't worked for years, probably haven't been wound up since Dad died, that was six years ago. It's the same with everything in this house, it's disgraceful. I've got to spend a lot of money now to get these clocks restored and back in working order. Why do you always leave it for someone else to spend the money? Why don't you look after things properly?' Sam looked at the grandfather clock for a moment. 'I don't think I really want this anyway, it's full of woodworm. I don't want that in our house.'

'Well leave it here then and I'll take it next door. I rather like it as it is anyway,' replied Duncan. 'Let me know what it's worth and I'll give you the money for it.'

'In its present condition about fifty quid, it needs putting in a different case, it's awful. Don't bother, I'll leave it here. You can keep it, gratis, free and for nothing. It can rot away with everything else in the house. It's so damp and cold in here.'

'It's a nice clock. It's only a bit of woodworm,' said

Duncan. 'It's probably the common furniture beetle, goes by the scientific name of Anobium punctatum, a woodboring beetle. In its larval stage it bores into wood and feeds on it…'

'Well it's certainly made a meal of this!' shouted Sam as he looked again at the grandfather clock shaking his head. 'There are several boring things in this house, the woodboring beetles and you. How do you know all this garbage, have you got nothing better to do than memorise all these obscure facts?' He heard his mother's voice in his head – *don't be rude to Duncan, dear*.

Duncan ignored the criticism and turned his back again to look out of the front room window.

Emma, who had been upstairs looking at the bedroom furniture, entered the room and appeared distressed. The furniture had suffered the same fate. Everything was infested with woodworm and the once highly polished wood was faded with years of exposure to the sun and damp. The furniture, like the clocks, had once belonged to Granny McAllister and had been handed down to their father many years earlier. They were once cherished family antiques, clocks that worked and chimed, their gentle ticking a source of comfort to those in the house. They were now reduced to shadows of their former beauty and the beautifully carved furniture now only fit for firewood.

*

When everyone had left Duncan returned to fifty-nine Stonebridge Road next door, sat at the table, opened a bottle of beer and poured it into a glass, then rolled a cigarette. As he sat deep in thought pondering on his predicament he had a strange feeling, that uneasy feeling you sometimes get when you suspect you are being watched. With his beer glass raised from the table his arm suddenly became rigid. He slowly turned his head and then he saw it, a horrible sight – two piercing silver eyes staring at him from a jet-black face. Duncan became transfixed, staring back into the bright eyes, neither Duncan nor the thing daring to blink, neither daring to move. Then there was a spine-chilling screech followed by a sudden commotion as the jackdaw flew directly in front of Duncan's face towards the grubby net curtains, scattering soot over the table as it passed. 'Damn you, blasted thing!' shouted Duncan as he suddenly stood up, knocking over his glass of beer on the table pursuing the jackdaw to the window. He drew back the net curtains and opened the window. The jackdaw turned and flew towards the closed curtains at the opposite end of the room depositing more soot, closely followed by Duncan frantically waving his arms. The bird turned again and flew straight towards Duncan, who ducked and turned to see the jackdaw flying out of the open window. It landed on the front garden wall and started to preen itself, shaking the soot from its feathers. As Duncan shut the window the bird's silver eyes stared at him, it flapped its wings and screeched as if laughing at him before flying back up to its nest in the chimney pot.

Duncan returned to the table, mopped up the beer on the table and looked in despair at the large pile of soot in the fireplace that had been brought down the chimney. He opened another bottle of beer and resumed his contemplation. What was he to do? The thought of his mother's house next door being sold worried him. What disturbed him more was the prospect of a builder buying the property, ripping it apart, modernising it and changing it. Then he considered the practical problems. The items from the house his mother had bequeathed to him were the largest and the most valuable. She had wanted him to have the Steinway concert grand piano and his father's 1965 Jaguar Mk2, which was last used in 1984 and had sat dormant in the garage of the old family home for the intervening 34 years. It was a double garage and the other half was occupied by Duncan's old 1960s Alfa Romeo, which had been pushed into the garage before its metalwork succumbed to the ravages of the British weather. His own garage next door at number fifty-nine was a single garage and housed Reginald Ramsbottom's old Jaguar E-Type. He had three cherished cars and needed three garages. He dropped his cigarette end into the empty beer bottle and tried to think of a solution. After several minutes the only solution he could come up with was a bit radical but it had to be done. He'd keep the old family home and leave his new possessions where they were.

He'd leave everything as it was – everything.

CHAPTER 21

'You can't do that!' exclaimed Sam and Emma in unison when Duncan revealed his radical plan to them as they were gathered around the table in the front room of the old family home the following day.

'I can. I've done my sums and can afford to give you both your third each of the value of the house; well, just about, and the bills won't amount to much. I'll just walk through the hole in the fence every day to have my lunch here and keep an eye on the place. I can keep both cars in the garage and leave the grand piano where it is.'

'Why don't you just sell the cars?' asked Sam, stunned by his brother's latest revelation. 'Let's face it, they don't work anyway, sell the piano, then we can sell the house which is what Mum wanted. A removal firm could get the grand piano out, or Steinway might even buy it and take it away, after all, they put the blasted thing in here. Getting it out of the house would be their problem. They can probably dismantle part of it. It must be worth thousands. You could invest the money or spend it on improving next door.'

Duncan began to wave his arms about, the first sign he was starting to become agitated, 'I don't want to sell the cars and I don't want to sell the Steinway. I want to keep them. I want to keep the house. I'm going to keep it as a holiday home.'

'A holiday home!' shouted Emma. 'But it's the house next door for heaven's sake!'

'Who says people have to have holiday homes on the coast, in Cornwall or some nice spot in Dorset? If I want to keep the house next door as a holiday home then I will.'

'Dad once called you soft in the head,' said Sam, still in a state of consternation. 'He was right. Think of the cost.'

'We're going round in circles. I've already said I can afford it, I've done the sums.'

Kendrick was sitting in an armchair listening and observing. He had always taken an interest in the family, not only because he was part of it, but over the years they had become such a rich source of material for his forthcoming book. Emma's mother had been a dear sweet lady but had led a difficult life married to Bernard, a belligerent and cynical man with a piano playing compulsion; one brother, an extroverted English teacher who sometimes imagined himself teaching in a non-existent school in the Lincolnshire Fens and tried to write poetry and her other brother, an introverted obsessive thinker with a penchant for detail and what seemed to others to be obscure and irrelevant facts. Kendrick considered the years of being mollycoddled by his mother had had a strange effect on Duncan. He wasn't interested in anything outside his 'world'. He had become detached from reality and seemed incapable of rational thought.

He rarely went out and didn't have any friends believing in his guiding principle that a friend in need was a pain in the arse. His world was the two houses, numbers fifty-seven and fifty-nine Stonebridge Road, and he didn't want that to change.

The family discussions had become a source of fascination for Kendrick. After the death of their father, should Emma and Sam have been more forceful with their recommendations that the house be improved to make their mother's life more comfortable? Possibly yes. She'd had the opportunity to change her life but she'd rejected all suggestions made by them, her decisions seemingly swayed by the intervention of Duncan.

Kendrick was intrigued by Duncan's determination to buy the old family home, considering it ludicrous for him to do so. Sam and Emma had started to put forward an excellent case why he shouldn't, but they always seemed to give in as if there was a general consensus that "we mustn't upset Duncan". Maybe that attitude stemmed from their mother's years of protecting and cosseting him. Now they were doing the same.

Yes, they are a strange breed, thought Kendrick.

It was impossible to sway Duncan from his plan, his mind was made up. Over the next few weeks, after Kendrick had finished the probate, Duncan had sorted his financial affairs and presented Emma and Sam with a cheque for their third of the value of their late mother's house, although how he'd managed to raise the money nobody was quite sure, but nobody asked.

As time passed the house became even more neglected and, as winter approached, more damp and cold. The grandfather clock, the tapestries and furniture bequeathed to Sam and Emma remained where they were. Indeed, apart from the French clock and Mrs McAllister's jewellery, nothing was removed from the house. Everything remained the same, as it had always been. Even her crochet shawl remained on the back of her chair and her slippers by the fire.

It was Duncan's house now and he seemed content, if not determined, to leave the house exactly as it was. It became a sort of shrine, as if his mother was still there.

Maybe she was, in Duncan's mind.

CHAPTER 22

Number fifty-seven and number fifty-nine Stonebridge Road, both now under the ownership of Duncan McAllister, were in startling contrast to each other. They were both built during the mid-1950s of an individual design. Number fifty-seven, the old family home, was an attractive house, at least when viewed from the outside, its yellowish coloured bricks contrasting with roof tiles of a deep red colour. Before it had become overgrown the front garden had contained a large semicircular border containing small bushes, a laburnum tree near the driveway gates and an almond tree near the smaller hand gate from which a path led to a front porch and an attractively glazed front door. In the front garden was a large stone wishing well with a tiled pitched roof, which was often a source of fascination with people walking by, who often stopped to admire it.

A hedge in the front garden separated it from number fifty-nine, Reginald Ramsbottom's old house. This was a depressing red-brick building with rounded corners and large windows. The windows also had a curvature in keeping with the rounded contours of the brickwork, a poor attempt in the design to resemble a scaled-down version of a more grand Art Deco type of property of the 1920s. The front door compared to the one next door was plain, with a single vertical glass pane in its centre. Above the front door was a semicircular concrete slab jutting out from the brickwork with a rather industrial-looking light on its underside, its glass bowl filled with dead insects and condensation. The front garden was mainly laid to lawn with a rickety brick wall and a hedge separating the garden from the public footpath. Rusty black wrought-iron gates opened onto a short gravel drive leading to a single garage with rotten wooden doors covered with flaking white paint.

Entering the house through the front door was like a gateway to a different world, like stepping back in time to the 1950s, and one was struck with the depressing nature of the place. If it wasn't so filthy inside some would look around and think it had potential, but most would turn round and wipe their feet on the doormat before leaving immediately. Having entered, those who chose to stay would see that the hallway led into an open-plan kitchen with grubby original 1950s wooden kitchen cupboards showing bare patches where the paint had peeled off over the decades and a filthy gas cooker that looked as old as the house, the top of which was littered with spent matches that had been used to light it over the years. Another original feature was the red and cream tiles that covered the entire ground-floor area. Only the front room had rugs on the floor, mostly threadbare but nevertheless gave the illusion of warmth and homeliness. The front room was sparsely furnished with items that had once resided in the summer house next door – a heavily carved dresser, some worn-out armchairs and an old upright piano. Attempts to remove the old wallpaper had been abandoned and bare plaster and patches of stubborn wallpaper remained defiantly on the walls. A door from the kitchen opened into a pantry with the same red and cream floor tiles and a grubby tiled work surface. On the wall above the work surface, small, thick, obscure glass panes gave some light from the garden. Oh what some people would give for such a pantry. This one however, not being used for its intended purpose was filled with car parts, old stepladders, oil cans, extension cables and an old lawnmower. The woodworm-ridden shelves on the walls were home to tins of grease and rusty old biscuit tins full of nails, screws and nuts and bolts. From the pantry there was a door leading to the overgrown back garden, a wilderness or, as Duncan preferred to call it, a "paradise of rustic charm".

Duncan McAllister had always lived modestly. He enjoyed (if enjoyed is the right word) a comparatively uncomplicated existence, at least uncomplicated compared to most. He deprived himself of not so much luxuries, but basic necessities that most people have; things like proper heating, a microwave, a washing machine and a television. His meagre existence was not burdened with what he considered distractions like holidays, relationships or unnecessary insurance policies. He appeared content to live unconventionally, as a recluse, almost as a hermit, with his own company, his piano, his books and cheap whisky.

He seemed to relish the challenges of enduring the misery of the cold winter months, walking round the house in his overcoat and scarf and sitting in front of a fan heater on the lowest setting in an attempt to keep warm, as if he was trying to prove something to somebody. What exactly he was trying to prove and to whom Sam had not been quite sure and he often had a feeling of bewilderment at his brother's miserable existence. For some, who had no choice, that lifestyle would be considered normal. However, for him it didn't have to be like that, he had a choice. He was a highly intelligent person but seemed to have adopted a willingness to live in a cold, damp and dirty house that desperately needed updating, just as the old family home next door did.

Strangely, when one visits old stately homes dating back centuries, one is often struck by the grandeur and opulence of a style of living that was available to a lucky few. The Victorian period also looked comfortable, at least for some, those known as the "middling" sort. Even primitive man living in a cave had a modicum of comfort and the means to combat the cold by sitting by the warmth of a fire. It was baffling to the rest of the family why Duncan, intelligent and reasonably well off with two houses, a valuable E-Type Jaguar in the garage and a Steinway grand piano in the house next door chose to live in the way that he did.

Reginald Ramsbottom had also existed there in a similar depressing and reclusive way. Both he and Duncan were people of considerable intellect and yet both, both of them bachelors, seemed to have been drawn downwards into a life of squalor, both reluctant to make improvements to the property or to the quality of their lives. Maybe the fact they were bachelors was the problem. Neither having entered into a matrimonial alliance had had the benefit of the guiding influence of a good woman, without the love and companionship that a stable relationship could, and should, bring.

Everyone in the family apart from Duncan had considered Reginald Ramsbottom a bit of a crank. Now Duncan seemed to have taken on that mantle from him, along with his house, almost as if one went inseparably with the other.

Nothing much changed in his life over the next few years until he retired from his part-time position as a librarian at the college in Lincoln and now, having an abundance of spare time, he became obsessed with Scottish history in addition to his constant search for rarely used words. He spent several hours a day researching the origins of the McAllister name and its association with other Highland clans. He started to learn Gaelic from a book and developed a strange accent, a poor attempt at a Scottish accent which sounded like a strange combination of Billy Connolly and Kenneth McKellar. He started wearing the tartan of the McAllister clan around the house (though never daring to venture out in public) and collecting ancient Scottish clan weaponry such as broadswords, claymores and old muskets, pistols and shields. These he displayed on the grubby walls of his front room, which in his mind, with his fertile imagination, became a grand entrance hall of a remote Scottish castle somewhere in the Highlands. To others, the unfortunate few who were invited inside fifty-nine Stonebridge Road, it was the front room of a 1950s detached house in South Lincolnshire, the walls of which were adorned with strange objects of warfare placed in juxtaposition, a vision of disorganised chaos, which left most people wondering why he hadn't removed the peeling 1960s wallpaper before he had decided to display the items in his strange collection.

'He only phones me when he wants something,' Sam said to Alistair McAllister as they pulled up on the driveway of the old family home. Duncan had requested assistance to push his precious E-Type back into the garage. Having managed to start the car and reverse it out onto the driveway and spend several hours tinkering, or "fettling" as he preferred to call it, the car had refused to start again and he was unable to push it through the deep gravel on the driveway back into the garage.

On the rare occasions Sam called to see his brother he was never sure which house he would be at. He tended to spend the nights at whichever one he fancied, have his breakfast at one and his lunch at the other, but Sam was never quite sure which one, so calling to see him was a process of elimination. They walked up the front garden path of number fifty-seven, cursing as seeds and grass stuck to their trousers as they negotiated the overgrown weeds and bushes that had encroached onto the path. Sam knocked on the front door of the old family home and waited. He knocked again – no sign of movement through the grubby frosted glass in the door. 'Oh well, he must be next door,' he said. Having retraced their steps along the overgrown path, Alistair McAllister closed the rusty wrought-iron front gate and looked at his hands stained with rust and flakes of peeling paint. They made their way up the gravel path to the front door of number fifty-nine. Sam rang the front door bell ,which didn't appear to work, so he banged loudly several times on the front door. While they waited they looked up at the two houses, both of which appeared as depressing as ever. All the curtains were closed and the windows covered with condensation, the bins near the front doors were overflowing and both the front gardens overgrown, giving both properties an uninhabited appearance. *Maybe they should be*, thought Sam. *Nobody in their right minds would live in either.*

There could be no other front door like the front door of number fifty-nine Stonebridge Road. Being the original door and now nearly seventy years old, its white paint was faded and peeling. The large central glass pane in the door was cracked with clumps of moss growing in each corner. Horizontal metal bars could be seen through the grubby frosted glass in the door, Duncan's attempt at improvised security. After a long delay there was movement in one of the front window curtains followed by the blurred outline of a figure through the frosted glass as Duncan approached the door. Then a strange voice in a peculiar Scottish accent was heard. 'Just a wee moment oot there. I'm on m' way.'

There was then the sound of bolts being drawn back, heavy chains being removed and keys inserted into several locks. The door creaked as it opened slowly to reveal Duncan McAllister dressed in full Highland regalia. He was adorned in a kilt complete with sporran, a tartan blanket thrown over his left shoulder, a bonnet of similar tartan, thick white socks and a pair of worn-out brown carpet slippers, an unusual addition as he hadn't a carpet. The two onlookers, both stunned at the bizarre spectacle in the doorway, were unable to move for several seconds when invited into the house.

'You'll no' be wantin' a dlink, would ye? Or do ye fancy a cup o' tea, or a wee dram?'

'Er, no thanks,' Sam replied as they stepped slowly into the house.

'Well, I'll no' be long. I'll just goo an' change' he said as he climbed the stairs.

Sam and Alistair McAllister looked on in astonishment as Duncan climbed the stairs lifting his kilt up above his knees as he negotiated the bare wooden staircase.

'I'll have to mention this strange new behaviour to Kendrick,' remarked Sam as he and Alistair McAllister stepped into the front room. 'It really is most unusual. I wonder what he'll make of it.' They walked slowly around the room, pausing occasionally to look at the strange items on display, the ancient weaponry hanging from the walls, a half-empty whisky bottle and glass on the table together with a .22 air rifle with telescopic sights and a tin of pellets next to it.

When Duncan descended the stairs and entered the room he was in his more usual attire of black threadbare trousers and an old sports jacket.

Sam looked at him rather disapprovingly. 'Duncan, why is there an air rifle with telescopic sights on the table?'

'Och well, I've got a wee problem with squirrels just now. The wee beasties are getting into the roof. I've got starlings nestin' in the roof as well. They make a bit of a row in the mornings but I do ne mind them. I canny stand squirrels though. They've got to goo. Aye, they've got to goo.'

'It all sounds a bit barbaric to me, shooting squirrels. If you kept the trees a bit lower maybe you wouldn't have squirrels. Some of the trees are as high as the house, no wonder they're getting in the loft. The trees must annoy the neighbours as well, blocking their light.'

'I like the trees just as they are thank ye. I do nay like squirrels.'

'What's that sticking up your chimney?' Sam asked looking at the fireplace.

'That's a chimney sweep's brush.'

'But you don't have open fires anymore. Why have you got a sweep's brush shoved up there?'

'I've had a wee problem with jackdaws nestin' in the chimney so I've shoved that up there to stop them a comin' doon. The brush is right at the top in the chimney pot so they canny get in.'

Sam sensed that Duncan was getting frustrated with the questioning and becoming agitated.

'Last question,' said Sam. 'Why were you dressed up in that Scottish garb just now and why are you trying to talk in a Scottish accent?'

'That's two questions,' he replied raising an eyebrow. A protracted piercing stare followed, after which the elevated eyebrow was suddenly lowered rather mechanically, resembling the movement of an old semaphore railway signal.

'Och well, as ye will probably be aware, I've been doing the research into the family name. Did ye not know we're descended from an old Highland clan? The name McAllister originates from the Gaelic name Mac Alasdair, son of Alasdair. We owe our ancestry to the Scottish clan Donald. Aye, we're a branch of the clan Donald. Pillaging, raping, cattle rustling Highlanders we were. Aye, it's difficult not to get... well, sort of drawn into the history of it all.'

As they all shuffled back towards the front door Sam was struck with his brother's strange behaviour. It was as if fifty-nine Stonebridge Road had become a parallel world, an alternative reality. Maybe it really was a Scottish castle in his mind where he could live in a sort of dream world. Perhaps it was the same at number fifty-seven, believing his mother was still there. Perhaps that's why he'd left the house exactly the same as when she *had* been there. Perhaps that's why he cooked his meals there every day, to sit at the table with her as he had done every day since their father's death. Maybe, in his world, she *was* still there.

The similarity with his own imaginary world at the South Lincolnshire Academy of Practical Studies was striking, although he reassured himself that when he was "there" it was a sort of entertainment, a sort of release from the stresses and strains of everyday life. In Duncan's case, it was all rather strange, all rather macabre.

Strangely, as soon as they left the house Duncan reverted to his normal vernacular Lincolnshire accent and started behaving more... not normally, that would be asking too much, let's just say more conventionally.

It had been several years since Alistair McAllister had seen the old Jaguar and he started to walk round the car admiring it. Duncan, sensing he was taking an interest, followed him and started to give technical details. 'Inboard rear brakes are a bit of a maintenance issue on these. It's the 4.2-litre engine with a compression ratio of about 9.0 and a firing order of 1.5.3.6.2.4.'

'Oh,' said Alistair McAllister, who appeared to be uninterested.

'It started earlier so I took it for a short drive, just round the roundabout, but it started to misfire and splutter a bit so I came straight back. Now it won't start at all.'

'Oh,' repeated Alistair McAllister as he looked along the road at the roundabout, which was about two hundred yards from the house. 'It didn't get very far, did it?'

Duncan's delivery of technical details continued as the three of them pushed the car through the deep gravel into the garage. As Duncan closed the rotten wooden garage doors he started to talk about the hours he had spent balancing the triple carburettors and his disappointment in the car refusing to start. Alistair McAllister and Sam soon became bored and started to walk away, Alistair muttering to himself, 'He's like a walking talking workshop manual.'

Duncan overheard and seemed to get the message. 'I know. I'm boring. Come and have a look round the back.'

He opened the side gate and they wandered through to the back garden, treading carefully over empty oil cans and broken television aerials that were strewn on the narrow path between the two houses. The fence between Duncan's two back gardens had completely fallen down in places and he'd created a precarious walkway over the rockery, which he used when visiting number fifty-seven.

Both back gardens had been neglected for years, their manicured charm a distant memory replaced with knee-high grass and overgrown bushes and trees. In the centre of the garden there was the remains of a bonfire that Reg had had years ago, the area littered with scrap metal – old brake discs, VW hubcaps and spark plugs from a car.

'He'd have needed a lot of heat to burn that lot,' said Alistair McAllister, sniggering as he walked towards the skeletal remains of the derelict greenhouse. Only the ivy covered wooden frame of the greenhouse remained, the glass long since gone. A large elderberry bush had taken root in the greenhouse, extending upwards well above the kitchen window and, together with the ivy, almost completely covered the glass of a bedroom window above.

A hole had been cut in the ivy where the greenhouse door had once been, forming a sort of archway. Alistair McAllister walked in. 'What's this?' he asked his uncle.

'It's an old safe. It belonged to Reg. Must have come from his shop,' replied Duncan.

The safe was about two feet high, very rusty and looked very heavy.

Alistair tried the door – it was locked.

'I've found a lot of old keys around the house, none of them are for this', said Duncan.

'Have you ever wondered what's in it?' asked Alistair McAllister.

'Not really, it can stay there for all I care. It's not doing any harm. Anyway it's too heavy to move. No one's going to steal it.'

Alistair McAllister and Sam looked at each other in astonishment.

'There's an old safe in your garden,' said Sam, 'in what's left of a greenhouse. It used to belong to someone who had a jewellery shop and you're just going to leave it there unopened'.

'Yes that's right, it's probably empty anyway, like the story of the old empty barn – there was nothing in it' he said sniggering.

'If there's nothing in it, why is the door locked?' asked Alistair McAllister. 'I could cut the hinges off with a big disc cutter, or I could drill a hole and put a small inspection camera in to see what's there.'

'Yes, well sometime perhaps. It can stay there for now.'

With the car now safely back in its garage and their task completed it was clear that Duncan was becoming frustrated with the questions and small talk. 'Well, thank you for your help. I expect you'll both be wanting to get off now,' he said as he led them both round to the front of the house.

As they drove home they were both deep in thought; Alistair McAllister thinking about his strange uncle and Sam thinking about the equally strange old neighbour Reginald Ramsbottom and the occasion as a fifteen-year-old when he'd spied on him through the knot hole in the fence as he'd locked the safe door in the greenhouse and returned the key to its hiding place under the flower pot.

'When I was a schoolboy and Granny McAllister came to stay she would always ask Reg to bring round his trays of jewellery, the remains of what was left of his stock when he closed his jewellery shop. She would spend hours looking through trays of rings, earrings, necklaces and brooches. She always bought something. I think he used to keep his old stock in the safe. Maybe it's still in there. Or it could be full of money. I know one thing, if it was in my garden I'd want to know what was in it.'

'Me too,' said Alistair McAllister.

CHAPTER 23

Duncan McAllister's ownership of both properties had become a source of bewilderment and frustration for the rest of the family, coupled at times with anger, outrage and exasperation. For the immediate neighbours it became a source of intrigue and curiosity, particularly for Beatrice Bassett. She would often sit in her porch with a glass of her favourite sherry, observing through her binoculars the activities of Duncan McAllister at the two properties opposite, not that there was much to observe. He seldom went out and, apart from infrequent grass cutting and hedge trimming, was rarely seen in the front garden of either property. From her window seat she was often puzzled by his appearance in the front bedroom window of one house, only to reappear at the front bedroom window of the neighbouring house a few minutes later without having been seen to walk from one property to the other. Similarly, she occasionally observed him entering one property through the front door and appearing again shortly afterwards when exiting the front door of the neighbouring house. She became intrigued by Duncan

McAllister and took an almost obsessive interest in observing his strange movements. She thought he looked such a nice man, a little scruffy perhaps and rather shy, but nevertheless a pleasant-looking character.

Her sister, Mrs Brierley, unknowingly became a source of information and intelligence gathering for Beatrice. She regularly divulged details of private conversations she'd had with Sam in her school secretary's office where he would often seek sanctuary during his lunch hour to escape the banal conversations in the staffroom centred around reality television and football. Since the death of his mother Sam often discussed with Mrs Brierley the years of control she'd had over Duncan, his frustration with his brother over the retention of the old family home and the way it had remained unchanged.

Beatrice Bassett was still an attractive woman. Her facial features were the exact opposite of her sister's rodent-like appearance. Beatrice had a large, wide mouth, a large, wide smile and beautiful small white teeth, in contrast to her sister's rat-like incisors. She had normal-sized ears and eyes compared to her sister's large ones and, more importantly, she had no moustache. Having been widowed twice she felt somehow comforted that both her deceased husbands now resided in the churchyard next to her house but Beatrice Bassett was lonely. Beatrice Bassett needed male companionship. She was looking for a relationship and a possible candidate for husband number three. Now Duncan was no longer tied to his mother's apron strings, he was free, he was available. Perhaps he too craved companionship and female company. Could she befriend him? Could he be trained and nurtured? Could he be moulded? Would he be willing?

Her observations continued over the following weeks and months, as did her intelligence gathering courtesy of her sister. She resigned herself to get to know Duncan better, but opportunities for interaction were scarce. Their paths never crossed. There was however one opportunity – bin day. Having two properties, he had two wheelie bins, which she had noticed he always retrieved promptly after being emptied. The next day was bin day. As she looked from her window she noticed he had already moved the bins out onto the grass verge and was a little disappointed that she had missed his appearance and a possible opportunity of engaging with what she now considered her quarry. The following morning when the bins had been emptied she would take her opportunity – she would pounce.

The following day she took up her position in her front porch to enjoy the first sherry of the day in the early-morning sunshine. As the bin lorry stopped outside her house the driver gave his usual cheery wave, which she returned with a smile and the raising of her sherry glass. After it had driven away she didn't have long to wait before the side gate of number fifty-nine started to open noisily as its bottom edge was violently pulled free of the gravel path. As Duncan McAllister walked slowly up the path towards the hand gate, Beatrice Bassett emerged from her concealment. She timed her approach to perfection, reaching her wheelie bin simultaneously with Duncan reaching his on the opposite side of the road.

'Good morning, Mr McAllister,' she shouted. 'How do you find yourself this morning?'

'Oh dear. As well as can be expected thank you, Mrs... er Bassett.'

Beatrice Bassett checked for passing traffic and energetically skipped across the road.

'Please call me Beatrice. May I call you Duncan?'

'Er yes. I suppose...'

'I was so sorry to hear about your dear mother Duncan. Your brother Sam told my sister Brenda Brierley. She's the secretary at his school. I know you were very close, quite literally I suppose, living next door to her. I lost my second husband shortly before your mother passed away. We're still close as well – he's buried in the churchyard next door, just the other side of the stone wall, near to his predecessor, husband number one. I talk to them both regularly when they come and sit on the stone wall of the churchyard. One is an elf, the other's a goblin. Do you believe in fairies and pixies, Duncan? The churchyard is full of them in the evenings.'

'Well I... oh dear,' he replied, looking at Beatrice Bassett with a look of astonishment.

'Still, I always say you can replace a husband but you can't replace a mother. My last husband always used to say the graveyards are full of people who thought they were indispensible, now he's one of them. Ha! You must pop in some time and try some of my home-made scones.'

'Well er... yes. Thank you – perhaps sometime.'

'Do you prefer cream or jam, or maybe you like both?'

Duncan looked rather blankly at Beatrice Bassett with his mouth open, unsure what she meant.

'On the scones, dear,' she said nudging his arm – 'cream or jam?'

'Oh I see. I've never really given it much thought. Jam I suppose,' replied Duncan who normally had a bland and uninteresting diet that didn't include such extravagancies as scones, cakes or pastries of any kind, things he considered self-indulgent, decadent and bad for his health.

'Then jam you shall have, dear. Jam it is! You can have anything you want, dear,' she said squeezing his left forearm with both hands, raising an eyebrow and smiling suggestively, 'anything at all.'

Duncan McAllister suddenly felt uncomfortable, threatened and terrified by this overpowering woman he'd lived opposite to for years but didn't know or had hardly even spoken to before that day. He mumbled something unintelligible to Beatrice, turned, grabbed an empty wheelie bin in each hand and scampered across the grass verge running into the front garden through the small gate of number fifty-nine. Both wheelie bins struck the brick gate pillars and remained overturned on the pavement. Duncan paused and looked over his shoulder – he would have to retrieve them later when it was safe to re-emerge. He walked briskly through to the rear garden, closed the side gate and breathed a sigh of relief, feeling like a fly that had managed to escape from a spider's web as the spider approached to incarcerate it, or prey that had escaped the talons of a raptor and certain death.

Beatrice Bassett turned and walked slowly back across the road and into her driveway deep in thought. She shouldn't pursue her quarry with excessive vigour or tenacity – he must be gently coerced. She would have to move slowly, take her time. She was dealing with a man inexperienced with the ways of women, especially a woman like her. Progress, if any would, be slow. Maybe she could use one of her novelty coffee mugs to break the ice, to lighten the mood – the novelty mugs always worked.

CHAPTER 24

The time had arrived in Samuel McAllister's life when he, like others, often looked back and asked themselves "What have I accomplished in life? What have I achieved?' He often thought back to his teenage years in the 1970s, his beloved 1970s, the decade of his carefree days, the days of no commitment when thoughts of growing old seemed irrelevant. In fact, as a teenager, such things weren't thought of at all with his whole life stretching out in front of him, his dreams and future plans to realise – the yellow Lamborghini Miura and the red Ferrari Dino he had dreamt of owning parked on the gravel driveway of a manor house or a leafy vicarage somewhere he had often imagined himself living in. The life he had wanted had been a fantasy, a dream – the life his father had accused him of looking at through rose-tinted spectacles. Maybe only a lucky few fulfil their dreams and with the realisation that pensioner status was fast approaching and time was running out and what his mother had referred to as the 'twilight years' were drawing closer, his mood became subdued.

He'd changed over the years and on reflection it occurred to him that it had all started twenty years earlier on his fortieth birthday, that milestone in a lot of people's lives when the future seemed to be bleak unless you were part of what he considered the misguided faction of society that believed that life begins at forty. He had found it a depressing sort of day. He'd arrived home from work and opened birthday cards, no doubt sent with good intentions but interpreted by him as congratulating him on the occasion that probably half his life was now gone. Arrangements had been made to mark the occasion with a meal out, just himself, Morag and Alistair McAllister. He hadn't been able to summon up any enthusiasm to go out, to celebrate, no desire to be jolly or even pleasant. He just wanted to be miserable, to spend the sad occasion on his own with a glass of beer and a good book, or perhaps wallowing in cynicism or reliving the past and thinking what the future might or might not hold. He succumbed as he always did after being told by Morag not to be so glum and bad-tempered, not to spoil the occasion for others. He always succumbed. He always gave in.

They had a meal in virtual silence at their favourite country pub. Before they were married he and Morag had often visited the same country pub and had looked around at the clientele seated at the tables and comfy chairs and played "spot the married couple" – the couples sitting in silence, looking around observing others, their only conversation probably "would you like another drink dear?" no doubt followed by "no thank you, dear. Maybe we'd better be going". At the time Sam had thought, *God forbid we end up like that.* They had, on the occasion of his fortieth birthday.

Some had what they termed a midlife crisis, whatever that is. It hadn't felt like a crisis. It hadn't even felt like midlife. For him it was different. It was as if from that day he'd changed into somebody else. It was a sort of metamorphosis. A change into a different being, just as a caterpillar eventually changes into a moth or a beautiful butterfly, except he was neither. He wasn't really sure what he was. The previous day, still thirty-nine, he'd been a relaxed, happy-go-lucky, contented individual. The next day, his fortieth birthday, he'd changed into a carbon copy of his father, wallowing in belligerence and grumpiness and enjoying it. It seemed to give him a sort of dark perverse pleasure being miserable and knowing he was inflicting his misery on others, just as his father had.

His thoughts went back to the conversation he'd had with his mother when he'd told her he thought he was turning into his father. "God help us," she had said.

'God help us indeed,' said Kendrick when Sam relayed his concerns to him over a pint at the Nobody Inn where they often met after Sam had finished school. 'It's not unusual for men to try to emulate their fathers in many ways later in their lives. Indeed I've noticed on many occasions over the last twenty years several mannerisms and things you've said that remind me of your father. I've known you for many years and I agree with you that strangely, the change wasn't something that had been gradually building up. It was as if a switch had been flicked on your fortieth birthday. You became more cynical, more intolerant of other people's behaviour and more critical of society. It would appear that the older you get the more miserable and petulant you are becoming, as if it's a calling, as if it's your destiny.'

Kendrick paused briefly to eat a handful of peanuts and take a swig of his beer before continuing, speaking slowly in his soft, gentle psychiatrist's voice. 'Becoming cantankerous, belligerent, misanthropic or cynical isn't so much of an illness as a state of mind. Possibly as one journeys through life the more these questionable qualities develop and manifest themselves. You may have inherited these characteristics from your father. He had after all been the master of cynicism and petulance in the family. Now that mantle seems to have passed to you. God help us.'

Sam nodded in agreement, then wondered if he should be agreeing or not.

'Kendrick, you understand dreams. For some time I've been troubled by a recurring dream. I'm alone on a boat, a small river cruiser, on a river, a narrow river with trees on both banks arched over, almost joining in the middle. The trees form a leafy canopy over the river just as the overgrown trees do over the lawn and the summer house at the old family home. It's dusk and the light's fading quickly. There's a light on the front of the boat casting eerie shadows on the surface of the water and on the grassy tree-lined banks on either side. All is quiet and still. I look behind at the ripples on the water caused by the boat's progress, the ripples distorting the reflection of the full moon. As I turn and look ahead again below the leafy canopy I suddenly become aware that the river's in the garden of the old family home and there, straight ahead, is the summer house, the beloved summer house of my childhood, my recluse, my haven. As I approach, the door opens slowly and the boat passes through, not into the summer house but into a bright sunny day. There is a cloudless blue sky, the sound of skylarks and the scent of freshly cut hay. I approach a wooden mooring on the bank where I keep the boat. On the bank a group of people are standing with their arms outstretched as if they are welcoming me. As I get nearer I recognise the group. Both my parents are there with Granny McAllister, my other grandparents and Reginald Ramsbottom, all long since dead, all looking as they had in the 1970s. As I get nearer to the bank I pick up a coiled rope to throw, hoping that someone will catch it to pull me in. As the boat glides slowly towards the bank, the group, still with arms outstretched, seem to move backwards, further away. They aren't walking backwards but seem to be gliding back, almost floating in the air further away from me. Suddenly a strong current carries the boat further away down the river. My mother and father, still with arms outstretched, are saying something. I can't hear what they are saying. I can't understand them, just as I hadn't understood what they were trying to tell me before they died. The group continues to drift further into the distance, disappearing in all directions across the empty fields just as the tractors had in my dreamy thoughts of the imaginary school in the Lincolnshire Fens, drifting away until they become tiny specks on the horizon before disappearing. Then I wake up as the boat continues to drift away. What does it mean? Is it an omen? Is it a warning to change my ways?'

'That's very interesting,' said Kendrick. 'Sigmund Freud would probably have interpreted that dream as having a sexual connotation, the boat passing through the opening door into the brightness and beauty of what lies beyond.'

'It's a sodding boat, Kendrick, entering a building, it doesn't make sense.'

'Exactly, Sam, but it's not any old building. It's the summer house that you once loved, the building you just described as your haven where you spent your carefree younger days.' Kendrick had more peanuts followed by another mouthful of beer. 'Actually most of Freud's dream interpretations come down to sex. There's probably more to it than that though. The group of people standing on the bank, refusing to take your rope, are refusing to help. They move away as if they're saying, "You're on your own, sort it out yourself." It's all very interesting.'

Kendrick inhaled deeply, took his notebook and pen from his jacket pocket and started to make some notes, then looked at Sam over the top of his glasses. 'Is there anything else you want to discuss with me? I'm rather enjoying our little chat.'

'Well actually there is something else, Kendrick. I'm getting very intolerant of others. In the mornings I listen to Radio 4 whilst we have our breakfast and end up shouting obscenities at the radio when prevaricating politicians incapable of answering a simple question are grilled by the presenters. Then the sports news comes on when half-witted sportspersons and football managers are interviewed. You know how much I detest sports so-called personalities that no one has ever heard of,

Kendrick. Well, I've now added sports presenters to the list. On the television they all seem to have an annoying habit of speaking very quickly with a stupid grin on their faces. They always seem to talk utter garbage through a ridiculous permanent smile, maybe not so much a smile but a grimace or a "muscular spasm" as PG Wodehouse would have probably described it. With radio sports presenters I imagine them sitting in front of the microphone with the same stupid expression on their faces. In frustration I sometimes change the channel to Classic FM but as soon as I'm reminded repeatedly which channel I'm listening to, or the first irritating advertisement comes on, I start shouting obscenities at the radio again before switching off. "Do try to calm down," Morag is always telling me. "You'll make yourself ill." Strangely, my mother used to say that to my father.'

'Most interesting, Sam – proof, as if I needed more that you have a fixation with your late father's behaviour and his intolerance to others.

There were a few moments of silence whilst Sam considered Kendrick's comments, during which Kendrick consumed more peanuts and beer before continuing, 'Are you still planning on retiring early, Sam?'

'Yes, when I'm sixty-two, just a couple of years to go now, Kendrick. I've had enough. I'm old school, Kendrick, some would say old-fashioned, believing in the old ways and old values. I detest political correctness and all those stupid equality and diversity courses I have to do. I hate them with a passion. I've always called a spade a spade, now I have to call it a digging implement. I was brought up in the sixties when the weekly family entertainment was *The Black and White Minstrel Show* and Alf Garnet in *'Til Death Us Do Part*, programmes that now I suppose would be considered offensive. Who has the right to decide what's offensive and what people watch? I find a lot of things and a lot of people offensive but I keep my views to myself, well, most of the time. I've had my time, Kendrick. I resent change and the openness of modern society. The world we live in now is depraved with the lowering of standards and values. Yes, I've had my time, besides, there's so much I want to do.'

Kendrick clicked his silver pen and put it on the table with his notebook. 'Yes, Sam, we seem to spend most of our lives working, then retire and then die, usually in that order. Others just carry on working, refusing to retire, and then die, missing out the retirement period, proclaiming that they'd be bored and have nothing to do.'

'The word "bored" doesn't exist in my vocabulary, Kendrick. There's no time to be bored, there's so much to do – great works of literature to read and wonderful music to listen to and play, yes, just as my father did. He was able to retire early to enjoy life and pursue his interests, even if he did only have one. We have bookshelves lined with wonderful books and novels – the entire works of Dickens, Sir Arthur Conan Doyle, P.G Wodehouse, Agatha Christie, Georges Simenon – the list goes on and on, Kendrick. I have a burning desire to read them all, one after the other, to lose myself in literature. If I could end my days with a good novel in my hands I'd be a happy man, well I wouldn't because I'd be dead, but you know what I mean. Great works of literature are to be read and enjoyed, not just to adorn a bookshelf for visual effect. I often snigger when people are interviewed at their homes or offices on the television news, always sitting in front of an impressive bookshelf. I imagine the interviewees carefully positioning their chairs before going on air, making small adjustments to ensure certain book titles are seen by the viewing audience. They probably haven't read any of the impressive titles but are no doubt keen to create the illusion of learning and sophistication, or is it an allusion? I never really know. I should do really.'

'Do try to calm down, you'll make yourself ill,' laughed Kendrick.

'How is your book coming along Kendrick?'

'Almost finished, Sam,' said Kendrick glancing down at the notes he'd just written in his notebook. 'I hope to send it off to the publisher soon. I can't decide on the title at the moment.'

'Any ideas?' asked Sam.

'Yes, a few. I thought of "Keep It in the Family" or "Family Matters" but my favourite so far is "Relatively Speaking".'

It was a reflective Sam McAllister who walked home from the Nobody Inn, his fears confirmed that he and Duncan, and probably the entire family, were featured in Kendrick's black notebook and the subject of some bizarre psychiatric study featured in his forthcoming book. Strangely, he'd found it somehow comforting to unburden his anxieties and concerns to his brother-in-law, without the psychiatrist's couch and without the psychiatrist's bill.

CHAPTER 25

A noticeable part of Sam's transformation from the age of forty, his metamorphosis into a facsimile of his father, was what he considered a necessity, almost a compulsion, to have a daily moan which, to the relief of others, usually took place in front of the bathroom mirror whilst engrossed in shaving, hair plucking, or the insertion of contact lenses. After all, there was so much to moan about, so many people worthy of his anger and wrath. Sometimes he stood in front of the mirror arguing with himself and on other occasions it was an argument with an imaginary person, or somebody he was likely to meet during the course of the day. Sometimes it was almost as if he was anticipating an argument with a particular person about a particular subject and he was going through some sort of bizarre rehearsal and learning his lines.

He stepped closer to the mirror to insert his contact lenses. After a trickier-than-usual insertion he opened his eyes wide and blinked slowly several times. He looked ridiculous. Why did he always have his mouth open holding his breath when he inserted his contact lenses? He looked like a beached halibut. He didn't need to hold his breath or have his mouth open, so why did he do it? He'd read somewhere it was impossible to sneeze and keep your eyes open, he found it impossible to insert his contact lenses and keep his mouth shut. There were so many mysteries to life, so many unanswered questions. He noticed a long hair emanating from the top of his right ear and moved closer to the mirror. Why hadn't he noticed it before? It was about half an inch long and must have been there for days, even weeks. He picked up the tweezers, gripped the offending hair and gave a sharp pull. 'Got the blighter', he said out loud as he released the hair from the grip of the tweezers into the washbasin below. He stepped forwards nearer to the mirror and began to scan his face for more rogue follicles, particularly grey ones that had appeared in his eyebrows. His hair was greying, which he thought made him look quite distinguished and sophisticated and at least he still had a full head of hair, something to be celebrated at the age of sixty, but grey hairs in his brown eyebrows were an embarrassment and had to be removed. Would there come a time in his life when grey hairs would dominate his eyebrows and the brown ones would require removal to avoid looking ridiculous? An interesting thought. Satisfied with his eyebrows he turned his attention to a hair protruding from his right nostril. As he guided the tweezers to their target he thought of the old neighbour Reginald Ramsbottom and the hairs that had sprouted from his nose and ears, and being determined not to acquire a similar conglomeration, he tightened the tweezers and gave a sharp pull. He moved closer to the mirror, the hair was still there, still protruding defiantly from his nostril. 'Blast the sodding thing. Missed the bugger!' he exclaimed. A second attempt at removal of the same hair usually resulted in frustration or excruciating pain. He decided against the challenge, or the pain. He'd try again tomorrow.

He picked up his electric razor and started to shave, remembering his father once suggesting that someone ought to invent a pill to prevent facial hair growth, adding that a man must spend several weeks, or even months, of his lifetime standing in front of a mirror shaving when the time could be better spent, in his father's case, playing his confounded piano or probably moaning about badly designed milk jugs, British Leyland, the unions or the Labour government. Maybe he moaned about Sam, the rebellious, disrespectful lout, the 1970s teenager with long hair, patchwork flared jeans and platform boots who looked at life through rose-tinted spectacles.

As he began to shave he remembered a forthcoming invitation he and Morag had to the Smedley-Barringtons for a barbecue. Mr Smedley-Barrington the headmaster had a barbecue obsession. Sam McAllister disliked many things but he detested barbecues. Every year, with the arrival of fine weather, the Smedley-Barringtons would invite selected members of staff, the 'privileged few', to the annual event in the immaculate garden of their equally immaculate suburban detached house to endure the delights of cheap sausages burnt to a cinder accompanied by undercooked and unrecognisable pieces of chicken. The Smedley-Barringtons' garden, like many others in the area, would be filled with acrid, oily, carcinogenic smoke as middle-aged men struck up their barbecues for the first time that year. They revelled in dominating the alfresco proceedings and suddenly became cookery experts, although for the rest of the year they would willingly leave that chore to their wives or partners in the kitchen, who sensibly used a serviceable and hygienic cooker, not the rusting, neglected metal appliance that resided in the garden inhabited by earwigs, moths and beetles. On sunny weekends the back gardens of suburban properties would echo to the sound of rattling cooking implements as a selection of undercooked meat was proudly distributed to unsuspecting family members and guests, many no doubt to succumb later to the effects of food poisoning.

He switched off the razor and examined his face in the mirror; running his fingers over his face he realised he'd missed a bit so he switched on again and moved the razor to the offending area, his thoughts randomly wandering again.

His grandmother on his mother's side was teetotal and once said she couldn't understand why a wine could be described as dry. She had once said, 'Wine is a liquid and is wet, so how can it be called dry?' Maybe if she'd ever drunk a dry wine she would have understood, but to the uninitiated, well, you could see her point. She had also questioned why cigarette and cigar manufacturers could describe their products as being "a cool smoke" in their television adverts in the 1960s and '70s. 'How can a cigarette or cigar be called a cool smoke when it's on fire?' she'd asked.

He switched off his electric razor and stepped back from the mirror to bring the reflection of his naked torso into view. The sight was not pleasing. What years before had been an enviable flat stomach was now a large round protuberance, the result of an overindulgence of beer, cheese, pizzas and careless living over the preceding decades. It had begun thirty years earlier in the nineties, unnoticed by him, but back then when Emma had asked him one day "when's the baby due?" he had dismissed her sarcasm, but now as he looked at himself in the mirror, he had to do something about it. He looked down. He could still see his feet and felt encouraged, but more intimate parts were obscured from view. He took a step back from the mirror and turned sideways to view his naked torso in profile. This was even more disturbing. Several adjectives came to mind – stout, plump, tubby, portly – but he settled for the lesser used one of corpulent. Yes, corpulent he most certainly was. As he gazed disapprovingly in the mirror at his torso in profile, its shape reminded him of part of a map of Eastern and Southern England. His stomach resembled the bulging East Anglian coastline of Norfolk, Suffolk and Essex whilst his genitals were somewhere in East Sussex. 'This has got to go,' he said aloud. 'Something must be done before my genitals reach the Isle of Wight. I must procrastinate no longer.'

On the landing, Morag paused as she passed the bathroom. The door was closed but she could hear Sam's voice from within. A few seconds earlier she had heard his electric razor, that had now stopped but she had clearly heard his voice – something about his genitals visiting the Isle of Wight. Well, if his genitals were going to the Isle of Wight he was surely going with them she thought. Then she heard his voice again. 'This has got to stop. I can't carry on like this any longer, it's got to stop'. Who was he talking to? He must be on the phone. Morag's fertile imagination took over. *He must have another woman. The swine – he's got a woman on the Isle of Wight. He's probably planning on leaving me, leaving me after nearly forty years of marriage for a woman on the Isle of Wight – but he's never been to the Isle of Wight.* She threw open the bathroom door to see Sam naked, standing sideways in front of the mirror.

'Who were you talking to?' she demanded.

Sam shrugged his shoulders. 'Just this guy in the mirror, I often talk to him in the mornings. Sometimes it's the only sensible conversation I have all day.'

Sam refused to accept the aging process. In his mind he still had the body and stamina of a 16-year-old. Until he gazed again into the mirror and realised he was deluding himself. His physical features were a shadow of their former loveliness. Some would consider him vain and pretentious. They'd be correct. He would also describe himself as a cynical and cantankerous old bastard. He didn't care anymore. *What's wrong with vanity and a desire to maintain youthfulness and what's wrong with having a good moan?* he thought.

He disliked frumpy, dowdy women and had great admiration for those of the fairer sex who maintained youthfulness in both dress and physical appearance as they aged – "glamorous grannies" who, rather like him, refused to give in to the aging process. Emma and Morag were in this category and he often looked at Morag after a couple of large whiskies and thought that in a poor light at a distance of twelve to fifteen feet she looked the same as she had thirty years earlier, well almost. He often observed aging but still glamorous and desirable women on the arms of their male partners who were in a state of decrepitude and physical decay. With women maybe it was the make-up, or in some cases surgery, or maybe just the desire to make the effort to retain a youthful appearance and an element of glamour whilst their husbands had given up and succumbed to the inevitable. He wondered if women looked at their male partners in the same critical way. What was the male equivalent of frumpiness? Was it what he was looking at in the mirror? The enlarged stomach area, the greying hair, the enlarged ear lobes and uncontrolled hair growth from the nose and ears, even the shape of his nose had changed and its colour too. His mother would have described it as a drinker's nose. "Bet he likes a whisky," she used to say if she saw a man with a large reddish nose that resembled a strawberry. Perhaps it was clothing. Frumpy women always wore clothes that were dull, unflattering and old-fashioned. Was it the same with men? Sam at the age of sixty still wore jeans and shirts of a style that his son Alistair McAllister would probably consider wearing himself, but Sam wouldn't have been seen dead in the style of clothing *his* father had worn. Some of his father's old suits resembled demob suits after the Second World War. They probably were. Regardless of the time of year he had always worn heavy leather shoes. They had always appeared to be the same shoes, never replaced or renewed but always the same highly polished squeaky leather shoes. His father had always worn braces, never a belt. As he'd aged his body had appeared to shrink in size and stature. Having reached his mid-eighties the tops of his trousers seemed to almost reach his armpits and when worn with braces he took on the appearance of a circus clown. His old thick string vests that were worn regardless of the weather probably ended up at knee level. From the viewpoint of a woman was the start of male frumpiness a change in the style of their partner's clothes? Was it the transition from tight-fitting jeans to thick corduroy trousers or perhaps the stubborn retention of the old woolly jumper that was full of holes and decades old, rather like the continued use of the old pair of comfortable slippers that couldn't be discarded? Or was it sandals worn with socks?

He finished his daily moan, stepped back from the mirror and felt somehow refreshed and purged of tension, ready for the stress of the day ahead.

Morag had returned to the kitchen. He heard the kettle boiling, looked in the mirror and smiled, not to admire his dental array, but in response to the sound of the boiling kettle in the kitchen. He pictured Morag in the kitchen below, 'tuned in' to the sounds in the bathroom above, pausing as she consumed her porridge to boil the kettle and make his tea so that it was on the table at the correct temperature when he descended the stairs and joined her at the breakfast table. Invariably his toast would pop up out of the toaster at the precise moment he entered the kitchen. Things were timed to perfection. Things just happened that way, they always had – the ever dependable Morag. It was rather like being married to a gentleman's gentleman, like a dependable Jeeves, except she wasn't Jeeves, she was Morag and she was special.

He realised he'd been in the bathroom far longer than

it would normally take to wash and shave and imagined his father knocking on the bathroom door shouting, 'How much longer are you going to be in there? We're on a water meter you know!'

CHAPTER 26

A knock at the front door of fifty-nine Stonebridge Road was reluctantly answered by Duncan McAllister, who having first peered through his grubby net curtains had undone several locks and chains on his front door to reveal a strange-looking young lady on his doorstep. She had bright-red hair, black lipstick, black mascara, black earrings, black studs in her nose and ears, a ring in her bottom lip and was wearing black fishnet tights, a short black leather skirt, a black leather jacket and highly polished black leather boots.

'Afternoon, mister. You Duncan?'

'I am he who you refer to. Who pray are you?'

'I be Geraldine Brierley. Beatrice over the road do be my ant.'

'Your ant?'

'Yeah. I be her niece.'

'Oh I see,' said Duncan. 'She's your *aunt*.'

'Yeah, that's what I said. She were wondering if you could give her an 'and. My boyfriend's over the road 'n' all and we need to get her new mattress what she's had delivered up the stairs into her boudoir.'

Duncan was a little taken aback by the use of the word "boudoir" so sought clarification. 'You mean her bedroom?'

'Yeah, that's what I said. Well, she calls it her boudoir cos she's posh.'

'When?'

'Soon as.'

'I'll be right over.'

'Ta.'

Duncan put on his grubby faw-coloured raincoat, old hobnailed boots with no laces and his cloth cap, left the house and locked the front door. He crossed the road safe in the knowledge that he wouldn't be alone with the overpowering Beatrice Bassett and walked up her driveway. He entered her large front porch pausing for a moment as he looked at the folded daily newspaper on her wicker table with the crossword half completed, a sherry bottle and empty glass and the shoe rack by the door displaying several pairs of colourful high-heeled shoes. Beatrice was not a wearer of sensible shoes, always high heels, and when traversing rough terrain or deep puddles she stepped cautiously, rather timidly resembling the first tentative steps of a newborn foal. Duncan removed his grubby fawn-coloured raincoat and cloth cap, laying them over a chair, stepped out of his old hobnailed boots with no laces and rang the front doorbell. Through the glass door he saw Beatrice Bassett bounding towards him.

'Duncan darling. How kind of you to help. I need two strong men to get my new mattress up the stairs.'

Beatrice led the way through to the kitchen where the strange leather-clad young lady was sitting at the table with what Duncan presumed was her boyfriend, an equally odd-looking character in a T-shirt exposing heavily tattooed arms and wearing a baseball cap the wrong way round. Duncan was always suspicious of men with tattoos who wore T-shirts in inclement weather and baseball caps the wrong way round. It said something about their character, but he wasn't sure what.

'This is Rupert my niece's boyfriend,' said Beatrice.

'How do, matey,' said Rupert.

'Good afternoon, Rupert,' replied Duncan thinking that Rupert was an unusual name for someone with heavily tattooed arms wearing a T-shirt on a cold day and a baseball cap the wrong way round.

'I'll put the kettle on while you and Rupert take my new mattress up and then you can try some of my home-made scones.'

The new mattress was leaning against the wall at the bottom of the stairs. Rupert went first, pulling followed by Duncan pushing. At the top of the stairs they turned left into the front bedroom. For Duncan, entering Beatrice Bassett's boudoir was like crossing a threshold into an unfamiliar world. The walls were a subtle shade of pink, the curtains a cream colour with red roses and the headboard of the king-size bed was a deep red buttoned velvet. Having struggled to lift the mattress onto the high bed Duncan stepped back and was briefly startled to see his reflection in the large mirrored doors of the built-in wardrobe at the bottom of the bed. On the large white dressing table were scent bottles, hairbrushes, jars of creams, a large powder puff, a sort of shaver and some odd-looking gadgets, the personal accoutrements of a lady the purpose of which he wasn't sure about. They returned to the landing, slid the old mattress down the stairs, left it leaning against the wall in the hallway and both returned to the kitchen.

'It's so kind of you to help with the mattress, Duncan. Do help yourselves to my home-made scones. I do like a good firm mattress, don't you, Duncan? Nice and firm, much better for a good night's sleep and better for the physique and, well everything really,' she said with a meaningful smile. 'They should be changed every few years before they go all soft and spongy. I don't like them soft and spongy, far better to have a firm one, much better for one's back.'

'Yes, I suppose so,' said Duncan although he'd never really given it much thought. He reluctantly accepted a mug of disgustingly weak tea from the pierced niece. He looked disapprovingly at the large steaming mug on the table in front of him, trying to decide which side to drink from to avoid the numerous chips in the rim that could be harbouring germs. He decided to hold the handle in his left hand and drink the wrong side. The tattooed nephew and the niece with the piercings didn't look the sort to notice or even care. He wasn't really a mug sort of person, always preferring to use bone china cups and saucers from one of his mother's numerous collections. There was an air of anticipation from those gathered round the table as he lifted his mug and took the first sip of his tea. He declined the jam and cream that was passed round the table by the tattooed nephew and took a bite of his dry scone followed by another larger gulp of tea, which was accompanied with sniggering from the nephew and niece, Beatrice Bassett managing to keep a straight face

Not this time, she thought, *maybe next time, surely next time.* Duncan reluctantly finished his dry scone and again raised his mug of tea to his lips. The expectation of the anticipated effect was almost too much for the onlookers as they sat and watched. Duncan appeared cross-eyed as he stared into the mug, having taken a large mouthful of tea, which revealed a ceramic erect penis standing proud about an inch from the bottom of the mug. His facial expression was one of shock and horror. Tears rolled down the faces of the others present as they laughed hysterically at the spectacle. Duncan didn't see the joke. He was shocked that he'd become a victim of someone else's depraved humour. He slammed the mug down onto the table, scraped his chair back on the tiled floor and walked briskly from the kitchen, pausing briefly in the porch to step into his old hobnailed boots with no laces, and put on his grubby fawn-coloured raincoat and cloth cap. He ran from the house as fast as he was able to without losing his boots with Beatrice Bassett in close pursuit.

'Duncan, Duncan. Come back,' she shouted. She stopped at her porch door as the fleeing Duncan ran down her driveway and into the road, looking on in horror at the disaster that was about to unfold.

As he turned right at the roundabout into Stonebridge Road in his double-decker bus, the driver Mr Dennison cursed as an empty plastic bottle rolled down the stairs from the upper deck and then continued to roll along the floor to the rear of the bus. He stopped at the bus stop outside Beatrice Bassett's house although there was no one waiting. He looked at his watch. 'Early again' he said to himself shaking his head as he walked to the rear of the empty bus to retrieve the annoying bottle. His whole life had been dogged by being premature – apparently he had been a premature baby, he'd had premature hair loss, suffered from premature ejaculation (although he considered that freed up more of his time to do more worthwhile things like gardening and word puzzles) and he had high blood pressure, which would probably result in his premature death. Everything was premature. He even arrived at most of his bus stops too early. 'Time for a quick smoke,' he mumbled as he stepped off the bus and stood under the bus shelter out of the rain.

*

Agnus Day was driving the Daimler hearse after a visit to the crematorium and was singing "Rock of Ages" to herself and cursing as the rain started to fall. She also turned right at the roundabout into Stonebridge Road and as she approached Mr Dennison's stationary bus she moved onto the other side of the road to pass by.

Mr Dennison's cigarette halted halfway to his lips as he turned his head, aware of a blurred figure running from the house by the bus stop into the road directly in front of his stationary bus. He heard a horn followed by a screech of tyres on the damp road. Agnus Day was almost past the bus when the figure of a man wearing a grubby fawn-coloured raincoat and cloth cap running with his loose boots wobbling on his feet appeared directly in front of her. She complimented herself on her quick reactions and, having composed herself, drove away slowly wiping her brow as Mr Dennison looked on shaking his head.

Having returned to the kitchen Beatrice Bassett looked into the empty mug, then at Geraldine. 'You stupid girl!' she shouted. 'It's the wrong mug! It should have been the titty mug, not the willy mug.' She had tried to plan things so carefully using one of her novelty mugs to break the ice, to lighten the mood and create a giggle and it had all gone horribly wrong.

Having entered what he considered the safety of number fifty-nine Stonebridge Road, Duncan McAllister locked, bolted and chained the front door, his house now becoming his fortress protecting him from the outside world and the dreadful Beatrice Bassett and her strange guests. He leaned against the door and breathed a sigh of relief before moving into the front room where, from the window, he noticed the tattooed boyfriend and pierced niece emerging from Beatrice Bassett's front door and walking towards their rusty old Vauxhall on the driveway. The light of the late November afternoon was fading and Duncan closed the curtains, blocking out the reality of the world outside and his view of Beatrice Bassett's house.

When Agnus Day arrived home later that afternoon she poured herself a large brandy to help calm her nerves after her traumatic experience. She took her brandy upstairs and ran a hot bath, spending some time deciding which bubbles were more appropriate to her mood – "stress relief" red bubble bath or "muscle soak" blue bubble bath. She opted for the stress relief. She had after all had a stressful day culminating in what could have been a tragic accident. Indeed it could have been embarrassing for Graves and Day. She imagined the front page of the local paper – "*Hearse on return journey from crematorium runs over and kills pedestrian outside local churchyard*". She lit some scented candles, switched on her portable CD player and reclined in the luxury of her bubbles to the relaxing tones of Rachmaninoff's second piano concerto.

The man had seemed vaguely familiar though she couldn't place him. Where had she seen him before? Then she dozed off.

CHAPTER 27

It was the time of year when lunchtime conversations in the school staff room seemed to revolve around sport, usually football. Sam detested most sports. It was all balls, or rather all about balls; the kicking, throwing or hitting of a spherical object that he so detested, all done in the name of sport, an activity that was alien to him but seemed to dominate other people's lives. He did however consider bowls and snooker more favourably. They were different, rather like darts, more of a relaxing leisure activity than a sport, participated in by intelligent, right-thinking people, particularly snooker, a game requiring a considerable mathematical acumen. He'd never quite understood the national obsession with football. Sam considered it a game that attracted the primitive tribal faction of society with their singing, chanting and, from the more moronic element, the tormenting of the opposition to provoke a violent response. His aversion to football and his indifference to who won which game had become well known amongst his colleagues. When Mr Bugby the sports teacher once asked him which football team he supported, Sam had thought for a moment whilst he recalled the name, then replied 'Hamilton Academicals', although he didn't support them, or indeed any other team, but had always been fascinated by their name. In the unlikely event that he would ever support a football team it would probably be that Scottish team. He visualised learned old men, academics as the name suggested, university lecturers in the arts and science with long grey beards wearing black mortar boards, monocles and black gowns meeting up on Saturday afternoons to kick an inflated pig's bladder around a wet field in some remote area of Scotland. After the match he imagined them visiting a nice cafe or gentleman's club where they'd discuss the cosmos or the Hadron Collider over some Darjeeling tea and toasted teacakes. Grimsby Town was also a possibility. Team supporters who walk to a match with an inflatable haddock under their arms must at least have a sense of humour.

As the conversation in the staffroom moved predictably to a forthcoming major football tournament, with Mr. Bugby irritatingly predicting the winning team, the final score, who would score the goals and in which minute, Sam decided to visit the school secretary's office and seek solace in Mrs Brierley. It had come to something when Mrs Brierley had to be approached for an intelligent conversation.

'Your brother Duncan had a lucky escape yesterday, didn't he?'

'Did he?' replied Sam, unaware of the strange events that had taken place the previous day.

'Oh yes. He was helping my sister Beatrice in her bedroom, left in rather a hurry and nearly got run over by a hearse as he crossed the road.'

'Helping your sister in her bedroom? That doesn't sound like Duncan,' said Sam sniggering.

'I think it was her new mattress. He was helping her get it up, well, the mattress up the stairs, you know. Anyway he left in a bit of a hurry and crossed the road back to his place and nearly got hit. Agnus Day was driving the hearse and missed him by a gnat's whisker. My friend Mrs Blewitt was talking to Mr Dennison the bus driver at the bus stop after it happened. He saw it all. Agnus was quite shaken apparently – well you would be, wouldn't you?'

CHAPTER 28

Dusk was starting to fall on a late November afternoon and Duncan, having regained his composure after the embarrassing affair with Beatrice Bassett's mattress and subsequent near-death experience two days previously, had settled back into his strict daily routine. Like a janitor or a caretaker of a museum he wandered round the old family home ensuring all was well. He drew the curtains and switched on the table lamp in the hall to give the impression to passers-by that someone was at home. Satisfied that all was as it should be, he returned to number fifty-nine via the gap in the broken fence in the rear garden. He paused before entering his back door to gaze up into the clear sky with stars starting to appear and the full moon rising above the sweep's brush that still protruded from his chimney pot as a jackdaw deterrent. It was going to be a cold frosty night. He shivered as he entered the back door thinking he'd have an early tea and settle down with his latest Sherlock Holmes novel. He removed one of several mackerel from the fridge, put it on a plate and started a rather one-sided conversation with it as he peeled some potatoes, discussing with the mackerel the weather and the state of the economy. He apologised to the mackerel as he put it under the grill and stood close to his aging gas cooker for warmth as he brought the potatoes and minted peas to the boil.

He ate his tea at the small kitchen table whilst listening to the BBC World Service. There was just enough room for his dinner plate amongst the unopened mail and car parts that littered the tabletop. He finished consuming the mackerel as the shipping forecast started at 17:20 and moved onto his customary second course, walnuts washed down with a large malt whisky. He had discovered several bottles of malt whisky after his father's death, the finest malt that Sam had bought his father for birthdays and Christmas over the years. Unknown to Sam, his father had stopped drinking it many years before his death having read in their 1950s medical book that it was bad for his prostate. Sam had continued to buy it, his father had continued to stash it away and, having discovered the hoard, Duncan continued to consume it.

On winter evenings in the past his favourite pastime was to sit in front of a warm fire with a good book, but with his chimney still blocked with the sweep's brush his fireside evenings had been substituted with sitting in a tatty red and yellow striped deckchair in front of his aging gas cooker. He lit the main oven, left the oven door open and moved his deckchair a little closer to the cooker to enjoy the warmth, picked up his copy of *The Sign of Four* and poured another Scotch. After reading a few pages he started to doze, imagining himself as Dr John Watson in the warmth and security of Sherlock Holmes' study at 221B Baker Street, the intelligent and stimulating conversations they would have together as they discussed their latest case seated in front of the crackling fire and… was that pipe smoke he could smell?

The earth hadn't moved for Beatrice Bassett for a long time but it certainly did that evening, the blast causing her to spill her sherry as she stood up to move from her porch to the warmth of her living room. Before her hand reached the light switch the room lit up, indeed the whole house and the surrounding area lit up with the flash from the fire ball emanating from number fifty-nine Stonebridge Road. Her house continued to be illuminated well into the night by the flashing blue lights of fire engines, an ambulance and police vehicles attending to their grisly tasks, as she lay in her bed, comforted by her new mattress and the warmth and luxury of her pink boudoir. She found it impossible to concentrate on the eroticism of her romantic novel, her mind occupied with poor Duncan McAllister from numbers fifty-seven and fifty-nine and what might have been if her delinquent niece had used the titty mug instead of the other one.

*

The subsequent investigation by the fire service revealed that the aging gas cooker had been the cause of the blast. They concluded from its age that it was most likely unserviceable or a gas ring had been left on. It was unclear whether Duncan McAllister's demise was a result of asphyxiation before the blast occurred, the blast itself, or being struck by flying debris, possibly a car cylinder head or gearbox that he'd been repairing on the kitchen draining board. So little was left of him it was hard to tell.

There was little left of the house itself, just a pile of rubble where it had stood. Amongst the rubble was Sam's old green Puch racing bike now mangled almost beyond recognition, Reginald Ramsbottom's mother's hairbrush still defiantly containing long white strands of her hair, now singed, and dozens of video cassette boxes that had fallen in from the bedroom above and started to melt in the raging fire. A mackerel thrown from the fridge had survived relatively unscathed and stared down from the curtain rail with an amusing expression on its face, almost one of relief that it had avoided the grill and had witnessed the end of its tormentor.

The fire had spread quickly to the adjoining garage, the precious E-Type now a burnt-out shell sitting on its four tyre-less wheels, its glass blown out by the blast of the exploding petrol tank, its final journey likely to be to a metal recycling centre, possibly to be reincarnated as a Nissan or something useful such as tin openers or manhole covers. It would probably be joined by the Mk2 Jaguar and the aging Alfa Romeo in number fifty-seven's garage next door, both flattened by falling concrete and masonry.

Apart from the garage at number fifty-seven, the old family home had fared slightly better and was at least still recognisable as a house, although now just a shell without most of its windows. Two days later, with the windows boarded up and having been declared safe to enter, Sam, Emma and Kendrick opened the front door and walked into the hallway. They stepped over the grandfather clock which now lay horizontally on the floor, and carefully walked along the hallway, their feet crunching on the broken glass from the front door and broken picture frames. As Kendrick attempted to open Bridget McAllister's old safe in the cupboard under the stairs Sam occupied himself walking from room to room, rooms all full of memories. He hesitated before opening the door to the lounge. Oh, what he would give to enter that room to see his father seated at his grand piano. What he would give to smell the aroma of coffee, cigar smoke, whisky and wood fires. He opened the door, somehow hoping that it would be that way, the way he remembered, but the room was dark and cold, the curtains drawn and it smelt like the rest of the house – musty, damp and unloved. The Steinway grand piano, covered in dust and plaster that had fallen from the ceiling, had fallen silent long ago.

There was a loud cheer from Kendrick as the safe door opened, having tried various combinations of Bridget McAllister's and Duncan's birthdates. Sam and Emma gathered round as Kendrick reversed on all fours from the cupboard under the stairs clutching the contents of the safe – Duncan's will, his expired passport, some bank books and a large brown envelope containing five hundred pounds in old twenty-pound notes bearing the image of Sir Edward Elgar, which were no longer legal tender. These were stuffed into plastic bags and taken home by Emma and Kendrick to be sorted.

Over the following days after the house had been cleared Kendrick arranged for the sale and collection of the only thing that remained – the Steinway grand piano. It appeared impossible to remove it without demolishing part of the house as the French doors through which it had entered the house in the 1960s via the back garden had been replaced with a single door. On the day of its collection its three legs were removed, it was tipped on its side onto several trolleys and wheeled outside through the door onto the lawn in the back garden. Because of the 1970s kitchen extension and the proximity of a large apple tree it was impossible to manoeuvre it round a ninety-degree bend to go down the side of the house so a mobile crane was waiting on the road to lift the grand piano over the roof of the house onto a waiting flatbed truck. Beatrice Bassett at the house opposite was observing from her porch, taking a keen interest in the proceedings. As the crane driver raised his jib with chains and straps hanging from a large hook, a small crowd gathered on the grass verge at the front of the house in anticipation of something interesting about to happen, although they weren't sure what. A few minutes later when the straps were secured the crane driver started to lift and the crowd raised their hands to shield their eyes from the bright sunlight as the grand piano slowly appeared pointed end first over the roof. A murmur of "ooohs" circulated through the crowd as the dark object appeared over the rooftop, swinging slowly from its straps. Sam watched from the back garden as the piano briefly hung motionlessly directly over the roof of the house, secretly hoping the straps would break, hoping it would plunge through the roof, through his old bedroom, back into the lounge below, smashing to pieces in a stubborn and defiant refusal to leave the room where it had resided for nearly sixty years. He was almost disappointed when it did eventually make it onto the flatbed truck and, having been secured and sheeted down, was driven away to be lovingly restored, to no doubt one day grace someone else's lounge, to deprive some other child of their sleep until the small hours, or perhaps to be returned to the Pavilion somewhere on the south coast from whence it originally came.

With the grand piano gone, the crowd dispersed and Sam entered the old family home for the last time. The hallway was now bare. There was an outline of the grandfather clock on the faded mouldy wallpaper where it had stood for decades, the strange silhouette now the only evidence of its past existence. He thought fondly of the old clock, the clock his mother had wanted him to have, the clock once cherished by past generations, now discarded having been ruined by years of neglect, damp and woodworm. Even the mouse that had once made its home in it had moved out years before. As Sam stood looking at the wall remembering the clock's former beauty, he recited his latest poem:

'A little wee mouse once lived in a house,
'The house was dirty and cold,
'He lived in a clock, a grandfather clock
'Against a wall that was covered in mould.

'No one lived in the house apart from the mouse
'And he could stand it no more,
'He packed up his things and gave a sigh
'As he made his way to the door.

"'I really can't stay, I'll move away
"This house is damp and cold,
"I'll live somewhere else where it's warm and dry
"Away from the dust and the mould.

"'I'll go and stay with my auntie,
"My lovely Auntie Grace,
"She lives over the road in the churchyard,
"She's got a nice little place."'

'He arrived at her nest by a headstone.
'Where someone was laid to rest,
'She was really pleased to see him
'As she rarely had a guest.

'She listened at length to his tale,
'Of his life in the grandfather clock,
'The damp and the dust and the woodworm,
'It came as quite a shock.

"'You must stay with me, my nephew"' she said,
"'It really would be nice,
"'It's warm and tidy and cosy too,
"'Just right for two little mice."'

Maybe he should have taken the grandfather clock six years earlier. At least back then it was worth saving, worth restoring. He had only taken the French clock to have restored: "It's Louis XVI" his mother had said. "No, it's a Victorian copy," the restorer had said.

When Duncan announced his determination to keep

the old family home, maybe Sam and the rest of the family should have acted more forcefully, insisting the house was cleared and sold, but the usual adage from Emma won: "We mustn't upset Duncan. We can't leave him with an empty house." With most normal families in the same situation the clearing and sale of the house would have been the normal sequence of events and, after all, what their mother had wished. Or was it? Maybe she left her darling Duncan the Steinway concert grand piano, that gargantuan lump of iron and maple, nine feet long and weighing nearly half a ton, together with his father's old Jaguar, knowing that he would never want to be parted from either, knowing that he'd want to keep the old family home to house them – after all, he couldn't keep them anywhere else.

Maybe she had predicted, even engineered in advance, the strange state of affairs that had occurred since her death. It was almost as if she had wanted him to keep the house, to let it remain as it was, as it had always been, unchanged, knowing that it would bring her darling Duncan comfort in believing that she was almost still there.

But now there was nobody there, his parents both gone, Duncan gone, even the once ubiquitous woodlice and clothes moths were gone, their dried and shrivelled remains that were scattered on the floors and window ledges the only evidence of their past existence. The termites and woodworm were triumphant despite Duncan's attempts to eradicate them with his home-made concoctions of creosote and paraffin. They had won against the odds. They were the only survivors. The only ones left.

CHAPTER 29

Stepping carefully over what was once a rockery, now a pile of rubble, Sam negotiated the gap in the fence from the overgrown back garden of number fifty-seven to the overgrown back garden of number fifty-nine. He paused where the old greenhouse had once stood, and there, entombed in ivy and brambles, was Reginald Ramsbottom's old safe, still defiantly standing where it had stood for over sixty years. He dropped to his knees and started pulling away the undergrowth, wincing and cursing as brambles scratched his hands and a piece of broken terracotta plant pot cut his finger. He continued his search, frantically sweeping away the leaves. Then he saw it – the brass key. He picked it up and blew off the dirt and the snail shit, inserted it in the door and tried to turn it. After a few attempts it turned. He grasped the handle, pulled and the safe door creaked as he slowly pulled it open. His first glance into the darkness of the safe was disappointing, just a few damp and decomposed jewellery boxes, which, having been entombed for decades, fell apart as he dragged them out, their contents spilling onto the ground – two old Rolex watches, a string of pearls, some old black-and-white photographs of Reg's mother, some old car keys on a Volkswagen key ring, three signet rings and a small bundle of old twenty-pound notes bearing the image of William Shakespeare. Not the treasure trove he had secretly hoped for during the brief period of anticipation before he had opened the door, or that he'd imagined in his younger days as he'd spied on Reginald Ramsbottom through the hole in the fence, but nevertheless things of rarity, things of beauty and things of value. Then he saw an envelope stuck to the inside of the safe door, discoloured and mottled by years of damp. He pulled the envelope free, the faded print identifying it was from a long-established solicitor in the town. Intrigued, he opened the envelope, taking care not to tear the fragile contents – "The last will and testament of Reginald Ramsbottom". There was a lot of legal jargon that he didn't understand before he came to the main points. Apart from five thousand pounds bequeathed to Bridget McAllister, Reginald Ramsbottom had left the remainder of his estate, including his house, to be divided equally between her three children. 'Bloody hell,' muttered Sam to himself as he stood up, folded the document, returned it to its grubby envelope and put it in his jacket pocket.

'Come in,' shouted Emma as Sam knocked on her front door, a white wooden coach bolted door with a large lion's head door knocker in its centre. Sam entered to the sound of rustling paper to find Emma and Kendrick seated at the table in their front room.

'Morning, Sam,' said Emma. 'We're looking through Duncan's paperwork and starting to sort things out.

There are people we need to notify of Duncan's death. Kendrick's going to sort out the bills that need to be paid, notify the bank, sort out his pension and make the funeral arrangements. Things like that.'

'Righty ho,' said Sam. 'Déjà vu.'

'What was that?' asked Emma.

'Déjà vu. We've been here before.'

'What do you mean?'

'You said exactly those words when you sorted out Mum's affairs six years ago, almost to the day. Spooky, isn't it?'

Emma ignored Sam and continued sorting through the pile of letters and paperwork on the table, tearing off addresses and personal information from documents. She put some of the scraps of paper into a pile on the table and gave Sam a disapproving glance.

'I'll shred this pile,' she said, 'and all this paper can be thrown out.'

'Recycled,' said Kendrick, who still had a passion for correctness and recycling.

'Quite correct, Kendrick. Recycled,' replied Emma.

'I found these,' said Sam as he emptied a carrier bag containing his finds from Reginald Ramsbottom's safe onto the table. Unsure whether Emma and Kendrick were aware of the existence of the safe, he explained. 'They were in an old safe in the garden at number fifty-nine, where the old greenhouse used to be. Reg used to keep his jewellery in it.'

Kendrick examined the rings, pearls and watches in detail with a small magnifying glass he always carried in his waistcoat pocket, mumbling to himself, reminding Sam of Fagin in *Oliver Twist*.

'And this,' continued Sam as he drew the tatty envelope containing the will from his jacket pocket and passed it to Emma. Having read through it she shook her head slowly and passed it to Kendrick. As he perused the document Sam sat at the table and gazed out of the window, with all the old questions surrounding Reginald Ramsbottom spinning round in his head; why had he moved from Northumberland to the same town in South Lincolnshire when he retired? As if that wasn't strange enough, why had he bought the house next door? Why had his relationship with his father changed? For years they'd been the best of friends but then Reg had become the object of his father's scorn and ridicule. Sam and Emma had always had a good relationship with Reginald Ramsbottom and together with Duncan they had thought fondly of him – a good neighbour and family friend. What had been their mother's influence over Reginald Ramsbottom? He *had* made a will, the one Sam found in his old safe, the one Kendrick was reading, but why had he changed it? For years Sam had believed his mother had influenced and controlled Reginald Ramsbottom, just as she had Duncan. Had he changed his will as a result of that influence, to leave Duncan as the main beneficiary, apart from the generous donation to the church of... whatever it was called? The same old unanswered questions haunted him. There was nobody to ask now. Everybody was gone.

Kendrick shrugged his shoulders. 'A photocopy of Reg's second will was found in your mother's safe in the cupboard under the stairs,' said Kendrick as he retrieved the document from a pile of papers on the table and passed it to Sam. 'It's dated 2001. Duncan dealt with the probate as you know. The will you found in the old safe in his garden was dated 1986, so the one I found must have superseded the one you found. To be correct Mr Ramsbottom should have added the clause "I hereby revoke all wills and testamentary dispositions heretofore made by me" or something like that, or destroyed the old will, but he obviously didn't. Why make a second will fifteen years later?'

'I think Reg left Duncan his house so he could live next door to Mum and look after her in her later years,' said Emma rather unconvincingly.

Sam gave her a look of astonishment. 'Reg died in 2001, seventeen years before Mum. How did he know what the future would hold? For all he knew she could have died before Dad, or even before Reg himself, so that theory doesn't make sense.'

'Anyway,' continued Emma, 'Reg's earlier will has come full circle. Duncan's left us the house anyway.'

Sam looked at Kendrick for support, who had returned to his Fagin pose, looking through his magnifying glass at some pearls and grunting with satisfaction. He looked at Emma over the top of his glasses and said in his slow, deep, calming voice, 'Yes, my dear, but there's nothing left. It's a pile of rubble. It's a building plot.'

'Exactly,' said Sam. 'Duncan hadn't even insured anything, the houses, the cars, everything's gone.'

The funeral was a quiet affair, just a few family members who, with the passing of time, were becoming fewer by the year. He was laid to rest in the churchyard across the road from his two houses, making his final journey courtesy of

Graves and Day in a Daimler hearse driven by Agnus Day, the same Daimler hearse that he'd spent so much time underneath fettling and maintaining, the same that had almost caused his earlier demise.

Characteristically, he hadn't left any instructions for his final departure, leaving it to others to sort the arrangements, including the expense. In this case the absence of instructions was probably fortunate, as if his lifelong obsession to avoid unnecessary expenditure had included his own funeral he would most likely have left a request to be carried across the road in his coffin.

Although he had never been mastered, trained or subjugated by Beatrice Bassett it was rather appropriate that his final resting place was in the churchyard next to her house, close to her two late husbands' graves. Maybe he would join them on the stone wall of the churchyard, appearing as a pixie or a goblin. From there he could watch disapprovingly the comings and goings of builders at his two old properties on the opposite side of the road, workmen with sledgehammers, wheelbarrows and cement mixers, rebuilding the houses, houses that would have proper heating, wiring and plumbing, houses that would be comfortable and warm, both features that he would have considered extravagant and unnecessary. His often used maxim "Think of the cost. Think of the mess" was never more appropriate with the destruction of his two properties. Throughout his life he had somehow managed to avoid expense and mess, leaving both for someone else to put their hands in *their* pockets to put things right – "Someone will sort them out, someone else will pay."

CHAPTER 30

It was the last day of term before the summer holidays and the last day of what Sam considered his insignificant career as an English teacher. He had been able to realise his dream of early retirement, although not at the early age of fifty-five as his father had. Still, he and Morag could now slow down and enjoy life and he could pursue his interests, his books and his music. They'd get an allotment and he'd start home brewing, take up fly fishing and learn the banjo again. There was so much to do, but now, being freed from the work ethos and with no commitments and a slower pace of life, they had plenty of time.

As he sat at the breakfast table listening to Radio 4, an interview with one of the usual prevaricating politicians was followed by the sports news with the presenter jabbering on about some football match taking place on the other side of the world with thousands of English supporters intending to travel. He swore and switched the radio off. He considered an irritating feature of the football supporter was their willingness, if not determination, to help destroy the planet by jetting off halfway around the world in their thousands to watch a football match that was televised. Maybe it was considered by them a matter of national importance. It was only a game, hardly worth releasing hundreds of tons of carbon into the atmosphere for. Sam cared about the planet. He wasn't sure why, he'd be long gone. He'd leave the car at home today and cycle to school. He'd do his bit.

*

He had never been quite sure how his last day in the job would feel, although he'd never really given it that much thought. There was the usual relaxed end-of-term atmosphere in the school. Most students would be returning to move up a year at the start of the next term, others would be leaving to start work or apprenticeships and others would be moving on to further education. Maybe he'd meet some of them again at SLAPS, the South Lincolnshire Academy for Practical Studies, the world of his imagination, his alternative reality that he still visited.

At lunchtime, in the staffroom he was presented with a sponge cake baked by Mrs Brierley, still the school secretary, still trying to be posh and still working approaching seventy due to her daughter Geraldine taking over the pig farm and apparently making a pig's ear of it. Following the presentation of the sponge cake, an eminently forgettable arrangement of Nat King Cole's "Unforgettable" was given by the 'Phyllis Stein Four' string quartet in the staffroom followed by a dreadful rendition of "For He's a Jolly Good Fellow". It was an assault on the senses, a cacophony from hell. The overenthusiastic bowing of her lower cello strings had made the sound of a rhinoceros breaking wind, not that Sam had ever heard a rhinoceros breaking wind, nor had any desire to, but he imagined that's what it would sound like. Phyllis Stein was the only original member of her quartet, the other three had either got fed up with her megalomaniac personality and wild histrionics, died of boredom, or sensibly taken up a proper instrument like the banjo and had been replaced by her most promising students who knew no better.

Phyllis Stein and Mrs. Brierley were the only original staff members remaining from the time Sam joined all those years ago. His replacement as head of the English department was to be taken by a former student called Blenkinsop who was moving down to Lincolnshire from a school in Yorkshire. Could it be *that* Blenkinsop? Surely not him. Well good luck to him if it was. Maybe Blenkinsop had looked up to Sam in a similar way that *he* had admired his old English teacher Mr Evans and decided to follow in *his* footsteps.

After an impromptu speech he was presented with a thesaurus and a carriage clock in recognition of his years of service. This presented Sam with a problem. Being impossible to cycle home five miles with a large sponge cake, a thesaurus and a carriage clock, he telephoned Morag to bring the car to collect him, thus cancelling out his day's contribution to saving the planet. He'd have to try again tomorrow.

Morag drove home with Sam carefully cradling his sponge cake in one hand and his carriage clock in the other. Not being far from Stonebridge Road, Sam requested they go past the old family home even though it was no longer there. He had avoided the area for about two years, unsure what emotions would be stirred. Not until now, the day of his retirement, had he a desire, whether through intrigue or curiosity, to return.

'Stop the car, Morag,' said Sam as they turned right at the roundabout into Stonebridge Road.

'Where?'

'Just along here, before the bus stop.'

As Morag pulled up, a car reversed out of Beatrice Bassett's driveway. The driver, a pleasant-looking grey-haired man, probably in his late fifties, waved to Beatrice, who looked rather dishevelled as she stood in her porch in her dressing gown. She gave the driver a cheerful wave in return and blew a kiss. The car drove away and Beatrice Bassett remained in her porch and sat in her wicker chair with the late afternoon sunlight glinting on her sherry glass as she raised it to her lips. Had she found romance? Was the gentleman caller a casual acquaintance or had the omnipotent Beatrice Bassett a potential candidate for husband number three firmly in her grasp? He'd probably never find out. Now he'd retired, his source of information in Mrs Brierley would be discontinued. Maybe Beatrice Bassett had introduced her new gentleman to her novelty mug collection to soften the mood. He hoped her new acquaintance had stamina, endurance and a sense of humour – he was dealing with an expert.

On the opposite side of the road were two newly built properties of individual design. Both were attractive and desirable houses, just as the old family home and number fifty-nine had once been before they had come into

Duncan's ownership and their subsequent decline into ruination and destruction.

A young boy, probably in his early teens, suddenly ran from the front gate where the old family home had once stood. Sam watched as the boy ran along the pavement and entered the front gate of the house next door, just as Sam had done as a boy to chat to Reginald Ramsbottom as he'd washed down his cherished E-Type having returned from the Church of… whatever it was called in Hertfordshire. The young boy was met at the gate by a girl of similar age and together they ran back round to where the old family home had once stood, down the side of the new house into the rear garden. Sam imagined the garden would now be immaculate with a manicured lawn and attractive flower boarders, a far cry from the overgrown, uncared-for "rustic paradise" that his brother Duncan had left behind. He wondered if the summer house was still there, the cherished summer house of his childhood, or maybe it had been demolished to make way for a greenhouse or a hot tub. He hoped not. This is where his home had once stood, his childhood home, but now it was different, it was somebody else's home, a home to live on in other people's memories.

'How much longer do want to sit here?' Morag asked.

'Take me home now please,' he replied.

CHAPTER 31

Sitting on the wooden bench on their allotment watching Morag picking runner beans, Sam McAllister was thinking of what he considered the transformation that had taken place in his life twenty-two years earlier, the day he considered he'd changed into a different person, a cynical belligerent old git, a carbon copy of his father. Strangely, the arrival of the fifty-and-sixty year milestones had not been met with the same horror and trepidation as his fortieth. It was as if there was an acceptance that the peak of the hill had been reached at forty and it was all downhill from there. What was it about forty that was so depressing? Was it that often used label of "middle age"? Age is but a number but for Sam there was a frustration and regret that as the years and decades had passed there had been little achieved in life and time was running out. He had always wanted to achieve something in life but had never been quite sure what it was. Kendrick had told him once that passing on his passion and appreciation of literature to others and developing young minds should be an achievement and reward in itself, but Sam didn't quite see it that way. He would probably just be remembered by a headstone proclaiming – "*Here lies Samuel Bartholomew McAllister, cynic and cantankerous git – born 23 March 1959 and died… (to be decided)*".

He had often considered that there was nothing worse than being described as a "used to be" person unless you used to be something really important like the prime minister or an astronaut. He put himself in the "used to be" category. Maybe his little known secrets would pop up in conversations long after he was dead and gone.

'He used to be an English teacher and he used to write poetry, or at least he tried to.'

'Did he?' would be asked out of politeness.

'He used to be a musician.'

'Did he?' would be asked in disbelief.

'Oh yes – he used to play the piano and the banjo."

'Well I never,' would be said with a lack of interest.

"Used to be" always seemed to describe people who were once able to do things and then couldn't anymore, or weren't very good at whatever it was they used to do and had given up. "You won't get far in life if you give up," his father had said. He could hear his father's voice: "Rose tinted glasses again." His father had played piano in a 1940s dance band "Stars in Battle Dress". He wouldn't be remembered for that by anyone because he'd never told anyone, not even Sam, but Sam had the photograph from 1944. That was special.

He knew there was nothing remarkable about himself, in fact unremarkable would be a more accurate description. He had been much the same as any other English teacher in any other secondary school. Much of his life had been rather dull, uneventful and predictable, but comfortable nevertheless. His life was still enlightened with his dreamy thoughts of his imaginary parallel life at the South Lincolnshire Academy of Practical Studies where he could do and say what he liked without offending anybody.

As they began to walk the short distance back home from the allotment, Morag carrying a bag of runner beans and Sam burdened with his thoughts, he considered how lucky he was to have her. She was eminently sensible and dependable, rather like his mother had been. She was gone but that same stability, that steadiness, lived on in his life through Morag, the ever dependable Morag.

*

Now that early retirement had finally been possible the allocation of time proved more difficult than he had imagined. The dream of "can't wait to retire, to spend time doing the things I want to do" now seemed a fallacy. In reality, tasks and chores become spread out over greater time with the result that no surplus time is created. Now they had all the time in the world, but there weren't enough hours in the day. More had seemed to be achieved in his spare time when working. Also with retirement came aging, a growing fear of ill health, poor mobility and the intolerance of certain foods. When he was a boy his grandmother had once said, "I like cucumber but it doesn't like me." He had thought she was talking nonsense but she'd been right. With him it wasn't just cucumber – it was sprouts, onions, leeks, plums, baked beans and real ale. How can you spend your life eating and drinking things and then suddenly when you get older you can't enjoy them anymore? For now he'd carry on regardless and ignore the discomfort and endure the gastric torture. The future could be bleak though. The future could be a world of prescriptions, mobility scooters, stairlifts, Viagra and not being able to raise himself up from a chair without breaking wind. Time would tell.

One task per day was the new norm and that particular day's task was to clean the windows. Most people living nearby had a window cleaner. They also had gardeners and domestic cleaners. Sam, who had never been comfortable paying someone to do something he could do himself, cleaned his own windows. He looked up as he positioned the ladder under the front bedroom window, then he took a couple of steps back on the lawn to make sure it was straight. Satisfied, he started to climb with one hand on the rungs, the other holding the bucket, with a chamois leather slung over his left shoulder. Having reached the window he looked around admiring the view. Everything looked different from up there. All was well with the world; a beautiful morning, the distant church clock finished striking eleven, the sun was shining, all was peaceful, the only sounds the chattering of house martins sitting on the telephone wire and the distant bleating of sheep. *A good day to get a few jobs done and nothing to get worked up or angry about*, he thought.

As he wiped the window dry with his wash leather he heard the sound of the back door closing at the neighbouring house. The Reverend Snodgrass shuffled along his garden path with Moriarty his black Labrador. Sam looked down as the Reverend Snodgrass opened his front gate and stepped onto the footpath, unaware of his presence as he perched at the top of the ladder.

'Morning, Vicar,' said Sam loudly as he looked down from his elevated position.

The Reverend Snodgrass appeared startled and looked up, saying, 'Oh my goodness, a voice from above. How are you, Sam? What are you up to?'

'I'm trying to get nearer to God, Vicar.'

'That's one way of doing it.'

'If I fall off this ladder I probably will be.'

'Ever the optimist, Sam, ever the optimist,' replied the vicar as he walked away leading Moriarty. After a few yards Moriarty stopped and turned his head. Sam's eyes met Moriarty's, a long penetrating stare from the black eyes of a black Labrador. What was he thinking? What was his view of life? The world as seen by Moriarty. Having satisfied his curiosity he sniffed the air, turned and slowly walked away by the right paw. Sam descended the ladder rather precariously, bucket and sponge in his left hand, his right hand nervously grasping the rungs. Having reached the safety of the front lawn he breathed a sigh of relief.

He became aware of voices approaching as a group of smartly dressed people wearing rosettes appeared from around the corner, walking in his direction.

'Oh blast,' he said aloud. It was the local councillor doing the rounds in the village, canvassing for the forthcoming local elections accompanied by their Member of Parliament, obviously there for visual ballast. He hurriedly started to lower the ladder thinking he could escape through his side gate before they reached him. Having identified Sam as their next target, the group appeared to quicken their steps in an attempt to reach him before he disappeared.

'Damn and blast,' Sam said to himself, realising he was going to get caught.

The MP looked at the house number and consulted the list on his clipboard.

'Ah, you must be Mr McAllister.'

'Must I?' replied Sam, determined that the exchange would get off to a bad start.

'Do you live here?'

'Apparently yes. I've just cleaned the windows. I'm not in the habit of cleaning other people's windows.'

'Then you must be Mr Samuel Bartholomew McAllister.'

Sam sighed deeply, wishing he'd said he was the McAllisters' handyman and chauffeur and that his master, Samuel McAllister, was next door with the vicar's wife as the vicar had gone out, thereby starting a local scandal. He always thought of witty things to say after the event – always too late.

'I am he who is recognised by that cognomen, but usually without the "uel" and without the Bartholomew,' he said in a posh voice. He was starting to get bored with the exchange so thought by talking posh it would unsettle and frustrate his conversational opponents and they'd bugger off and annoy someone else. It usually worked. On this occasion it didn't.

The MP took a step closer towards Sam, who took a step back and raised his bucket slightly. 'I'd like to introduce Mrs Bollinger-Smith, our candidate who's hoping to be re-elected in the local election next month.'

'Good morning Mr McAllister' said Mrs Bollinger-Smith. 'Can we rely on your support in the forthcoming election?'

Sam ignored the question. 'Good morning, Mrs Smith.'

'*Bollinger*-Smith,' she replied, accenting the 'Bollinger' having first given Sam a meaningful glance, almost a reproachful look. 'Are you happy with everything in the village, Mr McAllister?'

To Sam, the question was like the raising of the traps at the Grand National or the release of the hare at a dog track – he was off. 'No we're not. You see that light over our front door. We have to leave that on most of the night so people can see where they're walking because there are hardly any street lights along this road. We pay nearly three hundred pounds a month council tax and have to leave that light on so people can see. We should have a discount on our council tax for doing that. We need more doggy dustbins for dog walkers, the road is full of potholes and there's no bus service. Do you want me to go on?'

Mrs Bollinger-Smith didn't. 'Well of course our funds are extremely restricted Mr McAllister, and we've had to make some cutbacks in services.'

'Maybe you wouldn't have to make so many cutbacks if you paid your chief executive a more modest salary instead of the obscene remuneration he receives. It's disgusting and I bet if he wanted a street light and a doggy dustbin outside his house he'd get one. You lot in parliament aren't much better either,' he said directing his wrath towards the MP. 'What a load of hypocrites you lot are. What's the name of the Downing Street cat you see on the BBC News going in and out of the Number 10 front door as if it owns the place?'

'Larry,' replied the MP meekly.

'Well, why don't you make Larry the prime minister and put him in charge of the country? He'd do a better job. Yes, make Larry the PM and surround him with a cabinet made up of cynical old bastards like me and maybe we'd get the country sorted out. This country's gone to pot. If you told someone in the 1970s that in fifty years' time Nissans would be made in Sunderland and MGs would be made in China they'd have thought you were deranged. The world's gone mad. We rely on imports from communist, autocratic countries ruled by despots for most of our food and energy, importing what we should be producing ourselves, things we used to produce ourselves. Where's the sense in that? What are the government doing about house building?'

The MP seemed to become more relaxed now that the subject had been changed and confidently said, 'Ah we're dealing with that, Mr McAllister. We've got plans to build three hundred thousand new homes this year, many in this area.'

'Well you're bonkers then, you won't get my vote. You keep building thousands of houses on green fields and farmland, land that we should be using for food production. You lot won't be satisfied until you cover the whole bloody country with concrete. It doesn't stop there. The more houses you build, the more roads, schools and hospitals you have to build. You're ploughing up thousands of acres of farmland and beautiful countryside to build that stupid new HS… whatever it's called railway line just so that someone can get from one overpopulated hellhole to another one a few minutes quicker. Why not improve the railways we already have? Another thing – we have droughts most summers, the more houses you build the more water we need. Two thirds of our planet is covered in water and we have droughts. It doesn't make sense. Instead of wasting billions of pounds building HS… whatever it's called we should be building desalination plants around the country so we can use sea water to irrigate and put back into reservoirs when they're low – like they do in Saudi Arabia. If Saudi Arabia can do it, why can't we? Sea levels are rising and at the same time we're running out of water, it's bonkers. We put a man on the moon over fifty years ago and we've still not sorted out the water problem. Daft, isn't it? It doesn't make sense. Anyway if you lot curbed immigration like you said you would at the last election and started kicking out the ones who shouldn't be here we wouldn't need so much housing. Next time you see Larry the cat why don't you ask him if he's got an opinion on any of the points I've raised.'

'Well it's been nice talking to you, Mr McAllister,' the MP said as the group started to walk away, having sensed they were wasting their time.

'I'm sure you don't mean that,' said Sam, starting to froth at the mouth. 'You don't like the truth, that's the trouble with you lot,' he shouted as the group started to walk away briskly. 'You're all hypocrites. You're all full of sh… colonic throughput!'

As the group disappeared into the distance Sam

smiled to himself, now rather glad he'd encountered them and put his points across so eloquently. Earlier he had been determined to have a peaceful and relaxing day and not get agitated or bad-tempered but he somehow felt refreshed and purified after his encounter, purged of something that had been building up inside him. What exactly it was he wasn't quite sure. Anger probably.

He picked up the ladder from the front path and started to manoeuvre it through the side gate into the back garden, unaware he'd entangled Morag's sweet peas in the end of the ladder and was dragging them behind him across the garden.

He sat down on the sunlounger and thought about his encounter with the prospective local councillor and the MP. Secretly they had probably agreed with him but were too full of their own self-importance, too concerned with their own existence to admit that he was probably right. Now he was retired, maybe he should consider going into politics himself. Maybe he could become an MP and try to make a difference, make the world a better place.

He closed his eyes, his face basking in the warm sunshine, and drifted off, allowing his thoughts to wander and his imagination to reawaken…

'The PM wants to see you right away, Sir McAllister, he's in the cabinet room. They're all having a working lunch in there.'

Sam rushed along the corridor. A security guard opened the door to the cabinet room and Sam entered. The prime minister was standing on the cabinet table next to an empty bowl, licking his lips.

'You wanted to see me, Larry,' said Sam.

The PM looked up, said nothing and then sat down on the table. He licked his paws and started to wash his ears.

'Is there something wrong, Prime Minister?' asked Sam. 'I was told it was important.'

The home secretary, Mrs. Beverly Babbington-Buttress, a distant relative his local councillor Mrs Bollinger-Smith, stood up and started speaking with a mouthful of tuna fish sandwich. 'Sir McAllister, the PM is very concerned about your recommendation for the proposed site for the desalination plant along the east coast. When it was decided to use a brownfield site, we didn't mean a whole town, certainly not Skegness. What about the donkeys that give rides along the beach? What will happen to the donkeys?'

'Don't worry about the donkeys, Mrs Babbington-Buttress. My wife Morag has agreed to start a donkey sanctuary and look after them. They'll be very well cared-for. The rail link from Skegness to the Midlands is an important consideration—'

'Get away, you brute!' interrupted the home secretary as the prime minister started to sniff the remains of her tuna sandwich. She picked up the prime minister and threw him on the floor. Looking a little disgruntled he walked slowly over to the large window, sat on the carpet in the sunshine and started purring.

Sam felt a hand on his shoulder, shaking him, followed by Morag's soft voice. 'Wake up, Sam. Your lunch is ready.

CHAPTER 32

Later that day, as he sat in the garden with a glass of non-alcoholic beer enjoying the last of the evening sunshine, Sam, as usual, was reminiscing. He thought about his childhood, the summer house at the bottom of the garden of the old family home, the old neighbour Reginald Ramsbottom and the strange events that had taken place since the death of his parents.

Although his father could be best described as having been a difficult man, he often thought fondly of him and wished he'd known him better. Considering he'd survived into his early nineties he'd done rather well, retaining his hair, his own teeth and most importantly his sense of humour. After his death, his mother's proclamation that "things will change, I'll start to live a little, spend some money on myself and the house" was a dream that she probably knew would never be realised – a delusion. Her life *could* have become more enjoyable and comfortable in her final years. Those dreams and aspirations could perhaps have become reality were they not thwarted by the intervention of his brother Duncan

– his mantra "think of the cost. Think of the mess. I don't think we want that, do we", 'we' meaning *him*. He became a controlling influence over her, just as she had once controlled him. *He* was the one determined that nothing would change.

Since her death one strange event had led to another, each one becoming increasingly bizarre. When viewed as a whole they represented a strange state of affairs that was received in disbelief when relayed to others, particularly those with a more sensible and pragmatic approach to life. Sam was often troubled by the events that had developed over the years, especially the retention of the old family home by his brother. He had seemed at ease with his decision and to keep their parents' house and Reginald Ramsbottom's house next door exactly as they were when their former owners had occupied them, to have kept them both almost as shrines, content to have allowed both houses to fall further and further into disrepair, their contents and the buildings themselves ruined by damp and neglect. Rather like Sam, Duncan had had a challenging upbringing devoid of paternal affection. He'd never particularly liked his father and his father had never particularly liked him. Maybe having acquired his father's most cherished possessions he had drawn some sort of strange rebellious pleasure in seeing them fall further and further into neglect, decline and decay.

Sam had found his brother's general existence perplexing. He had disliked what most others liked, disapproved of what most others approved of and had been intolerant of what others tolerated. For years he had seemed to have indulged in a kind of morbid pleasure in living the way that he had, depriving himself of basic comfort, dressing like a tramp, surviving cold winters without any sort of proper heating in the house when he could well have afforded to live differently. It was bizarre therefore that his unconventional method of keeping warm, sitting in front of a gas cooker with the door open, had led to his unfortunate and untimely demise.

Despite their best efforts to help him, the rest of the family had despaired at his general existence and in frustration had been inclined to think, *if that's how he wants to live, let him get on with it*. Their father would have given Duncan little sympathy. Sam could hear his father's voice again – "He needs to sort himself out. He's soft in the head. He can't hold a job down and he's been handed everything on a plate." Sam had written a parody of Winston Churchill's famous "Never in the Field of Human Conflict" speech – "Never in the history of mankind has someone accumulated so much, from so many, by doing so little". Why was it that he'd ended up like that? Was anyone to blame? If he'd been treated differently or brought up differently and not mollycoddled, cocooned and wrapped up in cotton wool (in the metaphorical sense of that expression) by their mother for so many years, *could* he have been different? Would he have been different if he'd settled down, got married and had a family instead of remaining a bachelor and living a lonely and reclusive existence? It was as if he had been punishing himself for something, depriving himself of pleasure, social interaction, warmth and comfort. It was all very well for others to say "if that's how he chooses to live let him get on with it" – that's how he chose to live because he didn't know any better, probably believing that he didn't *deserve* any better. The loss of a mother leaves a gaping hole in people's lives but to Duncan McAllister it was a void filled with misery and self-deprivation resulting in him not having a life, just a miserable existence.

*

Much had changed in the eight years Sam's father had been gone. If he was still with us he would find the world a very different place even after that relatively short time – the election of buffoons to the highest offices of state in most civilised countries of the world with more mindless morons waiting in line for their turn, a pandemic, arguments about climate change, electric cars, what he would consider to be the scourge of the 21st century that was called social media, the garbage on television that was considered public entertainment dominated by cooking, dancing and people trying to sing. People of indeterminate gender, men marrying men, women marrying women, boys who wanted to be girls and girls who wanted to be boys – what would his father think? He would probably say he was in a better place, better off out of it. Yes, much had changed since he'd gone.

In a way Sam was following in his footsteps with his petulance, his cynicism and his intolerance to other people and the world itself. During his childhood days, he and the rest of the family had despaired about his father's constant moaning, cynicism and belligerence but those qualities were now unmistakably manifest in him and had been for years. What were other people's views of him? Did people say "God help us" when he left the room as his mother had said of his father? He didn't really care what people thought. He enjoyed an almost perverse pleasure from criticising and being rude and intolerant of others.

Since he'd retired he had become concerned that time was running out. Too much time had been wasted in the past – working, striving to exist to pay the bills and the mortgage and no sense of achievement. For some time he had been giving a lot of thought to writing a book but had become disillusioned with the prospect of failure. Kendrick had once told him, somewhat reassuringly, that failure could be interpreted as an attempt to succeed. Kendrick was writing his book so why couldn't he? After all, he had the time now and he had the imagination. He could write about his strange family, the events of the last fifty years, the strange neighbour Reginald Ramsbottom and his brother's retention of the old family home, not that those subjects would require much imagination. He'd told friends of the strange events, the strange state of affairs. Everyone had told him, "You couldn't make it up, could you." Well he wouldn't have to. It all happened, well, most of it. He picked up his pen and started writing – "It was a sad day when Mrs McAllister passed away, a sad end to an unfulfilled and mostly dreary life". *No, that won't do*, he thought, tearing up the sheet of paper and tossing it over his shoulder. *Too depressing, readers would give up at the first page.*

He thought for a moment as if seeking inspiration and started again.

"As Samuel Bartholomew McAllister walked around the garden of the old family home in the damp chill of an October morning in 2018 he looked up at the house and recalled what it had been like in happier times…"

This book is printed on paper from sustainable sources managed under the Forest Stewardship Council (FSC) scheme.

It has been printed in the UK to reduce transportation miles and their impact upon the environment.

For every new title that Troubador publishes, we plant a tree to offset CO_2, partnering with the More Trees scheme.

For more about how Troubador offsets its environmental impact, see www.troubador.co.uk/sustainability-and-community